DON'T CALL ME SLYE

Other Books by Mark Slade

Going Down Maine
A Novel

Of Pain And Coffee
Sooths, Sayings & Soliloquies

Someone's Story
Observations in Verse

Hangin' With The Truth
A Novel

DON'T CALL ME SLYE

A Novel
Mark Slade

A FORTIORI ENTERPRISES

Copyright 2024 by Mark Slade

All Rights Reserved. Except as permitted by the U.S. Copyright Act of 1976, no part of this publication may be reproduced, distributed, or transmitted in any form or by any means, or stored in a database or retrieval system, without prior permission of the publisher. Exceptions allowed in the case of brief quotations embodied on critical articles and reviews.

As a work of fiction & poetry, this book is a product of the author's imagination. Places, events, incidents and names of persons living and dead are used and intended to be read in an imaginative manner.

A Fortiori Enterprises
P.O. Box 671
Cloverdale, CA 95425
Email: **afortiorienterprises@yahoo.com**

First U.S. Print Edition
2024

ISBN-13: 978-09885885-7-8
ISBN-10: 0988588579

Printed in the United States of America

Photograph by Melinda Riccilli Slade
Photograph Copyright: A Fortiori Enterprises
www.marksladestudio.com

The Poem, HANGIN' WITH THE TRUTH, from "Someone's Story"
Edited Reprint Courtesy of A Fortiori Enterprises

Cover Design: Morgan Riccilli Slade
www.morgansladestudio.com

To My Family

"Sometimes just sayin' it won't do it but doin' it will more than just say it."

Millie Mae Duncan   1877

DON'T
CALL
ME
SLYE

The historically bent tale of
the
Bandit Bob Slye
and the
Bandit Sally Mae Boudine

Historic Warning:
In various instances, historical facts, references,
dates
events, names and places have been intentionally
bent to
accommodate this story

ONE

The bullet ripped through the upraised right shoulder of Sheriff Jack O'Banyon, shattering the joint. The downtrodden deputy sheriff, called "Pignuts" by O'Banyon, quickly grabbed the halter of the Bandit Bob Slye's horse to steady it. The crack of a rifle echoed across the badland expanse on the outskirts of Deadwood, South Dakota, as the second shot blew O'Banyon's left shoulder away. The Bandit, seated on his horse beneath the hanging tree, with the noose drooped around his neck, did not have to look, as he heard the third bullet blast dead center through the sheriff's forehead, exploding the back of his skull into a burst of blood and bone, followed by the echo of the gunshot ricocheting off into the distance. *'King-Queen-Ace'...* The deputy watched as the Bandit Bob Slye rode away at a full-on gallop, dust spewing from his roan's hooves as they spit dirt and rocks into the air. The deputy, whose real name was Otis Thigpen, knew what he had to do next. For, he had just murdered Jack O'Banyon, the notoriously cruel Sheriff of Deadwood, South Dakota and released the Bandit Bob Slye who was about to be hung by the neck until dead from the sheriff's favorite hanging tree. In actuality though, Otis had not murdered the sheriff. He did, however, deliver a lead slug Coup de grace from his six-shooter, point blank into the body of the already dead sheriff – directly through the heart of the dastardly lawman. This was shortly after the bandit, Sally Mae Bodine, delivered the evil O'Banyon to hell with her *"King-Queen-Ace"* sharpshooter specialty that she had developed and perfected during her days with Buffalo Bill Cody's Wild West Traveling Show.

Otis watched as the two bandits met up at the top of a rise and waved back down to him and then quickly rode away. He sighed and started the business of shoving the overstuffed body of the sheriff into the open wooden casket he had hauled out to the hanging tree on a buckboard. But, not before letting go with a chaw of brown tobacco slurp onto the dead man's face. "You ain't never gon' to call me Pignuts again!"

Otis then retrieved the sheriff's favorite bloodstained English riding crop from his clinched death grip fist and tossed it into the coffin. "And you ain't never gon' to do what you done to them womens no more!"

The plain board coffin, that was meant for the Bandit Bob Slye, was now the burying box for Sheriff Jack O'Banyon.

Otis reached down and tore the sheriff's badge from O'Banyon's sheepskin coat. "And you ain't no sheriff no more!"

He then proceeded to nail down the boards, closing up the coffin real tight.

After years of abuse, Deputy Sheriff Otis Thigpen calmly sat down on the driver's box of the buckboard, took up the reins and clucked the horse into a turn back toward Deadwood. Leaving the empty noose hanging from the branch of the hanging tree to gently swing in the breeze.

===

As Otis Thigpen guided the coffin-laden buckboard along the rutted Deadwood main street at a leisurely pace, no one seemed to notice. They'd seen it all before and knew that the deputy was only headed to one place, Boot Hill.

Lucretia Marchbanks did give Otis a bright, "Mornin' Otis," as she headed for the restaurant at the Grand Central Hotel, where she held sway over all that was served out of *her* kitchen; especially, overseeing the daily results of her local favorite plum pudding.

Otis gave her a nod, as was their routine, and continued on to the end of the street, turning off and onto the path that led up over a hill to the graveyard where he had already dug the ditch to deposit the coffin that was to have held the body of the Bandit Bob Slye.

===

At the freshly dug ditch Otis slid the heavy burial box, not so gently off the buckboard, then shoved it to the edge of the hole. He then straightened up, spit an extra-large dark slurp of tobacco chaw onto the box and then shoved the coffin over into the ditch, where it landed with a thud upside down. "Good riddance!"

After shoveling dirt over the coffin and filling in the grave, Deputy Thigpen headed back to the sheriff's office where he planned to spend the rest of the day whittling out a wooden grave marker with the name of *The Bandit Bob Slye*.

THE BANDITS

TWO

Sally Mae Boudine slowed her horse and reined in. Bob had stopped behind and was slumped over his horse's neck. The stuffed-full carpetbag that Deputy Thigpen had used to gather the personal items the sheriff had taken from Bob was listing, from where it was tied to his saddle strings on the back of his saddle. "You doin' poorly there, Slye?"

Bob straightened up as best he could, but the pain from where the sheriff had shot him the day before in his left shoulder was getting worse. "Don't call me *Slye* there, Boudine," he admonished hoarsely.

Boudine slid from her saddle and retied the carpetbag. "That's right! The Bandit Bob Slye is dead and buried! I gotta do better with that. There's a creek a little distance up ahead. Think you can make it?"

"Got to," Bob gritted and urged the roan forward.

===

With the coming of fall, the air was getting crisp early. Boudine had helped Bob from his horse and settled him next to a tree whose branches hung down over a creek that meandered through the cottonwoods, where they had stopped to deal with Bob's wound.

"Lemme have us a look there, Slye... Sorry... *Bob*." With that, Boudine tentatively unbuttoned his bloodstained shirt and peeled it back from the bullet wound in his left shoulder.

"What's it look like?" Bob winced.

"Did that deputy get that pouch of yarrow grind to you when you was in the hoosegow?"

"Yes... I pushed it in s'best I could."

"Good. Probably, gonna save your life then."

"What's it..."

"Looks like you been punched real hard. S'all black'n'blue with a nasty hole in the middle of it."

"Did it go through?"

"Let's have us a look-see." Boudine started to pull back more of his shirt. Bob winced, "Ahh!"

"Okay-okay." Boudine carefully eased back his shirt from the back of his shoulder and studied the area.

"What?" Bob breathed out.

"S'all dark and blotchy there. But there ain't no hole that I can see."

"There be a lump or a bump then?"

"Lemme see..."

"Easy..."

"Yeah-yeah." Boudine gingerly used two fingers to feel the center of the discolored area. "Um... looks to be a hard bump right here."

Bob grimaced, "S'the lead slug. Gotta get it out 'fore it starts the poisoning."

"How the hell're we gonna do that then, Slye?!"

"You have to do it."

"Me? I ain't never cut on anyone like that a'fore!"

"I have. You saw me do it to my mother's Lakota friend, Ogaleesha, back on her homestead."

"I know, but..."

"I'll talk you through it."

"But what if you pass out or somethin'?"

"Then... you'll have to do it without me."

"Goddamn, Slye."

"Duncan, dammit! The name's Duncan from here on out!"

Boudine stuttered nervously, "Yeah-yeah! Okay-okay. Where do I start?"

"Boil up a coffee tin of water from the creek. You got any of that yarrow grind left?"

"Don't think so. Gave it all to the deputy to give to you."

"Maybe you should take some of that Chinese medicine for yourself," Bob muttered.

"Might you too then."

"No, won't need it."

"We'll see..."

===

Boudine had built a small campfire and was finishing boiling up some water in a coffee tin. "Now what?"

Bob's breath was coming in short pants, "Like what I did to my mother's Lakota friend Ogaleesha. Take your skinnin' blade and stick it in the boiled water, then cut a little opening on top of the bump."

"I know-I know! The injun woman that was really a man. I was there remember? I'm still thinkin' on that one."

Boudine pulled out her skinning knife from the leather sheath on her belt and stuck it into the boiled water. Then, setting the tin down, she sniffed, wiped her nose on her sleeve and slowly positioned the knife blade over the bump in Bob's bruised shoulder.

"I'm gonna cut now," she whispered and started a small slice into his skin.

Bob winced, "Not too deep."

"There's somethin' there, I can see it."

"S'the bullet. Ease it out with the tip of the blade."

"Startin' to bleed pretty bad there..."

"Get it done!" Bob breathed out.

"Okay-okay."

Boudine slowly set the knife tip into the wound and tipped out the lead slug onto the ground, "There! Got it, Slye! Got'er out!"

Bob breathed in and caught some air, then instructed, "Now, get the blade hot in the fire."

"Why?"

"You're goin' to close up both holes."

===

It was pitch black out. Boudine had set out both their bedrolls next to the fire, which she had built up higher. Bob was wrapped into his bedroll asleep. Boudine sat on hers next to him waiting.

Bob stirred, then raised his head and flinched. He looked at his surroundings, then at Boudine, "What happened?"

"You passed out."

"Oh..."

Boudine leaned a bit closer to Bob. "How're you feelin'?"

"Hurtin'," Bob uttered.

"I bet. I seared up them holes pretty good after you passed out. Smelled like a bacon fry."

"Thanks."

"You'll be good as new in no time." There was a wisp of concern in Boudine's voice.

"Hope so," Bob replied with some effort.

"Better get some rest then."

"You too."

"Can't."

"Why not?"

"Too much Chinese medicine, I suspect. Gonna be awake for days, I reckon."

Boudine then sniffed and wiped her nose on her sleeve. Bob rested his head back down into his bedroll and closed his eyes.

"I put some of my pee on your wounds," Boudine said quietly.

Bob's eyes opened wide. "You did what?"

"There ain't no yarrow around to make up a paste out of, so I..."

"I heard you, Boudine!" Bob uttered with some irritation.

Boudine said right back at him, "You tellin' me you ain't never heard about puttin' pee on a cut a'fore?"

"'Course I have!"

"Well, there'ya go then. I'd of used your own pee but I didn't feel like milkin' an old goat there, Slye." With that, Boudine began to chuckle at her own joke.

"Will you stop! It ain't funny t'all!"

"Okay-okay." With that Boudine started to stretch out on her bedroll.

After a moment, in the quiet, with just the crackle of the fire, Bob said, almost in a whisper, "I... I got somethin' to tell you, Boudine."

"What's that then, Slye... *Bob?*"

"When I couldn't find you in Deadwood and there was them wanted posters about with you on'em for robbin' a stagecoach, I..."

"They can't tell it was me, though. The posters had me in my full-on bandana mask!"

"That's true, but I figured you'd gone back to your old ways and..."

Boudine interrupted, getting agitated, "What is it you want to tell me then?"

Bob hesitated, let out a sigh, then uttered slowly, "I wrote me some letters to the Wells Fargo Office and the American Express Office and the newspaper that I..."

Boudine interrupted again, "That you was the Bandit Bob Slye and that you was sorry for robbin' and stealin' and told'em where all our loot was hidden! Ain't that right, Bandit Bob Slye?!"

Bob tried to hunch up on his good elbow. "How'd you know that, Boudine? I didn't tell anyone else!"

"'Cept the damned newspaper which I read, for crissakes!"

"But..."

"*But* nothin'! If it weren't for me, you wouldn't have a cow-flop to your name! And, if it weren't for me, you'd'a been hangin' on that neck-stretcher and buried deep up on Boot Hill now. An' if it weren't for me, you'd be all infected and lead poisoned and I don't know what else!" Boudine stopped for a moment and took a breath. Bob laid his head back down and stared silently up into the darkness. After a few moments, Boudine said, "Now, I got somethin' to tell you. When I seen that story of yourn in the paper, I skedaddled back to Scooptown and bought back that buckboard and the two mules we used to take our takin's up to Lakota Wind Cave in the hills."

"You did that all alone?"

"No, I found that old burned-out prospector we bought it off'n and offered him his rig and mules back free, if'n he'd help me clean out our stuff from the cave, which he did and..."

"Where is it now then?"

"Where no one would think to look for it."

"What about the old prospector, he could..."

"He's just glad he's alive. I put a pistol in his mouth and told him if he breathed a word, I'd tell the Lakota that he was in their sacred cave and that they'd show no mercy on'im."

"But, that ain't true."

"Does he know that?"

"No, I guess he don't."

"Well, there'ya go then. I also told'im about my expert *King-Queen-Ace* shootin' act I did in the Buffalo Bill Cody shows and, if he wanted to keep both his shoulders and forehead from bein' splattered all over, he'd better keep his trap shut. An' I give him a fair count of coins and one of the pistols we took off'n them American Express agents when we robbed the train out of Yankton. Also, give'im a case of cheap whiskey to boot. He was aces-high over that. Hell, he'll be sellin' off his mules and rig again 'fore the chickens come home to roost."

Bob breathed in, then said hoarsely, "I see..."

"Damn, Slye! That all you got to say?"

Bob sighed, then said in almost a whisper, "Don't call me Slye."

DEPUTY OTIS THIGPEN

THREE

A sharp, raspy voice jarred Deputy Otis Thigpen out of his snooze in the chair outside the sheriff's office, "You seen the sheriff there, Otis?"

Otis looked up at the always foul-eyed, pudgy face of the local Justice-of-the- Peace, Judge Raintree. "Ah... oh, 'lo Judge Raintree. I was just..."

The irritated judge interrupted Otis. "I said, have you seen the sheriff about?" The judge asked, quite nastily.

Otis stood up out of his chair and looked down on the shorter man. "No, can't say's I have. He ain't been about since yesterday, since we hung that bandit out there on the hangin' tree..."

"Odd.... You buried the body?"

"Yessir. All tucked in nice'n'neat up on Boot Hill. Anythin' I can do for you there, Judge?"

"No," Raintree snapped. "Just tell'im to look me up soon's he gets back. We got a hangin' comin' this way from over'n Scooptown."

"I will surely do that, sir, I will surely do that. You can count on me, Judge…"

Judge Raintree grumbled, "Mmmm," and started to walk away, then turned back and added tersely, "Best have a coffin ready."

Deputy Thigpen watched him leave, then spit a large slurp of tobacco chaw in the judge's direction. Then, Otis uttered, "Damn!" and skittered into the sheriff's office like he was in a big hurry.

Deputy Thigpen had suddenly remembered, the noose that was to hang the Bandit Bob Slye was dangling unused from the hanging tree limb where he had left it.

===

At the hanging tree, Otis maneuvered the horse and buckboard under the noose, stepped up onto the driver's box and pulled his well-used Bowie knife from the leather sheath on his belt. He quickly cut the empty noose away from the hanging rope and tossed it into the wagon, then slapped the reins on the horse's rump and headed back toward Deadwood.

===

Back at the last jail cell, in the dark corridor just off the front office, Otis shoved a plate of food under the barred cell door to the current occupant… a woman of ill repute. The kind that Sheriff O'Banyon favored arresting, for whatever reason he drummed up, when he felt the urge to whip on someone with his favored English leather riding crop and debase them, as Otis was ordered to hold their arms through the bars until the sheriff had finished.

"Where's the sheriff?" the prostitute demanded. "I ain't been charged with nothin'!"

Otis didn't answer, as he stood up in the narrow, darkened hallway and started to leave. "Hey there, Otis! Goddammit, answer me! I ain't done nothin'!"

"Probably so," Otis mumbled.

The prostitute stepped up and gripped the bars with both hands. "Look, I know what that sick bastard does with the likes of me in here!"

"Not on my account," Otis uttered defensively.

"He calls you *Pignuts* don't he there, Otis?"

"Not no more," Otis muttered under his breath.

"You can't keep me here! It's been two days. For crissakes, I ain't done nothin'! I ain't done nothin'!"

Otis paused, then, "If he ain't back by midday, I'll let you out." With that, Deputy Thigpen turned and left.

===

"Where're we headed?" Bob asked Boudine, as she took a look at his wounds under his soiled shirt.

"Damn, you really stink there, Slye!"

"Thanks."

"I took a look through that carpetbag the deputy give to you. It's got most of your stuff in it, as well as them homestead papers you said you was gonna get for that land next the Pickerings over there in Belle Fourche. Your Peacemaker's there as well."

"But, not the Winchester?"

"Nope... I took that when I made the deal with the deputy to save your sorry hide."

Bob hesitated, then said, "Thank you."

"Hell, didn't think I'd let that 1776 Centennial get lost did'ja? I give that to you for your birthday, remember? 'Bout the same time that rat sheriff dry-gulched you in the box canyon for killin' his wife."

"I didn't kill'er, you did!"

"I did not kill his wife, Slye! You got that wrong!" Boudine protested.

Bob tried to straighten up. "You did your *King-Queen-Ace* on'er! I was there!"

"Oh, I bet you were, *Bandit-Bob-Slye*! I truly bet you were!"

"But.."

"*But* nothin'! You think I'm the only one what knows that shootin' trick? I know I'm better'n most, but... I-did-not-kill-the-sheriff's-wife!"

Bob just stared blankly at Boudine for a long moment. Boudine straightened up and stood over Bob. "Lemme ask you this then. J'you actually see me shoot there, Slye? I mean, did you actually have your blue eyes on me with my six-shooter in my hand?"

Bob went quiet for a moment, then uttered, "No."

"Well, there'ya go then. Now, we're gonna get you cleaned up a'fore we head on out. I'll help you strip off those smelly rags and get you and them into the creek for a wash down.

You got a change of clothes still in your saddlebags. We got a lot of work to do, and you got to look presentable."

===

Deputy Otis Thigpen sat at a single table in the Grand Central Hotel restaurant, eating a breakfast of grits, ham and eggs and coffee. Another nearby customer got up and left his newspaper behind. Otis reached over and took it up to read the headlines.

"Anythin' interesting there, Otis?"

Otis looked up into Lucretia Marchbanks' bright, creased, black face as she readied a pour to freshen his cup. "Nothin' I ain't seen before, Aunt Lou... seems a bit of the dulls goin' on 'round here lately."

"Well, let's hope it keeps that way... but, as my pappy used to sing when thems were all pickin' cotton down there in them Georgia fields, about the man gon' bring the fury down on-ya, 'fore you least expect it. Or somethin' like that. Anyway, I ain't seen the sheriff around for a bit. He eatin' somewhere's else behind my back there, Otis?"

"Beats me. I ain't seen hide-nor-hair of'im since we hung that bandit murderer out on the hangin' tree."

"What was his name anyway? Didn't get to see'im 'fore the sheriff took him away."

"Name of Bandit Bob Slye. Least that's what I carved into the marker I put up there on Boot Hill."

"Well, curiosity's gettin' the best of me there, Otis. Why'd a plain ol' bandit want to kill the sheriff's wife?"

Otis chuckled a bit. "Well, Aunt Lou, you know the ol' sayin' about curiosity killin' the cat."

Lucretia filled Otis's coffee cup and turned to leave. "Well, there, Deputy Thigpen, as you can plainly see, I ain't dead yet," she chided with a crinkly grin.

"That's for sure, Aunt Lou, that's for sure," Otis said with a chuckle and started looking through the newspaper again. Lucretia stopped before heading back into the kitchen and said to Otis, "How many meals you gon' need today for the jail?"

Otis hesitated a bit, then, "Oh... ah... not a one today... jail's flat empty."

Lucretia said, as she pushed through the swinging door to the kitchen, "Well, ain't that somethin'. Now, that is somethin' new for 'round here."

Just then, the Wells Fargo Agent came into the restaurant and walked up to Otis. "Deputy! Been lookin' for you. The sheriff's horse is standin' out front of the sheriff's office and looks pretty banged up. Got the saddle hangin' upside-down around the belly. I looked in the office and there ain't no one there." Otis just stared at the little man for an awkward moment. "Well, ain't you going to do somethin'? It don't look right."

Otis snapped to and hurriedly took up his napkin and wiped his mouth. Got up from the table and headed out the door. "I'll take care of things, you go on your way," he said, as the door slammed back closed.

It was nearly dusk, as Otis drove his one-horse coffin wagon up to the barn next to the Sheriff O'Banyon's home. The sheriff's horse, that the Wells Fargo Agent spoke of, was cinched to the back of the wagon with its saddle stowed in the wagon bed, along with an empty coffin. Otis hurriedly led the horse into the barn and came hustling back to get the saddle.

The late afternoon light sifted through the dirty windows inside O'Banyon's home. Otis gingerly opened the front door and, as if someone were still there, quietly entered and closed the door behind him. He stood there for a moment, not knowing what he should do next. It was deathly still. Otis turned to the window and peered outside, making sure he wasn't being followed. Satisfied, he turned back. The smallish main room was fairly orderly but sparsely furnished. There was a roll top desk and a banker's chair. On the wall behind the desk was a gun rack with several rifles and shotguns in the carriages. Otis went to the desk and rolled the top back to reveal some papers and writing materials. Still nervously looking around, he quickly sifted through the papers but found nothing of interest. He then opened one of the large side drawers and peered inside, reached in and took out a good-sized locked metal box.

Otis set the box on a table beside the open kitchen area and stopped. He looked out the window again. Nothing. No sounds. Still, the hairs on the back of his neck and his forearms bristled, as a shiver went through his body with a sudden fear that Sheriff O'Banyon would burst in and catch him rummaging through his things and thrash him within an inch of his life. Even though he knew the sheriff was shot dead and deep in a grave up on Boot Hill under the name of the Bandit Bob Slye. The years of cruel abuse that he and others had taken from the evil brute had left its scars on him.

Otis used his hunting blade to pry open the metal box. He then took out quite a large bundle of stacked paper currency with one hand and a fistful of gold and silver coins with his other and stared at them. Again, his eyes darted furtively around, as if he'd heard someone coming. No one was. He hastily put the money back into the box, closed it, and held it under his arm as he walked over to what would be the door to the bedroom. Ever so slowly, he opened the door inward and quietly looked inside. He stopped short of going in all the way, when he saw the iron wrist shackles hanging from the top bar of the iron bed headboard. Then, he spotted the leather woven horsewhip and lengths of cut cloth hanging on a peg on the wall. The bed was unmade and some of the sheriff's soiled clothing was tossed in a pile on the rough-hewn board floor. Otis stood there for a moment more, imagining what hurtful things the sheriff's wife must have endured there. He then retreated quietly and closed the door behind him.

Outside, darkness was closing in. Otis set an armload of rifles and guns into the open empty coffin, along with the money box and other items he had taken from the house. He hurriedly set the coffin's top boards in place and pulled a grimy canvas covering over them. Satisfied that he had done what he had to do, Otis stepped up onto the wagon, sat on the driver's box, gathered up the reins and eased the horse into a circle toward the pathway leading back toward Deadwood. As he slowly passed a large wooden pole in the ground, over a head high, he stopped the horse and paused and stared at the iron ring attached to the top with the set of rusted iron wrist shackles looped through it.

The sounds of a woman screaming, "Please don't! Please! I'll be good! I'll be good!" Then the sharp snap of a horsewhip sliced through his brain, as his mind pictured O'Banyon lashing the prostitute's bare back again and again...

Otis put his hand to his mouth, as he remembered, then quietly took out his tin of chewing tobacco and scooped a dollop into his cheek. After a moment of chewing enough to wet it through, he spat a large slurp that arched over onto the whipping post and dripped down over it. He then lightly tapped the reins onto the horse's rump and headed away from the sheriff's home.

Driving the wagon over the rutted path that led back toward Deadwood, Otis suddenly pulled the horse to a stop and jumped down off the driver's box. He hurried to some bushes, bent over them and retched... as the darkness folded in around him.

===

Bob was cleaned up and dressed in his dry ordinary work clothes. Boudine had hung his washed-up gambler's duds over a tree branch and was fashioning a sling for his left arm. As she tied it off on the back of his neck she asked, "Still hurtin'?"

"I'll stand it."

"Want some of my Chinese medicine?"

"Told you a'fore. No."

She finished tying off the sling and came around in front of him. "It really helps."

"No!"

"Well, suit yourself. We got a ways to go yet."

Bob and Boudine rode side-by-side along a seldom-used trail. Bob fought back the pain from his wounds. "You didn't answer me about where we're headed."

"S'right," Boudine answered. "Wasn't sure yet where the best place would be. First thought we'd head back to your Ma's place over Fort Randall way but thought better of it because of her friend that there army fella."

"Sergeant Major Bartholomew," Bob interjected.

"Yeah, him. He had too many questions last time we seen him."

Bob stayed silent, waiting for Boudine to continue.

"So, I recollect that the Pickering's would be a better place for you to be healin' up. Ever since we gave'em that horse and that there Confederate Sharps Carbine we took off that road agent bastard we kilt..."

Bob quickly corrected her, "*You* killed!"

"Oh, that's right, you ain't never kilt no one. I keep forgettin' there, Slye."

"Duncan, dammit!"

"Yeah-yeah, anyway, they never questioned anything about us after that, so I thought it better we head their way. S'ides, you got that paper for the homestead land next to'em."

Bob went quiet, as they rode slowly along.

After a moment, Boudine asked, "You like my plan?"

"S'only one we got."

THE PICKERING'S

FOUR

Since Bob and Boudine's recent visit to the Pickering family homestead in Belle Fourche, near thirty miles north of Deadwood as the crow flies, Nathan Pickering had nearly completed adding the hand-hewn board siding and roof to the barn that Bob had helped him erect the frames for, when Boudine had decided she didn't want any part of settling down and left for Deadwood and parts unknown. At least that's what she had indicated to Bob.

As Abigail Pickering came up from the nearby river carrying two buckets of water, the Pickering children, Ben and his sister Sarah, lugged another sawed board over to where their father was climbing down off his ladder.

"Come get some water you three," Abigail called out. Ben and Sarah dropped the board and dashed over to their mother, as their hound woke from a slumber and scampered over to them.

"Me first," Sarah announced and took the ladle from one of the buckets.

Just then, their hound spotted something on the path to the riverbank and started barking a warning, as he advanced toward the path. The family all looked around. Boudine and Bob on horseback came into view.

"Oh, my goodness! Abigail started to say, "It's..."

"Bob and Boudine!" young Ben announced excitedly and ran to the two riders.

Boudine and Bob reigned up as Ben came running to them. Boudine uttered to Bob, "Let me do the talkin'."

Ben spotted the sling on Bob's arm. "You're hurt," he said and turned to his family, "Bob's hurt!"

===

Bob sat at the Pickering's kitchen table, as the others hovered around him. He let Abigail tentatively ease back his shirt. "Let's have a look-see here." Bob winced a bit as she gently peeled back the torn cloth pads Boudine had placed over the back and front shoulder wounds. Some of the scabbed over skin had stuck to the cloth. Abigail expressed some concern, "That's pretty mean lookin' there and it ain't smellin' too good neither." Then, Abigail ordered, "Sarah boil me some water then fetch me some cloth bandage I keep in the cupboard and the jar of camphor ointment."

Boudine spoke up, "Somethin' wrong?"

Abigail stepped back and said to Bob, "Might remove your shirt there, Bob."

Bob realized that it was easier said than done. "Might need a little help here, Boudine."

Boudine quickly started to help Bob out of his shirt. Abigail asked, "What'd you use on the wounds there, Boudine?"

"I would'a used yarrow grind had we had some, but we didn't so I used..." she stopped short.

Bob answered for her, "She used her pee."

Young Ben stifled a laugh.

Nathan Pickering scolded him a bit, "Ben, stop."

"Yessir."

Abigail looked over to Sarah who was boiling water in a kettle on the woodstove. "How's it comin' there?"

"Near done."

Abigail turned to Boudine, as Boudine gently removed Bob's shirt. "Doin' what you did was the right thing in a pinch, Boudine. I might've done the same thing if'n the need arose."

Ben stifled another laugh.

Abigail looked right at Ben. "Isn't that right, Ben?"

Ben flushed red a bit, then uttered seriously, "Yes ma'am..."

"Sealin' up the wounds with a fired hot knife was good thinkin'. But it don't always stop the infection from takin' over. So, we'll just make sure here that we give'em a good chance to heal up right.

===

An early morning fall frost dusted the buried mounds of those who had ended up on Boot Hill in Deadwood. Under an overcast sky, Deputy Otis Thigpen finished digging a shallow trench on the far side of the dreary graveyard. Next to him, was the coffin he had filled with the goods he had taken from O'Banyon's house.

Otis looked around apprehensively, then eased the covered wooden coffin into the shallow ditch. He furtively looked around again, then started shoveling dirt into the ditch and onto the coffin.

===

As Lucretia Marchbanks walked handily along the boardwalk toward her restaurant at the Grand Central Hotel, she stopped and turned at the sound of Otis's coffin wagon heading toward the sheriff's office in the early morning light. "Hey there, Otis," she called out as she waved him down. Otis reined the horse and wagon to a stop. "You're up and about early there, Otis."

"Yes ma'am. Things to do," he uttered as he looked back over his shoulder.

"Be seein' you for breakfast then?"

"Most likely not today, Aunt Lou. Gotta hangin' comin' from over Scooptown way."

"Is the sheriff back then?"

"Ain't seen'im yet."

"Well then, there's a gentleman name of Seth Bullock been lookin' for him and you as well I suspect. Asked me to pass the word."

Otis glanced around nervously. "Don't know that name. He say what he wanted?"

"Just that he wanted to speak to you both as soon's he could and that it was important. He looked like a pretty dapper well-off man. Seems he's been seen around with Al Swearengen over t'the Gem Theater and t'other important townsfolk. Seems there was a big meetin' yesterday with'em all. That's it, s'far as I know. But somethin's goin' on there, Otis. I can feel it in my bones."

Otis's expression darkened noticeably. "I best be gettin' to it, Aunt Lou."

Lucretia took notice. "Alright then, you take care, Otis," she said with some concern. "You take care, hear?"

"Yes ma'am."

With that, Otis reined the horse and empty coffin wagon toward the end of town, as Lucretia Marchbanks watched him go.

===

Nathan stood with Bob next to the entrance to the new barn. Out of earshot, the children were gathered on the front porch of the Pickering's cabin at the feet of their mother, who was seated in a thatched rocking chair reading aloud to them from a book.

"How're you feelin' there, Bob?" Nathan inquired rather guardedly.

"Better'n before. Abigail knows her medicine business."

"She does. She does that, indeed... her father was a healer back in the day."

"Oh? I didn't know that."

"Yes, indeed... lucky for us. Yes, indeed," Nathan said stiffly.

Both were silent for a long moment, then Bob said, "Nathan, I'm supposin' you want to know more about what happened to us."

"Well, I'm thinkin' it might be more serious than just runnin' up against a road agent... or, then again, it might not be. Maybe, just none of my beeswax, but I do have my family to consider here."

"You do, Nathan, you do." Bob looked over at Abigail and the children who were deep into their book learning with their mother. Bob paused and walked into the open barn. Nathan followed.

"There is such a possibility that there is more to the story. But I can assure you that there ain't nothin' that can reflect on you or your family in any way."

Nathan looked at Bob and waited for more.

Bob looked over at the chair and worktable set out in the middle of the barn. "Do you mind if I have a seat, Nathan? I'm feelin' a bit..."

"No-no!" Nathan said with some alarm and hastened to pull the chair around for Bob. "I'm sorry there, Bob! I shouldn't have been so…"

Bob sat rather stiffly onto the chair. "S'all right. You have every right to know."

Nathan pulled up a nail keg and sat down to listen.

SETH BULLOCK

FIVE

"Goddammit, Pignuts! Pull'er tighter! The bitch is tryin' to wiggle away from me!" *A drunken Sheriff Jack O'Banyon roared from inside the dark jail cell. On the other side of the bars, Otis held tight to the prostitute's wrists and pulled on them through the bars tighter. The woman's dress and undergarments were torn away. O'Banyon laughed loudly and patted her bare buttocks. He then reared back and brought his trusty bloodstained English leather riding crop lashing down on the poor woman. With each slicing lash, she screamed and pleaded louder and louder for him to stop. Her screams and cries of distress echoed through the jail.* "Pull harder, Pignuts! Pull harder you piece of dog shite! Pull harder!" "Hello?... Anyone here?... Hello?...

"Are you back there, Sheriff?"

Otis blinked his eyes open from a dead sleep dream, where he was laid out on a cot in an open jail cell.

"Are you back there, Sheriff O'Banyon?"

A man's voice had entered the jail cell hallway. Otis snapped out of it and jumped to his feet. "Who's there?" he called out, as he tentatively entered the hallway and spotted the outline of a man standing in the office doorway, with the noon light shining behind him.

Otis stopped. "Sheriff ain't here. Who be askin' there?"

"I'm Seth Bullock. I'd like to speak with..."

Otis interrupted and approached the entrance. "Have a seat in there."

The man retreated into the sheriff's office. Otis followed.

Otis indicated a chair in front of O'Banyon's desk. "Set yerself there." Otis circled around and took a seat in the chair behind the sheriff's desk. As Otis eyed the man sitting in the chair opposite him, he could see that Seth Bullock was a rather imposing individual in his neatly tailored dark suit and well-groomed appearance, including his large trimmed black mustache. In the most authoritative voice he could muster, Otis asked, "Who might you be and what do you want of the sheriff?"

Seth Bullock stifled a smile and said seriously, "I'm Seth Bullock and I might ask you the same thing, sir. Although, I see by your badge there that you must be the deputy here."

"I am that, sir. Deputy Otis Thigpen," he announced and nervously cleared his throat.

"I see," said Bullock, as he studied Otis for a moment, then he stated, "Well, Deputy Thigpen, I am rather new to these parts and I am here setting up several new business ventures. I've been working with the town's leaders toward these endeavors and, also getting to know who is who in Deadwood."

It did not go unnoticed to Bullock that Otis seemed very uneasy. His hand was trembling a bit, and he was beginning to sweat profusely.

"The sheriff ain't here," Otis repeated.

"I can see that. I understand from my conversation with the lady who runs the eating establishment at the Grand Hotel..."

"Aunt Lou," Otis interjected.

"Oh, she said her name is..."

"Aunt Lou! That's what she's known as." Otis wiped a bead of sweat from his brow.

Bullock adjusted himself in his chair. "Well, she did tell me that Sheriff O'Banyon has not been seen for several days now and..."

"Two days!"

"Ah, yes, he..."

Otis snapped, "He ain't been seen near two days now."

"I see. Well, Deputy Thigpen, can you tell me when was the last time you saw the sheriff? I understand his horse showed up here and..."

"Who're you to be askin' all these questions? You the law or somethin'?"

Bullock's expression hardened some. "Not yet, Mister Thigpen. But soon."

Bullock stood and said, "Mister Thigpen, I'm not going into the changes that are going to take place here in Deadwood just yet, but I can assure you that some changes are about to be made."

Otis just blinked and said nothing. Bullock then told him in no uncertain terms, "I want you to lead me out to the sheriff's home. You will be paid for your time." With that, Bullock left the office with a shaken Otis Thigpen sitting there behind Sheriff O'Banyon's desk.

===

Bob and Boudine watered their horses at the Pickering riverbank.

"You did what?!" Boudine exclaimed out loud.

Bob hushed her up. "Easy there, Boudine. I didn't say I told Nathan everythin' we were about, but he was getting itchy about how I got wounded. Sayin' we was held up by a road agent didn't seem to be holdin' water."

"Holy shite, Slye, how much did you tell'im?"

"Will you just simmer down there some? I just told'im enough to stop him from askin' more. He ain't a stupid man, Boudine. Remember, he already figured out how we got that horse we gave him back when we met up with them on the trail when they was travelin' here."

Boudine seethed, "Well're you gonna keep me in the dark here, Slye, or am I gonna have to reach down your throat and pull it outta you?"

Bob looked back at the pathway to the Pickering homestead then took a breath. "One thing I didn't say was anything about me bein' the Bandit Bob Slye, if that's what you're thinkin'."

"Well, I sure as hell hope not."

"But you got to stop callin' me Slye, you hear? They hear you call me that and..."

Boudine held up her hand, "I know-I know! I'm workin' on it. Now, what the hell did you tell'im?"

Bob sighed, took a breath, and said in a lowered voice, "I lied to the man..."

Boudine stepped back in mocked surprise. "Oh-my-God! May the heavens open up and lightnin' come down and strike you dead!" Then she said with a sarcastic chuckle, "I sure as hell hope you did!"

"This ain't funny, Boudine."

"I ain't laughin' there... *Bob*..."

He hesitated for a moment until Boudine said, "So, what was this big lie you told'im?"

"I told'im I was bushwhacked on the trail to Belle Fourche by a drunken gambler who I'd cleaned out at the tables in Deadwood the night before and that you drew down on'im and sent him to his eternal hell."

Boudine's horse bobbed its head up from drinking down its thirst. Boudine patted its head and just studied Bob for a moment, then said rather quietly, "Sort of what happened to Wild Bill Hickok."

"Only I didn't die."

Boudine gathered up the reins of both horses. "What'd you say about me then?"

"Nothin' else 'cept I was lucky you'd decided to come along this time."

Boudine turned the horses around toward the path back to the Pickering's, "So, you didn't tell'im I took the sheriff down with my *King-Queen-Ace* shots..."

"No... no, I didn't."

They headed back toward the homestead.

"Good... that's a good thing."

===

It was late afternoon when Otis pulled the coffin wagon to a stop next to the barn at Sheriff Jack O'Banyon's home. Without saying a word Seth Bullock, who was following quietly from behind, reined in his horse and dismounted. He stepped out in front of Otis's wagon and looked around. The post with the iron ring at the top and the rusted wrist shackles looped through it caught his eye.

"What's this here?"

Otis hesitated...

"Well, Otis, what is this used for?"

Otis's eyes darted around, then he uttered under his breath, "It's the whippin' post."

"Speak up, I didn't hear you."

Otis cleared his throat and said, "It's the sheriff's whippin' post..."

Bullock studied the post for a moment, then turned toward the house across the open yard. "Get down and follow me," he said firmly to Otis, who again hesitated then got down from the wagon and followed Bullock to the hitching rail in front of the house. Bullock wrapped his horse's reins around it, stepped up onto the porch and headed for the front door. Bullock knocked on the closed door. It opened slightly. He slowly pushed on the door, opening it further. Otis instinctively backed away a step. Bullock then opened the door fully and said to Otis, "Follow me."

"Nossir," Otis said.

Bullock turned toward Otis. "What's wrong?"

"I ain't never been inside before," Otis answered nervously.

"Well, you're with me. Come."

"Nossir! Sheriff O'Banyon never would let me inside his home."

"You've never been inside, all the time you've been his deputy?"

"S'right. He never allowed it."

Bullock hesitated, then said, "Well, I'm ordering you to be with me as a witness to anything I might find in there. Hear me, Otis?"

Otis blanched, looked quickly around, then tentatively followed Bullock inside.

Bullock stood in the middle of the sparsely furnished front room of Sheriff Jack O'Banyon's house. Otis watched nervously from just inside the opened front doorway. Bullock went to the roll top desk that Otis had left open. He then looked into the large side drawer that Otis had not closed. Then Bullock looked up at the empty gun rack on the wall behind the desk. "Gun rack's empty. Desk looks rummaged in." Bullock turned around and indicated the closed bedroom door. "That the bedroom?" he asked Otis. Otis hesitated. "Oh, that's right. You've never been inside here before… right Otis?"

Otis answered in a near whisper, "Yessir."

Bullock eased open the bedroom door and stepped inside. Otis didn't move. After a moment, Bullock called out, "Come in here, Otis."

Otis timidly came to the bedroom doorway. Bullock gestured to the wrist shackles hanging from the iron headboard and then to the horsewhip and cloth bindings hanging from the peg on the wall. "I want you to see what I'm seeing here, Otis." Otis was silent. "Did you know about the goings on here, Otis?" Otis gulped but didn't answer. Bullock pressed him, "Otis, it's important. If you know something, tell me."

Otis managed to offer, "I've heard stories..."

"So have I, Otis. So have I."

Outside the house, dusk was beginning to settle in. Bullock stepped down off the front porch. Otis closed the front door. As he stepped off the porch, Bullock indicated something toward the edge of the clearing, nearly blocked by overgrown weeds. "What's that mound over there? Looks to be a grave of some sort."

Otis said, "'Tis the missus..."

"The sheriff's wife who was murdered?"

"Yessir."

Bullock took a few steps closer. "There doesn't seem to be a marker."

"That's the way the sheriff wanted it."

"So, did you bury the coffin, Otis?"

Otis took a moment to answer, then uttered, "No coffin."

Bullock was quiet for a bit, then said, "I see." He then gathered his horse's reins from the hitching post and started toward the barn. "Walk with me." Otis followed along.

Inside the small barn, Bullock walked up to the stall where the sheriff's horse was kept. Otis stood nearby. "This horse needs watering and feed."

"I'll see to it."

Bullock looked down into the stall. "When was the last time you swamped out this stall?"

"T'wasn't my job. T'was the missus job."

"I see. Then, I suggest you bring it to the livery in town. I'll see to it that its keep is taken care of. Bring the tack as well. Never know, the sheriff might actually show up."

"Yessir.'

"Otis... what was the name of the killer?"

Otis was taken aback... "I..."

"The killer who murdered the sheriff's wife. What was his name?"

"Ah... they called him Bandit Bob Slye."

"And he was hung by the sheriff?"

Otis seemed perplexed by the questions. "Yessir."

"Was there a trial?"

Confused, Otis hesitated.

"Otis, was there a proper trial?"

Otis flinched a bit, then said, "It was Judge Raintree what signed the hangin' paper."

"That was it?"

"Yessir."

"You were there?"

"Yessir."

"And you were at the hanging as well?"

"Yessir... out at the sheriff's hangin' tree."

Bullock took this in, then said, "And you buried the killer up on Boot Hill, I presume."

"Yessir, I did. That's what I do."

"This Judge Raintree.... Is he a real judge?"

"Sir?"

Bullock brushed it off. "Never mind. Tell me, Otis, how long have you been a deputy sheriff?"

Otis tried to hide a gulp then answered with, "'Bout when the sheriff showed up in Deadwood."

Bullock walked to the open barn door. "It's getting late. I should get back before dark." He then turned back to Otis. "Otis, there are going to be quite a few changes in Deadwood, starting right away. First, I have been assigned by the town leadership to take over, temporarily, the job of Sheriff of Deadwood. I will be at it until the new marshal, name of Wyatt Earp, arrives. Have you heard of Marshal Earp?"

Otis replied quietly, "Nossir."

"Not sure exactly when he'll be arriving. Supposed to be coming in from Tombstone, I've been told. So, the law will be up to me until he does. Now, I understand that before you were hired by O'Banyon, you did not have any law experience, is that correct?"

Otis didn't answer...

"Have you ever arrested anyone yourself, since you started wearing that deputy badge?"

Otis couldn't quite grasp what was happening.

Bullock turned and walked out of the barn. Otis followed. "In fact, I was given to understand that you worked as a swamper and did odd jobs at the Gem Theater and brothel, as well as some of the other brothels in town. Am I correct?"

Otis had trouble catching his breath. Bullock walked to his horse and continued talking. "With this new arrangement, we won't be needing your deputy services any longer. Please stop by the sheriff's office tomorrow and turn in your badge. I will pay you for your time today and anything you are owed up to this point."

Bullock mounted his horse. "With regard to O'Banyon, he is no longer the Sheriff of Deadwood. So, if he doesn't return, or if he does, it really doesn't matter. Also, if you want your old job back at the Gem, I'm quite sure Al Swearengen will hire you on again. Seems he's been having trouble keeping a good swamper on and the working girls are complaining that their rooms and potties aren't being cleaned enough after they get through with their doings. I'll be staying at the Gem until I find a more permanent living arrangement, so you can usually find me there if the need be. Also, I imagine the job of tending to Boot Hill can still be yours if you wish. Thank you for your time, Otis. You've been very helpful." With that, Bullock headed his horse back onto the trail toward Deadwood.

Otis stood next to his coffin wagon in shock.

===

Bob and Boudine sat at the Pickering dinner table. Abigail said to Bob, "That wound of yours seems to be coming along. Should be healed up in no time. I'll have another look-see in the mornin'."

"I can't thank you enough for all you've done."

Abigail brushed it off. "Don't be silly. T'ain't nothin'. But I do wish we had a bit more room for you instead of putting you up in the barn."

Nathan Pickering interjected, "I believe Bob here has a bit of good news for us."

"Oh?" said Abigail.

"What-what?" said the children together excitedly. Bob glanced at Boudine, who was expressionless, then said, "Well, I did take your advice, Nathan, and took out the Homestead Claim papers on the parcel next to yours and..."

"We'll be neighbors!" Ben shouted. Sarah jumped up and ran around behind Boudine to give her a big hug. Boudine tried but could not suppress a smile.

"Oh, my goodness, that is wonderful news. Praise the Lord!" Abigail pronounced.

===

Seth Bullock sat at a table in the Grand Central Hotel Restaurant in Deadwood, having breakfast with Calamity Jane, the famous trick shot artist.

"Are you planning on staying in Deadwood, Miss Jane?"

"I suspect I will be stickin' around some. Gettin' a bit tired of the travelin' show life. Also, without Wild Bill Hickok, it ain't quite the same for me of late."

"You were quite close then?"

Jane took a breath, then added, "You could say that."

Lucretia Marchbanks came by with her coffeepot. "Freshen' up?"

Bullock put his hand over his cup. Jane nodded yes.

As Lucretia poured, Seth asked her, "By the way, ma'am, have you seen that Deputy Otis Thigpen around?"

"Nossir, I haven't. Not since yesterday mornin'. Gettin' a bit worried 'bout him of late."

"Why's that, ma'am?"

"He's been actin' a bit out of sorts since the sheriff went missin'."

"I see. Well, if you do see him, please tell 'im I'll be at the sheriff's office until around noon. He was to meet me there."

"Yessir, I surely will." With that, Lucretia went about refreshing coffees for other customers.

Concerned, Bullock pulled out his pocket watch and checked the time.

"Something wrong?" Jane asked.

"Hope not."

===

Bob stood with Nathan at the boundary of Bob's homestead location, in a wooded area, where Ben pounded a stake into the ground with a large wooden mallet. Nathan was quite cheerful. "Well, sir, this be your first provin' up on your own homestead. If I were a drinkin' man, I'd offer up a toast of congratulations."

"Thank you both. It is a start that is for sure."

"Would you still be thinkin' about buildin' a tradin' post then?"

'It is still a thought, but I better be lookin' for a spot to build a cabin first." Then, he referred to his wounded shoulder. "Well, at least lookin' for a spot anyway. Won't be buildin' much 'fore this is healed."

Nathan held up a hand, "Don't you worry none. I owe you a frame-up like you helped me with on the new barn."

The clatter of Abigail's triangle meal call came ringing out from the Pickering home. Ben dropped the mallet and broke into a run toward the sound.

===

"Sorry, I'm late." Boudine said, as she came bustling through the front door of the Pickering cabin. Bob was seated at the table eating lunch with the rest of the family. Boudine unloaded a pouch full of fresh killed game hens onto the sideboard next to the sink in the kitchen area.

"Oh, look at those! Bless you, Sally Mae! Now, you set yourself right next to me here before all these vittles gets cold. We can feather those after we eat."

The distant rumble of a storm was heard. Nathan said, "We'd better batten down the hatches. Sounds like there's going to be some weather upon us around nightfall. I'm thinkin' you folks better settle into the schooner wagon 'til this blows over. We haven't had rain since we got the roof on the barn to test for leaks. Ben and I will make sure the bonnet is secured and..."

Ben butted in with, "And make sure there ain't no more skunks in there!"

Abigail admonished her son, "Ben!"

"Well, there were..."

Nathan stifled a chuckle, as well as Bob.

===

In the dead of night, wind and rain whipped around the prairie schooner covered wagon. Suddenly, a huge bolt of lightning and a crack of thunder split the sky and shattered the darkness with a flash of blinding light over the homestead.

Inside the wagon, Boudine jolted from a sound sleep in her bedroll. "Holy Shite!" she shouted, as another thunderclap and lightning flash illuminated the wagon's canvas bonnet. Bob rolled over and uttered, "That was close."

Boudine scooted up to the front opening and pulled back the cloth covering to look outside, as yet another bolt of lightning struck overhead. "Someone's out there!" she exclaimed to Bob.

"What?"

"There's someone out there in a buckboard!"

Bob hunched himself up beside Boudine, and looked out through the opening, as a flash of light crackled across the dark sky. "See. Right over there. See'im?"

"Maybe he needs help."

"You stay right here. You ain't helpin' nobody with that shoulder. I'll see to it." With that, Boudine grabbed her pistol, wrapped her poncho around herself and climbed out of the wagon into the downpour.

The lightning had traveled away some and left only a few stutters of light behind. Boudine walked cautiously toward the silhouetted driver and horse. He was seated on the driver's box of a buckboard, hunched over as the steady rain splattered down on his soaked hat and tattered poncho. Boudine held her pistol near waist high, ready to shoot should the situation call for it. "Who be there?" she called out over the receding thunder.

"It's me, Miss Boudine... Otis Thigpen..."

"Who is it?" Bob called out from the covered wagon.

Boudine answered as she approached the buckboard, "Says he's Otis Thigpen."

Bob gingerly stepped through the wagon flap and down onto the ground.

Boudine lowered her pistol and stepped closer to Otis. "What the hell're you doin' way out here, Otis?"

As the thunder and lightning flashes clattered off into the distance, Bob stepped up in the darkness beside Boudine. "That you there, Otis?"

"Yessir, Mister Bob. Yessir, it is."

"What're you doin' way out here then?"

"Just asked'im that," said Boudine.

Otis fumbled for an answer, just as Nathan came out onto the front porch of his house holding up a lantern and shouted over the swirling wind and rain, as the family hound joined him and started barking. "What's all the commotion there?"

Boudine answered quickly and called out to him, "It's alright here, Nathan. Just a man we know lookin' for shelter."

"Well, he's welcome to put up in the barn there. I'll see you all come mornin'. Have to help Abigail calm the children." With that Nathan and the hound went back inside.

===

Inside the darkened barn, with Boudine's help, Otis started unhitching the horse from his coffin wagon. He spoke nervously, "Things be changin' fast in Deadwood. A man name of Seth Bullock took over as sheriff and there be a marshal name of Wyatt Earp comin' soon to take over the law."

"First off, Otis, these folks here are good Christian folks. They know nothin' about who we really are and what we done. All they know is that Bob here got wounded in a gunfight with a drunk gambler and that's it, you hear me? They know nothin' about the sheriff gettin' kilt and they know nothin' about my *King-Queen-Ace* shootin' that did the killin', you understand me there, Otis? They don't know nothin' more'n that!"

"Yes ma'am, I understand."

"We'll be talkin' more come daylight. Just keep your mouth shut about anythin' else, you hear?"

"Yes ma'am."

"Is anyone chasin' you, Otis?" Bob asked.

"No... not yet."

"What's that mean, *not yet?*" Boudine quickly asked.

"I left before nightfall, and it started stormin'. No one knows I'm gone."

"Alright, then this'll keep 'til mornin'," Bob said and started toward the barn door.

As Boudine turned to leave, she said to Otis, "Not a word, you hear?"

"No ma'am, not a word."

Boudine stopped at the barn door and turned back. "Why're you carryin' a coffin there, Otis?"

"Jes-jes some things I might be needin'," he stuttered.

Boudine left and closed the barn door behind her.

===

The early grays of dawn crept up over the Pickering homestead. A rooster let out its first crow of the day. Otis

Thigpen had already risen and rolled up his poncho and was leading his horse between the wagon shafts to hitch it up when he froze at the sight before him. There, standing in the slightly opened barn doorway, with the dim light behind him, stood young Ben Pickering staring at him.

"Are you a sheriff?" Ben asked Otis apprehensively. A bewildered Otis replied, "Wussat?"

"Is that a sheriff's badge you're wearin'?"

"Deputy," Otis muttered, as his hand went up to the badge still pinned to his shirt. "Well... not no more it ain't."

"Then why're you wearin' it then?" Ben asked abruptly.

"Forgot to take it off," Otis told him, then started to unpin the badge.

"Can I have it?" Ben asked flatly.

Otis finished unpinning the badge and said, "Don't see why not. T'aint no good to me no more." He then handed the badge toward Ben who quickly grabbed it and ran out of the barn. Otis stood there for a moment then turned back to hitching up the horse.

Bob and Boudine walked toward the barn, as Ben came scooting out and passed them without a word. "Mornin' there,

Ben," said Bob, as Ben skittered behind the cabin into the semidarkness. "Always in a big hurry, that one."

Boudine and Bob entered the barn as Otis finished cinching up the leathers to the horse. "'Mornin' there, Otis," Bob said.

Otis mumbled, "'Mornin'."

Boudine added, "So... are you gonna tell us what the hell's goin' on with you or are we gonna have to hogtie you and..."

Otis snapped at Boudine, "Already tol'ja there's big changes takin' place in Deadwood!"

"What changes, Otis?" Bob asked.

Boudine interjected, "You said somethin' 'bout a new sheriff."

"Yes ma'am, that be the case."

"Who is he?" Bob asked.

"Name of Seth Bullock," Otis said, then paused.

"Well, come on there, Otis, who is this Bullock?" Boudine prodded.

"He be a well-to-do businessman who the other townsmen put him in charge, because Sheriff O'Banyon went missin'. Least that's what he told me out at the sheriff's house day last."

Flabbergasted, Boudine exclaimed, "You what? You talked to him?"

"Yes ma'am, he made me take'im out to the sheriff's house for a look-see and for me to tend to the sheriff's horse."

"Dad-blasted!" Boudine uttered.

Bob put his hand on Boudine's arm. "Easy..." Then to Otis he asked, "What else did he say?"

"He made it be known that I was not a deputy no more and that Mr. Swearengen would hire me on at the Gem Theater as a swamper again and a rat catcher."

"What else?" Boudine demanded.

"He-he asked a lot of questions about what the sheriff was up to and how much I knew 'bout what he did with the women and what happened to his wife."

"What'd you say, Otis?"

"Nothin'. He saw the missus's grave and..."

"Shite!"

"Wait," Bob said to Boudine, then he asked Otis, "Was that all?"

"Nossir, he wanted to know about the hangin' and if I buried you up on Boot Hill, I mean the Bandit Bob Slye."

Just then, Nathan entered the barn. "Well, who do we have here then?"

Bob stepped aside from Boudine and Otis and introduced Otis to Nathan. "This here's a friend of ours from over Deadwood way, Otis Thigpen. Otis, this is Nathan Pickering. He's been a big help to us."

As Nathan shook hands with Otis, he asked, "Well, you're a ways from Deadwood there, Otis. Where 'bouts you headed?"

Otis gulped a bit, then uttered, "Not sure's'yet. Maybe Spearfish or Lead..."

"Well, sir, 'can't say's I blame you. Deadwood can be a nasty place indeed."

"Yessir... yessir, it can be..."

Nathan stopped for a moment, then eyeing Otis asked tentatively, "Ah... have we met before? You do look a bit familiar."

Ben peeked in from outside and listened unnoticed by the others.

"Don't reckon we have, sir..."

"He's a deputy sheriff!" Ben blurted out.

They all turned toward Ben who stepped into the barn and pulled at the badge pinned to his shirt. "See!"

"Ben, you..." Nathan started to say.

"It be okay. I give it to him this mornin'. I forgot to take it off, since I ain't a deputy no more."

Nathan turned to Otis. "That's it. We did meet once or twice at the Deadwood Sheriff's Office. We tried diggin' for gold in the hills for a short bit, until our minin' equipment was stolen. I remember going to the sheriff's office to report the theft and you were there. And I believe it was you who told me that'd be like lookin' for a needle in a haystack tryin' to find out who the thieves were."

"Well... yessir, that would've been 'bout the size of it. T'were'n't much sense tellin' you different."

Nathan brightened as he spoke, "Look, we owe you a debt of thanks for helping steer this family away from a debtor's path onto a much better road. Now, you unhitch that wagon and spend some time here so's you can get your bearings. I'll tell Abigail to set another place. With that, Nathan headed toward the barn door and good-naturedly commanded Ben, "Scat, you!"

THE GEM

SIX

Al Swearengen, owner of the Gem Theater, gambling hall and brothel, stood on the planked walkway in front of the theater entrance talking with Seth Bullock. "Otis's been here most of his life. Was dropped off here when he was just a nipper. Mother was a workin' girl far as I knew. Not here, but from somewhere's else. She wanted a job, but my clientele don't cotton to women with kids. So, she just up and left him here right on this spot. Some of the ladies took turns watchin' over him and I give him a job catchin' rats and swampin' out the rooms for his keep. T'was the Madam here and Lucretia Marchbanks over at the Grand Hotel taught'im to read and write some so's he could get along. He never caused no trouble s'far's I know. Sheriff O'Banyon needed a hand over at the jail so I give him over and O'Banyon give him a deputy badge to make'im feel good, but he wasn't a real deputy.

Built a good coffin 'though. Tended to Boot Hill for extra wages."

"Well, Al, he seems to have up and disappeared. Along with O'Banyon. A bit odd I'd say."

"Oh, he'll turn up. He don't have no other place to go to earn a livin'. Pretty much a good-for-nothin'."

"Still, it's all a bit odd to me."

"Well, you are the new sheriff there, Seth. It's all in your bailiwick now," Al said with a chuckle.

"Yeah, thanks. When's Wyatt Earp supposed to take over here?"

"Hell, if I know. Maybe never. Haven't heard back as yet."

"Great... remind me to punch you in the nose for giving me this job."

"I'll do that, Seth, I'll do that."

With that, the two men parted ways with a mutual chuckle.

Seth stopped and called back to Swearengen, "By the way, the more I dig into this, the more I'm findin' out that O'Banyon was doing more than just a sheriff's business."

Swearengen turned and smiled a warning back at Seth. "I wouldn't dig too deep there, Seth, you might find somethin' you shouldn't." He then walked into the Gem Theater.

===

Bob, Boudine and Otis stood at the riverbank watering their horses. Bob asked, "Otis... just how'd you know to come here?"

Boudine spoke up, "Yeah, Otis, who tol'ja we was here?"

Otis's horse jerked at its reins and halter. Otis gave it more lead so it could drink easier, "No one told me where you was. When I gathered up Mister Bob's belongin's the day you was to be hanged, I saw them homestead papers of yourn an' figured that's where you'd all be headed. I didn't know 'bout these folks bein' next door to your claim. Just figured I might run into y'all someplace here-abouts."

"And then what, Otis? What was your plan then?" Boudine insisted.

Otis took a deep breath then answered, "I don't have one."

"So, why didn't you just stay there in Deadwood? Be a lot easier than tryin' to set up somewheres new."

Otis looked away for a moment...

"Otis?" she uttered.

"I... I took some things from the sheriff's house."

"You what?!" Boudine exclaimed loudly.

Bob stopped her and tried to calm her down. "Wait-wait! What kind of things, Otis?"

Otis suddenly became defensive, "Not nothin' I wasn't owed! Just things for all the shite I had to do all the time!"

Bob shushed both of them. "Alright-alright. Let's not get all heated up now. Just have an easy talk here, so's we can see what to do about all this. Let me ask you this, Otis... who else would care if you took your leave from Deadwood?"

Otis thought for a brief moment then said, "Guess Aunt Lou..."

"Who's Aunt Lou?" Boudine quickly asked.

Bob answered for him, "I know who she is. She ain't a worry. Who else, Otis?"

"Might be Mister Swearengen over at the Gem... maybe. An' that Seth Bullock who's gon' be the new sheriff. He was sure askin' a lot of questions of me an' I was supposed to meet him over to the sheriff's office to leave my badge an' he was gonna pay me what I was owed and ask Mister Swearengen to give me a swampin' job."

"That's it then?" Boudine asked.

"Think so..."

"Is that justice-of-the-peace still around?" Bob asked.

"What justice-of-the-peace?" Boudine asked impatiently.

"Roy Raintree," Otis answered. "He be the one what signed your hangin' paper."

"Dammit!" Boudine uttered.

"But Mr. Bullock said he weren't gon' be used around Deadwood no more."

"Why's that?" Bob asked.

"Didn't say, but he got a bit ruffled when he spoke of him and said as much... Asked if he were a real judge."

Bob and Boudine looked at each other for a moment.

"What're you thinkin' there, Bob?" Boudine asked.

"Just ponderin' for now. Just ponderin'."

With that, they turned the horses toward the Pickerings and started back along the pathway.

"I want to show you somethin', Otis," Bob said.

Otis and Bob stood next to the homestead stake that Ben had pounded into the ground to mark Bob's claim.

"This is it, Otis... one-hundred-and-sixty acres."

"All yours?"

"Yes, it is. All legally."

"What'chu gon' do with all this?"

"Well, prove up by buildin' a cabin first then maybe a tradin' post closer to the river."

Otis paused for a moment, then said, "That be quite a big undertakin'."

"That's why I have a proposition to make to you, Otis."

"Me?"

"Yessir... if you want, I'd like to offer you a job helpin' me get started here. Then, if you decide you like the situation, we can build you a place nearby of your own and, I'm sure the Pickerings would be happy for any help you could give them as well."

Otis seemed a bit overwhelmed, "What... what does Miss Boudine think about all this?"

Bob paused, then said, "Ain't spoke of it yet."

===

Abigail bustled a large bowl to the table where everyone had gathered for the noon meal, including a very quiet Otis who sat next to Bob. "This venison stew should stick to your ribs for the rest of the day." She then sat between Sarah and Ben, who was staring at Otis. "Now, before we give thanks," Nathan said, "I want to introduce you children to a brand-new acquaintance of ours here, Otis Thigpen."

Ben, not very successfully, stifled a laugh. "Ben!" Abigail admonished.

"Ben muffled, "Sounds like *pigpen*."

This made Sarah laugh. "Hush you two! You will both have a session with me after our meal and we will go over the importance of kindness and manners."

Otis quietly spoke up, "S'all right, ma'am, I'm used to it and... it does sound like *pigpen*."

Nathan interjected, "Well, now shall we all hold hands and give our thanks to our Lord and Savior, Jesus Christ."

A darkness came into Boudine's eyes as she quietly kept her hands to herself.

Then, as they all took turns ladling out the stew from the bowl, Bob said, "I have an announcement here. I have asked Otis to come to work to help me to start proving up my homestead. He has agreed. And also, should there be a need, he has agreed to give a hand to you all here when the need arises. Since money is of short supply, Otis will be working only for his keep and, after a cabin is built, I will help him build himself a lodging nearby on the new homestead land..."

All eyes were on Otis and Bob, except for Boudine, whose expression had become dark, as she stared off.

"Well," Nathan finally said, "I, for one, think this is a fine idea. Very fine indeed. Welcome, Otis! We welcome you here!"

Boudine stood with Bob in the woods apart from the Pickering homestead. "You did this without a word to me! What're you thinkin' with up there?!" she nearly shouted as she indicated his head. "We don't know nothin' 'bout him! We don't..."

Bob cut her off, "We know he helped save my life. We know he buried the sheriff up on Boot Hill with the name of Bandit Bob Slye over the grave. We know he gathered my belongings so's we could settle here. We know he met with the new sheriff and said nothin' about us."

Boudine cut in, "An' we know he stole from the sheriff's house. He could be hunted for all we know."

Bob hesitated then said, "Don't think so. They got more to think about over in Deadwood then one man leavin' town."

===

Seth Bullock, who now wore a new sheriff's badge, dismounted from his horse and slowly walked between the haphazard mounds of both marked and unmarked graves up on Boot Hill. He stopped when he saw the crudely, hand whittled marker; *Here lies the Bandit Bob Slye 1876*. After pondering for a moment, he looked around at the plots, noticed something at the edge of the graveyard, and walked over to it.

The shallow ditch, where Otis had hidden the coffin filled with the items taken from Sheriff O'Banyon's house, had drawn his interest. He scuffed some dirt at the edge of the ditch and saw that it was fresh.

===

Bullock sat alone at a window table at The Grand Central Hotel restaurant. Lucretia Marchbanks came over to take his order. "Well, sir, you are lookin' a might serious there, Mister Bullock, and I notice there that you must be the new sheriff everyone's talkin' about."

Bullock's expression didn't change. "Could you sit for a moment Miss Marchbanks?"

A bit puzzled, Lucretia said, as she sat across from Bullock, "Only if you start callin' me Aunt Lou like everyone else."

"Well, I was raised in a formal way, I guess. I'd like to find out more about Otis Thigpen. I assume he hasn't shown yet."

His seriousness took over Lucretia, "Nossir, ain't seen hide-nor-hair of'im. You suspect somethin's wrong?"

"I'm not sure what to suspect. I understand that you and some of the ladies over at the Gem Theater helped watch over him when he was a youngster."

"Yes, we did. He mostly slept at my place. Taught'im to read an' write some so's he could get along."

"That's what I understand."

"Sad little critter he was..."

Bullock paused and took out a note pad and looked at his notations, "Did Otis ever travel much?"

"Nossir, I don't think he never rode to anywhere's outside Deadwood, 'cept maybe for Sheriff O'Banyon's business."

Bullock started to ask another question, but Lucretia started in with, "You-know that O'Banyon was a real skunk! He treated Otis like a cur dog! Slapped'im around and yelled at'im right in front of anyone! Called'im, s'cuse me for sayin', *pignuts*!"

Bullock said calmly, "I see."

"He was somethin' terrible to his wife too. 'Tho there's some says they wasn't really married. Some say he took'er from the Gem as payment for a debt owed by Al Swearengen over there."

Bullock took a breath, then said, "Interesting."

"That bast... he never comes back here won't be soon enough, that's all I gotta say!"

"Well, I can assure you, Miss Marchbanks, he won't be working here in Deadwood any longer."

"Good to hear, Mister Bullock. I've got customers comin' in, I'll have'ta get my tail waggin' here." She started to get up. Bullock raised his hand to stay put.

"Just a couple more questions. Did Otis ever get into trouble?"

"Not a lick!" she answered defensively. "Nicest boy you'd ever wanna be around. Even with all the bad luck he started out with, I'd trust'im with my last nickel."

===

Inside the prairie schooner, Bob and Boudine had settled in for the night. Boudine had wrapped herself into her bedroll and seemed quiet until she said, "How's your wound feelin' there?"

Bob was finishing getting himself arranged. "Seemed better today. Still not workin' good enough as yet."

Boudine was quiet for a moment, then said, "I'm thinkin' goin' into Deadwood tomorrow or next day."

"What for?"

"Runnin' low on some things."

"Chinese medicine?"

"S'my business," she answered curtly.

"You might be thinkin' of stoppin' usin' that stuff. Can't be good for you."

"I'll be the judge of that," she said.

"Like you've said, Boudine, like you've said."

"Like I've said."

Bob turned over in his bedroll in the darkened wagon. After a moment, Boudine said, "Otis said Calamity Jane's back in Deadwood."

"What's that of importance to you? Thought you were on the outs with her, since you was let loose from your shootin' act."

"Some unfinished business."

Outside, the full moon became covered over by a dark cloud.

===

In the Pickering barn, Boudine finished cinching up the saddle on her horse and led it outside into the early morning light. Bob came out of the Pickering's house and met Boudine, as she mounted up. He handed her a piece of paper. "Here's a list of things Abigail needs, if you're of a mind. And here's a gold piece to pay."

"Never mind that, I'll do the payin'. Anythin' else?"

Bob pulled a postal envelope out of his pocket. "I'd like to have this mailed at the Wells Fargo Office. It's addressed to my mother care of Sergeant Major Bartholomew at Fort Randall. Just needs postage."

Boudine took the envelope and tucked it into her shirt. "I'll see to it." She then reined her horse around.

"Be careful there, Boudine."

Boudine let out a sarcastic chuckle and said, "Got this far din't I." With that, she spurred her horse toward the pathway through the woods toward Deadwood.

===

The diminutive Wells Fargo Agent adjusted the thick pillow on his banker's chair and hiked himself up onto his seat behind his desk, as the spring doorbell tinkled, and Seth Bullock entered the small office.

"Mornin'," Bullock said.

"Mornin'. What kin I help you with, sir?"

"Just want to introduce myself and..."

"You be Mister Seth Bullock the new sheriff."

Bullock chuckled a bit, "Guess word gets around fast here,"

"And, that shiny new badge you be wearin' there."

"And who might I be talkin' to here?" Bullock asked.

"Scotch South, at your service. Agent and postal clerk for the Wells Fargo Company."

"You have a bit of a brogue there, Mister South. From Scotland by any chance?"

"Father came by boat through Nova Scotia. Joined up with a travelin' circus show. Met up with a little lady person and I came about. I got the short end of the stick you might say."

Bullock paused a bit, then said, "I might have a smidgen of the Scottish in me as well there, Mister South."

"Scotty to those what know me."

"All right, Scotty, pleased to know you. Your reputation of knowing what goes on around Deadwood has preceded you, so I'm sure I'll be seeing you about matters from time to time."

"I understand Sheriff O'Banyon won't be returnin'."

"Looks to be that. Looks to be that."

"And looks to be Deputy Otis Thigpen has also taken his leave."

Bullock stopped at the door, paused and turned back to Scotty. "Do you find that a bit peculiar?"

"Yes, I do. Yes indeedy."

"Well, I do as well. Good mornin' to you, Scotty."

With that, Bullock left the office, and Scotty adjusted the black arm garters on his shirtsleeves.

CALAMITY

SEVEN

Doc Babcock looked up from the cluttered desk in the office-surgery in the front room of his house. The Deadwood Medical Doctor was well known in and around Deadwood, South Dakota and was trusted to do the best that he could with what little he had in medical supplies.

"L'o there, Doc."

Doc Babcock's face brightened at the sight of the person who had just entered. "Well, I'll be! It's you there!"

"Yep, it's me here."

"Calamity Jane, as I live and breathe!"

"You better be, Doc. You better be."

The older man rose out of his chair and dragged another chair toward Jane. "Here sit yourself down and tell me what's the matter."

Jane set the chair in front of Doc's desk and sat. "What makes you think something's the matter with me there, Doc?"

"Well, how long's it been since you've seen me?"

"Probably, since I left Ol' Buffalo Bill Cody's last show run around the country."

"I'd say so-yes, I'd say so. Been a long time."

Jane went quiet for a moment...

"Well?" asked Doc.

Jane cleared her throat. "Fuckin' stomach's been actin' up some."

Doc chuckled, "Still the same fowl-mouthed Calamity Jane."

"One an' the same."

"How bad is it?"

"Comes an' goes."

"You been eatin' regular?"

Jane paused...

"Drinkin' regular?"

"Both," Jane muttered.

"Well, then I suggest you cut out one of them and it shouldn't be eatin'."

"Thought you'd say that, Doc. Ain't there somethin' I can take?"

"There is, but I don't recommend it."

"Laudanum."

"That's right, but again, I don't recommend it."

"I'll take it," Jane said flatly.

===

The bell tinkled in the Wells Fargo Office, as Boudine entered. Scotty came out from the mailroom where he was sorting the day's stagecoach delivery. "Help you?"

Boudine reached into her shirt and took out the envelope Bob had given her. "Need postage for this here." She handed the envelope over to the little Wells Fargo agent.

Scotty looked at it for a moment and turned it over and back in his hand. "Fort Randall…"

"That's what it says," Boudine said flatly. "Somethin' wrong?"

"No-no, just that I have a letter here from Fort Randall for a Mister Robert Duncan." He indicated the envelope in his hand. "This wouldn't be from Mister Duncan goin' out to Fort Randall, would it?"

"What's it to ya?" Boubine quipped.

"Nothin' really, 'cept I ain't seen Mister Duncan since the last time he got a letter from Fort Randall some time ago."

Irritated, Boudine asked, "How much for postage there?"

"Don't get your feathers fluttered." Scotty went to his desk and ran his finger down a pricing chart. "Fort Randall be over three hundred miles from here. That'd be eighteen cents."

Boudine heaved a sigh and pulled a coin out of her pants pocket. "Here."

Scotty took the coin and looked at it. Bit it, then said, "Way too much."

"Then keep the damned change for crissakes! Just mail the damn letter!"

"You don't have to get testy there, I was just..."

"An' give me the letter for Mister Duncan. I'll take it to'im."

"Can't."

"What'chu mean, you can't?"

"He'll have to show up here himself, if'n he wants it. Thems the rules."

Boudine just stared at the little man for a long moment, then quickly turned toward the door. "Shite!" she muttered and left.

===

"That's a coffin in the wagon, ain't it?" Ben, who was still a bit standoffish but had the Deputy Badge pinned to his shirt, asked Otis, who was cleaning out a dung pile from his horse next to his coffin wagon in the Pickering barn.

"Not no more," Otis said, as he kept cleaning up the barn floor.

"What's it for then?"

"My things I took with me."

"Oh..."

Otis took the full bucket of horse dung toward the opened barn door. "Where's your Pa empty this?"

"On the pile next to the garden."

Otis headed outside. Ben hustled up beside him. "I'll show you."

Most of the vegetable garden had been plowed under for fall. Ben pointed out the fertilizer pile of dung and kitchen scraps for Otis and then asked, "When you was a sheriff..."

"Deputy Sheriff," Otis corrected.

"Did you ever shoot any bad people?"

Otis hesitated, then said, "No. Never did."

"How could you be a sheriff and not shoot no one?"

"Just never come about."

Abigail called out from the front porch, "S'he botherin' you there, Otis?"

Otis had finished dumping the horse dung onto the pile and looked over toward Abigail. "No ma'am, he ain't no bother 't'all."

"I showed him where you like the horse poop put."

"Anythin' you'd like done, ma'am?" Otis called to Abigail.

'No, I'm fine for now, thank you. But, if you're of a mind, we could use a bucket or two of water from the river later and don't let the boy get underfoot and be bothersome. You hear me, Ben?"

"Yessum."

"He's no bother, ma'am."

"Ben, you should see if your father needs help where he's been clearin' up more land yonder."

"Yessum."

With that, Abigail went back inside. Otis headed back toward the barn. Ben tagged right along. "Are you really going to build a cabin for yourself here, Otis?"

"Lots to do 'fore be doin' that."

"What was it like livin' in Deadwood?"

Otis's face clouded up and he didn't answer, then finally said to Ben, as they approached the barn door, "You best be going to help your Pa like your Ma said."

Bob hunched over at the eating table in the Pickering cabin, so Abigail could take a look at his healing bullet wound. Nathan was washing his hands at the kitchen sink. As she peeled back the bandage, she said, "It's lookin' so much better there, Bob. So much better."

Nathan wiped his hands with a hand towel and walked over. "Fine day's work comin' on today, Bob."

Bob let Abigail dress his wound with a clean bandage and replied to Nathan. "Let's say a half-day worth from me there, Nathan."

"Don't let my Nathan push you too hard there, Bob. You ain't a hundred percent quite yet."

Ben came bounding through the door with Sarah in tow. "Wash up, you two. Gettin' on luncheon time here," instructed Abigail.

"Will Boudine be returnin' 'fore dark then?" Nathan asked Bob.

"I suspect, but one never knows with her," Bob said, as he pulled his shirt back up and buttoned it. "Don't wait on her if'n she's late."

Nathan chuckled, "Abigail's dinner bell waits for no one."

===

"That you there, Sally Mae?"

Boudine stopped on the boardwalk in front of a dry goods store in the middle of town. She turned and said, "Hello. Jane."

At the bar next to the gaming tables in the Nuttal & Mann's No.10 Saloon, Calamity Jane and Boudine were being served up with whiskeys. Calamity Jane raised her glass to Boudine. "Well, here's to you, Sally Mae."

"Boudine."

Jane looked puzzled.

"That's what I go by now?" Boudine said flatly.

Jane continued with her toast, "Well-well. *Boudine* then. Here's to Boudine's new name," Jane said with a slight smirk and chuckle.

"T'aint funny."

Jane took a sip of her whiskey and set the glass down, as she eyed Boudine. "Hmmm... guess not. I can see by your hair growed out that you ain't that sixteen-year-old boy sharpshooter no more."

"Never was."

"You sure as hell pulled it off when you was with Buffalo Bill's show."

"'Til you an' Wild Bill had me throwed off," Boudine retorted.

"Whoa! Wait just a second there, Sally Mae."

"Boudine!"

"Allright-allright your bein' fired was all Bill Cody's doin'. Wild Bill and me had nothin' to do with it."

"Bullshite." Boudine muttered and took a healthy gulp of whiskey.

Calamity pulled up straight and looked right at Boudine. "Listen, it was all about Bill's business. He put a lot of money into all them banners and posters of me and Wild Bill as the main attractions. An' he was payin' the two of us top dollar for our acts. He figured that the folks who were payin' hard cash to come to his shows weren't comin' to see some snot-nosed brat out draw an' outshoot us."

"But I was."

"Yeah, you was good! Too good. And he warned you more'n once to ease up, but you didn't and that's why you was let go... and that's the sum an' substance of it."

Boudine fumed a bit inside, then took another gulp of whiskey and set the empty glass on the bar. Jane signaled the bartender for two more.

Jane and Boudine stood there in silence for a few moments watching the gamblers at the tables, as the piano player tickled the ivories and a couple of powdered-up working girls made themselves available to any early morning takers. The bartender filled their whiskey glasses and drifted away. After a moment more, Jane said softly, "That's where Wild Bill was murdered. Over that table next to the wall. Never had a chance. That little piece of dog shite, Broken Nose Jack McCall, just walked in an' plugged him in the back of the head. All because Charlie Rich talked him out of sittin' in his usual chair with his back to the wall. They hung the little rat-shite over there in Yankton."

Boudine sighed a bit, turned her back on the gamblers and hunched over her drink. "I visited'im last time I was here."

"Must've been right after they moved'im."

Boudine flinched a bit. "Moved'im?"

"Was first set down on Boot Hill, but the town started movin' some of'em over to Mt. Moriah Cemetery."

"Oh," Boudine muttered, "didn't know that."

Boudine's jaw started to work. Calamity stared off for a moment, then said, "I'm hopin' to be buried next to'im come the day."

Boudine looked at Calamity and then uttered, "You were with him back before weren't you."

"For a time."

"Some says you was married to'im."

"An' some says we wasn't."

A moment more passed, then Jane asked, "What about you? Who named you *Boudine*?"

Boudine went quiet. Jane took a belt of her whiskey, then continued, "Be a man then?" Jane asked Boudine, as she turned down the bartender's approach to fill another drink.

"Be a man what?" Boudine answered.

"Be a man what named you Boudine?"

Boudine shrugged.

"Sure as hell, you wouldn't name yourself that."

Boudine shrugged again.

"Still tryin'im on then?"

Again, Boudine shrugged.

"Good lookin'?"

She hesitated, then muttered under her breath, "Maybe..."

"Ha! Better not bring'im around me then." Jane chuckled.

"What?!"

"Hell, you remember how I am around men."

"An' you remember my *King-Queen-Ace* shootin'."

"Listen," Jane said, "where're you stayin' at now?"

"Over Belle Fourche way."

"I mean here in Deadwood."

"Ain't stayin' in Deadwood. Headin' out 'fore dark."

Jane signaled the bartender for two more whiskeys. Boudine started to object. "Look we ain't done talkin' yet. Been too long'a'time between... *Boudine*."

"Alright, one more then I gotta get crackin' and then hit the leather back," Boudine said.

"I'm thinkin'," Jane said, as the bartender filled their glasses, "that we might think about puttin' together a shootin' act between us. These folks here would turn out for that."

Boudine just looked at Jane for a bit, then sipped her whiskey.

"Well?" Jane asked.

Boudine took another moment, then asked, "Ain't you still goin' out with Cody's show?"

"Not since Wild Bill passed. I did try it once, but it t'weren't the same. Every place I looked, there he was. Just standin' there grinnin' at me."

Boudine nodded quietly, then asked, "How're you makin' it here, Jane?"

Calamity was taken aback by the question. "Whud'you mean?"

"I mean, how're you eatin' and drinkin' and sleepin' here in Deadwood? You can't be doin' your shootin' act all the time."

Jane seemed a bit thrown by the question. Cleared her throat. "Well... Al Swearengen give me a room over at the Gem."

Boudine paused, then asked, "For what?"

"Whud'a'you mean, '*for what*'?"

"Just what I says. You a workin' girl now?"

Calamity Jane looked away, then took a large swig of her whiskey. After a moment of silence, Jane looked right at Boudine and asked with more than some rasp in her voice, "Lemme ask *you* a question there, *Boudine!*. How've *you* been keepin' there, *Boudine*, huh? Still robbin' stages then, *Bou-dine*?"

Boudine stood straight and shot back with a harsh whisper, "What the hell you say, Calamity Jane?!"

"There's been more'n'one stage outta Deadwood that was held-up by a woman or ain't you heard?"

Boudine gritted back close to Jane's face, "No, I ain't heard, *Martha Jane Cannary!*"

"'Course you ain't heard, 'cause it t'was you weren't it?!"

Boudine hissed, "Bloody hell, Jane! You come up with the strangest shite!"

Calamity eased back from the confrontation a bit and took a breath. She downed her whiskey and signaled for another. "D'jou know there was a dead Rebel road agent found out on the trail to Belle Fourche some time back."

Boudine fiddled with her half full glass, then shrugged.

"Was kilt with the same three shots you used on the targets in Cody's shows." Boudine didn't respond.

Boudine straightened up and eased her whiskey glass away from her. Jane placed her hand firmly on Boudine's arm. "Look, all I'm sayin' is..."

Boudine eased her arm back. "I don't know what the hell you're sayin'. "

"Well, all I'm sayin' is, if I can figure it out, others can too."

"No one here in Deadwood knows me."

"S'right. But there's a lot of questions flyin' around about how the sheriff's wife was kilt an' why Sheriff O'Banyon disappeared, and how come Deputy Otis Thigpen suddenly up and left town right after that bandit was hung out there on O'Banyon's hangin' tree. Just seems a puzzlement, don't'cha think?"

Boudine stepped off the boardwalk in front of Nuttal & Mann's Saloon. Calamity Jane stopped at the boardwalk edge and said, "Sure you won't stay over? You can bunk in my room."

"Best not. Told the folks I'm with I'd be back 'fore..."

"I know, 'fore dark. Too bad, we could grab us a steak, then have us some fun."

"One thing," Boudine said, "where can I get me more of that Chinese medicine you give to me when we was workin' together?"

Jane paused, then said seriously, "How much of that shite're you usin', Boudine?"

"Only when I get the jitters and when the month comes on."

"Well, I been away from that for a time. T'was gettin' the best of me. Had me pukin', shittin' an' shakin'. And you better watch it or it'll get the best of you too. Anyways, there's somethin' new goin' around that my Doc told me about called Laudanum that's supposed to be better for-ya. I could ask'im if..."

Boudine waved her off. "Ain't got time for that. There a Chinese town here abouts?"

"Sure is. A pretty nice one as it goes too. Folks here and there get along pretty good with each other."

Getting impatient, Boudine asked, "Where's it at?"

Jane indicated, "Up t'other end of town that way. Ask for a man name of Wing Tsue. Owns a shop there. Tell'im I sent-ya. He'll get-ya whatever you need."

"Thanks."

Just then, Jane hopped down off the boardwalk and headed to the middle of the dirt street. "Hey, before you go, I wanna try somethin' with you." Jane stopped and turned quickly toward Boudine. "I wanna see if'n you still got as quick a draw as you used to!"

"Aw shite, Jane!"

"Come on there, *Bou-dine*! Let's see if you can still outdraw me or if'n you've dropped off a notch or two."

Boudine sighed then suddenly, in a flash, went for her holstered pistol, but Calamity Jane had her gun up out and fired an instant before Boudine, who did not fire her gun. The bullet snapped within a snake's breath of Boudine's ear and blew a hole through one of the windowpanes of the saloon behind her.

"Dammit, Jane! What the hell!"

"Shite! Sorry! But I was faster, that's for sure!"

Several patrons of Nuttal & Mann's came out of the saloon. A well-dressed man charged out of the Gem Theater and ran up to the two women. It was Sheriff Seth Bullock.

"What the hell's going on here, Calamity?"

"Nothin'! Just a little accident. Just havin' some fun here, Seth, s'all."

"You been drinkin', Jane?"

"Not much, just bein' playful with my friend here, haven't seen for some time."

Seth turned to Boudine and asked sternly, "And, who might you be?"

Jane quickly answered as Boudine holstered her gun, "This here's Sally Mae from over Yankton way."

Bullock addressed Boudine, "Are you a sharpshooter like Calamity Jane here?"

"No, she ain't. She's a... she's a broncobuster!"

Bullock looked askance at Boudine's diminutive size, "That right?"

Boudine hesitated then answered, "S'right. Not so much bronco bustin'. Mostly, trainin' horses."

"Haven't seen you around here before," Bullock said.

"Ain't been here much. Came on in to see if'n I could drum up some work."

"Well, ma'am, I'd say you're not off to a very good start. Seems your friend here isn't helping you out much. Someone could've been killed. Where'd you two happen to meet?"

Boudine glanced at Calamity who started to answer for her. Boudine cut her off. "I wrangled horses for the shows when they come to town."

Bullock said, "In Yankton?"

Boudine mumbled, "Yeah, an'... an' other places when I was nearby."

Calamity piped up, "Had us some times then din't we Bou... Sally Mae!"

The bartender who served the drinks at the bar shouted out to Calamity Jane, "Hey, Jane, you gonna pay for my window here?"

"Yeah-yeah, hold'yer johnson, I'll see to it!" She then said to Bullock, "So, Seth, you gonna arrest me or we gonna stand here chit-chattin' all day?"

Bullock's jaw started to work a bit, then he said forcefully, "Jane you are cutting it right close to the edge with me. You'd better straighten up or you'll be heading for some real trouble."

Calamity threw it back at him with a laugh, "Hell, I'll drink to that, Seth!"

Bullock glared at her, turned and headed back toward the Gem Theater.

Boudine watched him go, then asked, "He the new sheriff?"

"Oh yeah, just got the badge from the head townfolk. More of a businessman. Got a business partner name of Sol Star. They own the hardware store over yonder and some other bits and pieces around town. Gonna build a new hotel, I hear. Anyway, nothin' for you to worry 'bout. I got'im wrapped around my little finger, if'n you know what I mean."

===

Bob was asleep in his bedroll in the prairie schooner. The moon above outlined a shadow moving slowly along the wagon bonnet toward the opening. A silhouetted hand pulled back the flap and someone quietly eased in and snuggled up to Bob. He stirred. Boudine lightly shook him and whispered, "Wake up there, Slye... I'm feelin' good... I'm feelin' real good."

In the early morning dawn, Bob stood at the riverbank and set down one of the two empty wooden water buckets he'd been carrying. As he lowered one of them into the water, a voice came from the pathway. "Need a hand there, Slye?" Bob glanced over at Boudine as she came toward him. "Thought maybe I'd hurt your shoulder there after our little roustabout last night." She chuckled and sniffed then wiped her nose on her sleeve.

Bob pulled the full bucket up with his good arm and set it down, then lowered the second one into the river without speaking. Then he asked, "What kept'ya in Deadwood so long, Boudine?"

"Met up with Jane."

"Who?"

"Calamity Jane. The sharpshooter I told you about from the Buffalo Bill shows I used to be in. I told you about her and..."

Bob set the full bucket down. He didn't hide his mood. "The one who got you pushed out."

"Yeah..."

"The one who give you that Chinese medicine you're always usin'."

"Not always, Slye. Only when the need be."

"Suppose she give you more of it now."

"Shite, Slye!"

"And got you cussin' all the time."

"Dammit, Slye! What's all this now?!"

"First off, you're supposed to stop callin' me Slye, remember?"

Boudine gritted, "Shite. Sorry, I keep forgettin'."

"You keep forgettin' is gonna get us a wagon load of trouble, Boudine."

As they walked back toward the Pickering homestead, Bob asked Boudine, "You get all the stuff on Abigail's list?"

"Took it into her when I woke up."

"You mailed my letter?"

"'Course I mailed your letter. Damned thing cost eighteen cent! Could'a had me three beers and a jug of cheap whiskey for that."

"Thank you."

"But..."

"But, what?"

"There's more. There be a letter waitin' for you at the Wells Fargo Office."

"D'you bring it?"

"Sumbitch little shite wouldn't give it to me. Said only you could pick it up."

Bob sighed, "Yeah, I know'im. He goes by the rules."

"Straighter than a store-bought target arrow, he was."

"S'alright. Just doin' his job. Anythin' else?"

"Met the new sheriff name of Seth Bullock."

"Oh?"

"Well... seems Calamity shot out a windowpane over at Nuttal & Mann's Saloon and he got a little pissed off."

Bob just shook his head a bit.

"But that's not the whole of it..."

Bob glanced at her.

"They're fixin' to move some of the graves from Boot Hill over to Mt. Moriah Cemetery. Already moved Wild Bill."

This pulled Bob up short. The word almost caught in his throat, "What?!"

===

With the help of young Ben, wearing the deputy badge, Otis Thigpen threw some fresh cut brush he was clearing from Bob's homestead land into his coffin wagon.

"Otis, could you come over here for a minute," Bob said from several yards away, "Got somethin' to speak of."

"Can I come too?" Ben asked.

"Not this time, Ben."

"Growed up talk?"

"Yup... just keep goin' there. You're bein' a great help."

Otis walked to where Bob and Boudine were standing. Bob took Otis by the arm and turned him, as he and Boudine started walking further away from Ben.

At a distance, amidst several yellow pines, Boudine said to Otis in a low voice, "They be startin' to move the graves from Boot Hill over to the new Mount Moriah Cemetery." Otis glanced over toward where Ben was loading more brush into the wagon. "You know 'bout this?" Boudine asked Otis.

"They already had me move Mister Hickok over t'there sometime back. Don't know how many they was plannin' to move."

"They dig up Sheriff O'Banyon, we're up shite creek without a paddle!" Boudine exclaimed.

"Name of Bandit Bob Slye on the marker. They won't be movin' no bandits over to Moriah. S'only for respectable folks."

Boudine paused, then said, "I got a bad feelin' 'bout this. What about the sheriff's wife?"

Puzzled, Otis remarked, "She be buried over by the sheriff's house."

"But they could decide to move're and open the coffin an'..."

"T'weren't no coffin," Otis said.

"Jesus, he just dumped'er in a hole?"

Otis sighed, then remarked, "Had me do it for'im."

"So, you saw what she looked like then?"

"No. Sheriff'd wrapped her up in gunnysacks. All I did was dig the hole and..."

"So, no one seen how she was kilt then?"

"Don't think so. He said nothin' to me 'cept goin' after the bandit who he said done it."

Anyone in town say things about it'tall?" Boudine asked.

"No... not much. She t'weren't really the sheriff's wife."

Boudine looked at Otis with a peculiar look in her eye. "Whudda you mean there, Otis?"

"They wasn't never married. She was just a workin' girl over at the Gem that he liked to use. But, then Al Swearengen owed'im some big gamblin' winnings. So, the sheriff just up an' took'er as payment. No one never said no more about it."

Just then, Abigail's morning meal bell clanged out from her porch. Ben immediately dropped what he was doing and dashed in the direction of the Pickering's. Otis walked off as well.

As Bob turned to leave, Boudine hooked him back by his arm. "There'ya go then..."

Bob said, "How's that, Boudine?"

"I didn't kill the sheriff's wife, 'cause they was never married."

As the warm porridge bowl was being passed around, Bob said, "I'm thinkin' of goin' on into Deadwood tomorrow. Got a letter there an' I need a few other things."

Ben piped up, "Can I go?!"

"Ben!" Abigail said.

"Well now, wait," Nathan said, "I might have to go in as well. Need a keg of nails and a new scythe with all the clearin' goin' on here, and some lumber cut boards from the sawmill."

"But..." Abigail started to object. Nathan raised his hand. "It's settled than.
Ben and I will leave come dawn and follow Bob into Deadwood. All things being equal, we should be back by mid-afternoon. How does that sound?"

Otis said, "You might use my wagon there, should you find other things you need."

"Why that's very kind of you, Otis, the lumber cut boards would fit handily in it, now that you mention it. And, Bob, you could ride with us then."

Bob glanced at Boudine first, then said, "I believe I'll ride on ahead, if you don't mind. There's a possibility I might have to stay on a bit longer, dependin' on some things that need tendin' to."

Nathan paused a bit, then announced, "It's settled then. We leave at first light."

Boudine interjected with, "Whyn't Abigail an' Sarah go along with y'all? Otis and me'll hold down the fort here."

Sarah reacted with a plea to her father, "Please, Pa! Please can we go too?"

Nathan looked at Abigail for approval, then said with a grin, "Well, I suppose you both could use a new sun bonnet."

===

An early sun pushed up from behind the Black Hills that surrounded Deadwood, South Dakota. The sharp shadows of the decrepit crosses and rotting wooden grave markers, stabbed into the dirt mounds of the Deadwood Boot Hill, accentuated the forgotten souls last stop. Bob, dressed in his gambling duds and

Boss of the Plains black hat, with the hole that he himself had shot through it, during his gun battle with Sheriff Jack O'Banyon, sat astride his roan and looked down at the carved wooden grave marker of one "Bandit Bob Slye." He paused for a moment more, then looked around at what seemed to be some ongoing grave digging activity. "Kin I help'ya there, mister?" came a voice from across the haphazard graveyard. Bob looked behind him and saw a workman with a shovel and a pickaxe watching him.

"Mornin', sir. Lookin' for the grave of one William Hickok but can't seem to find it."

"Oh, we done moved ol' Wild Bill over'ta Mount Moriah Cemetery short while back. You know Wild Bill?"

"For a time..."

"Well, he deserved better'n this dump, so's we got orders to move'im over with the respectable folks."

"Well, that's good to know. Thank you, sir."

"You can't miss it. Got hisself a fine marker now. Seems folks come from near an' far just to visit'im there.

Bob steadied his mount and asked, "Plannin' on movin' more graves from here then?"

"Yep, don't know how many. Just get word now an' then on which ones and get to it. Hopin' ol' Otis gets back here soon. Handlin' all this by myself ain't a job for one, I can assure you of that. Sumbitch just took off to who knows where without a word to no one."

Bob indicated the Bandit Bob Slye's marker. How'bout this'ne here? Be movin' it as well?"

The gravedigger chuckled, "Hell no! 'Less the town big shites decide somethin' else. Ya never know with that bunch. They might just dig'im up and sell tickets. That be the bastard what killed ol' Sheriff O'Banyon's woman. They strung'im up good'n'tight. But, then O'Banyon up an disappeared. Seems a puzzlement s'all I can say."

Bob touched the brim of his *Boss of the Plains* hat and reined his horse back around toward the town. "Thank you, sir. Much obliged. I'll head over to Mount Moriah and pay my respects."

"Nice talkin' to ya. Don't get many visitors 'round this place."

"Well, look what the cat drug in. Ain't seen you in a dog's age!" A smiling Lucretia Marchbanks announced as Bob entered her restaurant in the Grand Central Hotel.

"You look better'n ever there, Aunt Lou."

"Come on over here to my special table and tell me all about your goin's on then." Aunt Lou led the way to a table for two by the window overlooking the main street. "Set yerself down whilst I dish you up some vittles."

Nathan Pickering sat on the driver's box of Otis's coffin wagon, next to his wife Abigail, as he guided the dead road agent's horse, that he had received from Bob and Boudine upon first meeting them, along the main street of Deadwood. Their children sat excitedly in the wagon bed. "Alright, I'm gonna park up there next to the General Store. Ben, I'd like you to set up here and watch over the horse for a bit. She ain't used to pullin' a wagon much. Abigail, you and Sarah kin go about your woman's business whilst I buy up this list of goods I have here."

Ben protested, "But..."

"No buts. Don't worry, you'll get your turn to look around."

"Now, tell me all about your doin's since I last saw you, Mister Duncan." Lucretia asked Bob, as she set out a full up breakfast in front of him and sat down with a cup of coffee.

"Bob to you, Aunt Lou."

"S'right," she smiled.

"Well, first off, I was able to square up a homestead over there in Belle Fourche."

"Well, ain't that somethin'. So, we'll be neighbors then."

"Yes, ma'am, looks to be."

But, what about your story writin' then? You did say you'd make me famous… remember?" She admonished with a twinkle.

"That I did, and I always keep my promises."

Nathan stepped down from the wagon, parked next to the boardwalk and helped Abigail down from the iron footstep. Sarah jumped down and grabbed her mother's hand, pulling her toward the walkway in front of the stores. "Patience, girl, patience now," she said with a laugh.

Ben set himself onto the driver's box, took hold of the reins and sulked. "Don't you go grumblin' there, Son, like I said, you'll get your turn." Nathan stepped up onto the board walkway and was nearly knocked over by a large drunken drover who weaved right into him. "Whoa, there!" he said and passed on into the store.

Seeing this, Ben looked around at all the dirt-covered drovers, cowhands and ne'er-do-wells with holsters and pistols strapped to their hips. A hung-over, played-out man wobbled out of a nearby saloon and just made it off the boardwalk before he upchucked and fell flat-faced into a pool of ox piss. Ben clapped his hand over his mouth at the sight of the man, as he stumbled to his feet and wobbled off across the rutted street. Ben then reached quietly into his pants pocket, pulled out the deputy badge Otis had given him and pinned it to his shirt.

Just then, a fully powdered, painted, cinched and pushed-up working girl passed by on the boardwalk and gave Ben a big playful wink. Ben immediately reddened and looked away.

"You say, the sheriff and the deputy have both disappeared then?"

"Yessir. Damnedest thing. Don't know what to make of it," Aunt Lou replied to Bob's question. "O'Banyon won't be missed at all. Mean ol' critter he was, but Otis, that's a real mystery to me. I helped brung'im up, you know, after his Ma orphaned him right on the front steps of the Gem Theater. He's real special to me."

Bob pondered this for a moment, then asked, "When does the Wells Fargo Agent show up?"

"Be there about now 'fore the first stage rolls in."

Bob hesitated for a moment then said quietly, "Aunt Lou, if'n I say somethin' to you without sayin' it, I want you to take it as gospel." He looked directly into her eyes, then said, "Otis is fine. He's safe."

The Wells Fargo Agent, Scotch South, handed Bob the letter he'd asked for. "Woman said she knew you, but we got rules to go by. Never know when you're bein' hoodwinked nowadays."

"S'right," Bob said and touched the brim of his *Boss of the Plains* hat. "Thank you."

"Looks like you got yourself a near miss there," Scotty said. Bob looked a bit confused. "That hole there in your hat. Bullet I'm guessin'."

"Like you said, never know when you're bein' hoodwinked."

"Nice badge you have there, son." Ben, seated on the wagon, held the horse's reins and gulped at the sight of an imposing Sheriff Seth Bullock wearing his new badge. "Might I ask where you came by it?"

Ben's eyes widened. "I...I..." He stammered.

"Deputy give it to'im." Nathan said to Bullock from behind him, as he deposited several items into the wagon bed.

"This wagon too?" Bullock asked Nathan.

"Yessir, traded'im up even."

Bullocks' face went dark. "And where is this deputy now?"

"Kingdom come s'far's I know. He seemed in desperate straits when he showed up at our homestead over in Belle Fourche. Next thing we knowed he just up and disappeared." Nathan looked right at his son Ben. "Ain't that right, Ben?"

Ben's throat went dry as a sandstorm, "Yessir," he managed to mumble.

Bullock studied Nathan for a moment, then asked, "Have we met before?"

Nathan brightened, "Oh, we sure as a winter's storm have met, Mister Bullock. You be the one who tried to buy me out of our homestead 'fore we even had time to breathe on it."

Bullock gritted a bit, "Oh yes, I remember now, t'was a good offer as I recall, Mister…"

"Nathan Pickering, and I told you to go straight to Hades, as I recall, Mister Bullock."

"Pa! Look at my new bonnet?" A pleased as punch Sarah rushed up and skipped around the boardwalk, followed by Abigail carrying some items. She eyed the sheriff. "Well, who do we have here, Nathan?"

Outside the Wells Fargo Office, Bob opened his letter. Although the return address was from Fort Randall, where his mother, Millie Mae Duncan, would have posted the letter, the letter was not from Millie Mae. It was from her friend Sergeant Major William Harrison Bartholomew...

Dear Robert,

May this letter find you sooner than later. I have some rather hard news about your mother. She came down with a very bad illness that nearly took her life. The doctors at the fort were unable to help her much at all. She insisted on me going to the Lakota Tribe reservation to fetch her friend Ogaleesha for her. It took some doing to get the Captain here to agree, but he finally allowed me to bring him and two Lakota escorts to the fort. They set up a tepee outside the fort and took your mother inside for several days. They burned something I have never heard of and filled the tepee with smoke and other Indian medicines they brought with them. I was sorely afraid this would bring an end to her. It did not. She became much better from the experience. She is still quite weak, but nevertheless better. As you know, I will be mustering out of the Army soon and we wish to be together after my release. The problem arises that your mother's small homestead is not a place for her any longer. I know she has the will but not the gumption at the moment to last out there, even with me around. You had spoken about moving into Belle

Fourche territory. Please let me know by writing me here at the fort how that endeavor is coming along. I hope to hear from you soon.

Sincerely,

Bill Bartholomew

Ben heard the first gunshot but not the second that slammed the lead slug into his chest and sent him crashing backwards into the wagon bed. He did not hear his mother's scream. He did not hear the cascade of gunfire as the two bank robbers leapt onto their horses with the money sacks and headed at a full gallop down the main street. He did not see the sharpshooter Calamity Jane aim her trusty rifle and bag both bandits in their backs. He did not see Sheriff Bullock also fire at the bandits and miss, hitting one of fleeing horses, sending it crashing and screaming in a sliding heap to the ground. He did not hear the wretched screams of the thrashing animal. He did not see Bob, who had seen everything from the boardwalk in front of the Wells Fargo Office, draw his Peacemaker, walk to the horse and put the wreathing animal out of its misery. He did hear his father say, "He's moving! His eyes are open!"

"Don't move'im!" Calamity Jane ordered. Let's get'im over to my doc's house. Just up ahead aways." With that, Jane jumped up onto the driver's box, took up the reins and headed the family on up the main street.

Nathan, Abigail and Sarah waited, huddled together on a well-used sofa in the small waiting area of Doc Babcock's home surgery. Abigail had one arm around Sarah and the other silently gripping Nathan's hand, as they stared at the closed door to the surgery. After a moment, Calamity Jane came out and closed the door behind her.

"You have one lucky sumbitch of a son there, s'all's I kin say!"

Abigail let out a breath. "Is he..."

"S'gonna be fine. Whoever give'im that badge should go to heaven with bangles on. Bullet stopped dead center of it. Gonna be one hell of a bruise for a bit, but he'll be up doin' chores again real soon."

Abigail did her best to stop the burst of tears with little success. She raised her arms to the heavens and clasped her hands together in sheer joy, "Praise the Lord!" she said just above a whisper, "Praise the Lord!"

"Doc says, you can see'im for a bit, but he wants'ta keep'im overnight, just to make sure," Jane said.

"How can we thank you miss... ah..." Nathan said.

"They call me Calamity Jane."

Bob was waiting on the front porch, as the Pickerings came outside. Sarah immediately spotted Bob, ran up to him and gave him a big hug. "He's gonna be alright, Bob! He got shot in his badge!"

Calamity Jane came out of Doc's house, as the Pickerings were finishing telling Bob what had happened. "I know, I saw it all from over at the Wells Fargo Office..."

"Who're you then?" Jane interrupted Bob with.

Nathan spoke up, "This be our friend Bob Duncan. This here's the famous sharpshooter Calamity Jane, Bob. She shot the two bank robbers right off'n their..."

"Bob said quietly, "Yes, I gathered that." he said to Jane as he touched his fingers to his *Boss of the Plains* hat.

Jane squinted a bit at Bob. "An' you be the one what named Sally Mae, *Boudine*."

Lucretia Marchbanks led the shocked Pickering family to a table with three chairs and drew up another for Bob, who stood behind them in the Grand Central Hotel restaurant.

"No need for a chair for me there, Aunt Lou, I won't be stayin'. That chair be for you."

Nathan drew out a chair for Abigail and then one for Sarah to sit in. "Where're you going?" Nathan began to ask Bob.

Bob interjected, "I'll take the horse and wagon over to the livery and then ride on back to the homestead."

"But..." Nathan started to say."

"It's all settled there, Nathan. Everything's taken care of here as well. You can check on Ben tomorrow and head back at your leisure."

Nathan began to reach into his pocket. Bob held up his hand, "No need. S'all done up. Stayin' here at the hotel under the watchful eye of Aunt Lou here will get you all fed and rested up. By the way Miss Marchbanks here is very famous for her plum puddin', ain't that right, Aunt Lou?"

"Right as rain," she said with a serious smile. "Don't you worry none. They be in good hands here with me."

"Go ahead and tell'em a few stories about Wild Bill Hickok and such, like you told me."

"Oh, I surely will and y'all can tell me about what happened out there today."

Sarah piped up, "My brother got shot right in his badge!"

===

Boudine advanced on Bob as he dismounted in front of the Pickering cabin in near darkness. "Where the hell've you been? Where's the Pickerings?"

"Long story."

Inside the cabin, Bob and Boudine sat at the dinner table with an oil lamp illuminating them. "Sumbitch!" Boudine breathed out, "And he's gonna be alright, then?"

"So, the doctor told your friend, Calamity Jane. They should be comin' on in tomorrow sometime."

Boudine took a breath, then asked, "What'd'you think of her?"

"Who?"

"Jane. What'd'you think of her?"

Bob paused, then answered with, "Good shooter."

"We know that. What'd'you think of *her?*"

"Same's all the others around Deadwood, I guess. Cusses a lot."

Boudine gritted a bit, then asked, "Anythin' else goin' on there?"

"They might be movin' more graves from Boot Hill over to Mount Moriah. Sheriff saw the badge Ben was wearin' was Otis's"

"Seth Bullock?"

"Yeah..."

"Could be trouble there."

"Maybe, maybe not. Nathan told'im Otis'd hit the road and he didn't know where he was headed."

"So, no one there knew you then?"

"Just Aunt Lou and the Wells Fargo agent, s'all."

"Who the hell's Aunt Lou?" Boudine shot back.

"Oh, that's right, you never been to the Grand Central Hotel. She's the colored lady who runs the eatin' place there. Name of Lucretia Marchbanks. She was friends with Hickok. That's how I come to eat there. Real nice lady and knows just about everything about everything that goes on in Deadwood."

"Oh..."

"She be lookin' after the Pickerings tonight."

"I see. Did you get your letter?"

Bob sighed a bit, then slipped the letter from his shirt pocket and held it for a moment. "Somethin' else we got to talk about."

Just then, Otis came in from outside with a quizzical expression on his face, "Set yourself down here, Otis... things to discuss..."

Inside the prairie schooner, the night's moon filtered down through the canvas covering onto Bob and Boudine wrapped up in their bedrolls.

"Otis, seemed pretty broken up when you told'im your friend... what's'er name?"

"Aunt Lou."

"Yeah, he seemed broken up about hearin' the story about how she brung him up."

"He's had some hard times."

"He didn't say nothin' about that sheriff askin' Nathan about where he was."

"Nathan said he was gone."

"Yeah, but he ain't gone. He be here and you said he could build himself a place on your homestead."

"Mmmm..." Bob uttered.

"What if Bullock comes here to see for himself then?"

"Don't think it matters much. Seems all Otis did was quit Deadwood. That ain't breakin' the law."

Boudine pondered this, then said, "What're you thinkin' he's got stashed in that there coffin he brought with'im?"

The sun was up and well on its way. Hens and roosters in the henhouse began cackling and crowing loudly, as eggs filled their nests. Bob walked out of the woods carrying a water bucket from the river and headed toward the Pickering cabin, soon followed by Boudine with another bucket. "When d'you think they'll show up?" she asked.

"Depends on how Ben's feelin', I reckon. Probably have'ta take it slow."

Boudine looked up at the sun and squinted. "Gettin' well on to high noon. I'm goin' in to see what I can rustle up for us all to eat."

Bob set his bucket on the front porch. "I'll go after Otis."

Just as Bob started across the yard toward the path to his homestead, he heard a wagon slowly approaching and stopped.

Sarah spotted Bob and jumped down off the wagon and raced toward Bob, shouting as she ran, "Bob! Bob!"

As Sarah breathlessly reached Bob, Boudine came out of the cabin. "Bob! Boudine!" Sarah blurted out, "Ben got shot right in his badge! Come see!" Sarah turned back toward the oncoming wagon. "Ben is a miracle! He's alive!"

Nathan pulled up to the front porch and stepped down off the wagon. As he did, he said quietly to Sarah, "Hush there, Sarah, Ben's sleepin' with your Ma back there."

"No, I ain't," came Ben's rather tired voice. He then poked his head up over the wagon side, then laid back down.

At the evening meal in the cabin, Nathan addressed Otis, who sat quietly with the others. Nathan finished up the saying of grace. "...and, Dear Lord, we wish to thank ye for sending Otis Thigpen to us. For without him, and his gift of that badge there to our son Ben, we would not be sitting here this evening celebrating his recovery. Amen."

"You should see his bruise, Otis! It's huge!" Sarah announced.

"Sarah, please!" Abigail admonished.

"Well, it is..." Sarah whispered.

Nathan continued, "I hope you will establish yourself here, Otis. It's folks like yourself that helps us all bear up to a hard and hopefully prosperous life out here in the wilds. As I've said before, if I were a drinkin' man, I'd salute you with a toast. But the best I can do is this water from our river."

Otis blushed a bit, but nonetheless, nodded his thanks.

Bob, Boudine and Otis stood at the riverbank, under the moonlight that sent its reflection onto the water's ripples. Boudine spoke up, "Otis, I think we gotta speak of a few things in case that Sheriff Bullock shows up here lookin' for you."

"Look, Otis," Bob added, "I have to be leavin' here for a while. Seems my mother has been quite sickly and I want to see her for myself over near Fort Randall where she lives on her homestead in a small soddy with her few farm animals."

Boudine added, "I be goin' with'im."

Bob reacted to her announcement... Boudine said, with a firmness, "That's it there, Slye! I be goin' along to help keep things level."

Bob just looked at her with a look that she knew all too well. "Sorry, I mean *Bob*." Then to Otis she said, "You should let us know what you have stashed in that there coffin you brought with you. Is there anythin' there that would get you in trouble with the sheriff? 'Cause if there is, we're gonna have to bury it somewhere before we leave."

Bob looked at Otis for a reaction. After a moment, Otis shook his head in agreement and uttered, "Yes."

Bob said, "Well, get it done then. Won't be good to waste time. Take what you need out of it and bury it off in the woods on my homestead. Hide it good. If'n you ain't done nothin' else to bring notice to you, then you ain't got nothin' to worry about. Sayin' you didn't want to live in Deadwood ain't no sin. We're gonna be gone for a time. More'n three hundred hard miles, as the crow flies from here. No tellin' what we'll run into on the trail or what we'll find once we get there."

"S'gonna be up to you here, Otis," Boudine said.

"Gettin' on toward fall. Countin' on you to help keep things here in good stead. I'll give you some gold money to tide things over."

Otis interrupted, "Don't need no money. Got my own."

"In the coffin?" Boudine said.

Otis didn't need to answer.

"All things bein' equal, we'll be returnin' 'fore the snow falls." Bob said. "These be good folks here. Don't run into their likes often."

Gathered around the fire pit in front of the Pickering cabin, with chairs set about the crackling fire under the stars, Nathan braced his fiddle under his chin. Abigail readied her concertina player in her lap. Nathan spoke up, "Even though this be a time for joy because of the miracle bestowed on our Ben here, I've chosen a few Gospel songs that we will dedicate to Bob's mother, Millie Mae Duncan, in hopes that she has fully weathered her sickness and that Bob and Boudine here will have safe travels, because us Pickering's feel strongly that y'all are part of our family." With that, Nathan drew his bow over his fiddle's strings to introduce *Precious Lord*.

THE TREK

EIGHT

"Don't get no easier, since we already done this a'fore," Boudine said, as she maneuvered her horse around rock outcroppings and sagebrush.

Bob uttered, "Nope."

"When we get closer to Scooptown, I wanna show you somethin'."

"No need to stop in Scooptown. Just slow us down."

"It's a ways this side. You'll see."

===

Boudine reined her horse up and turned toward a burned out, overgrown remnant of a sod house that had completely caved in on itself. "This be it," she said.

Puzzled and annoyed, Bob said, "This be what?"

"Remember, I said I took that ol' drunk and his wagon up to the Wind Cave to clean out our swag?"

"Yes..."

Boudine indicated a broken-down, brush-covered well next to the wrecked sod house. "There it is." She dismounted and cautiously walked to the well and looked down into it. "Still down there."

"But anyone could just take it."

"Don't reckon."

"Why?"

Boudine picked up a rock and tossed it down into the well. The ominous sound of many rattling tails buzzed up from below. "Snakes!"

"Nothin' like a pit full of hungry rattlers standin' guard over our loot to keep 'em away."

It was dusk when Bob and Boudine made camp next to a rushing stream well south of Scooptown. Both had stripped down and bathed in the clear, cold water.

"Jesus, this'll freeze your acorns off there, Bob!"

"Bit cold, ain't it."

"Hell, I'm gettin' out 'fore icicles form on my whatsit!"

"Me, too."

"But that don't mean we can't heat things up later, do it there, Bob?" she said with a shivering giggle.

In the dark, next to a small campfire, Bob and Boudine together beneath his bedroll spread out over them. "Feel good there, Slye?"

"Who?"

"Shite! *Bob*! Sorry! Anyway..."

"Yeah, I feel good."

As dawn broke over the rugged horizon, both Bob and Boudine brushed their teeth with bristle brushes and small jars of Dr. Peabody's toothpaste next to the stream. "Gettin' near Badlands comin' up," Boudine said and spit into the stream.

"Don't like the looks of them dark clouds over yonder."

"Pretty far away. Might blow south from us."

As they rode along, Boudine said, "Them scars of yourn healin' up pretty good."

"Seems to be."

"Didn't get in the way last night."

Bob didn't answer.

"Cat got'yer tongue, there Bob?"

Bob stayed quiet.

"Anyway, I brought along some yarrow grind just in case."

"Thanks."

"You goin' moody on me there?"

"Thinkin'."

"'Bout your mother?"

Bob didn't answer.

"She's gonna be better, I can feel it," Boudine said quietly, as they headed further on the outskirts of The Badlands.

The storm hit them with a vengeance! Bob and Boudine braced against the unrelenting squall, a mixture of cold rain and fall hail, as they held tightly to the reins of their horses and led them between a cropping of boulders to try to shield themselves from the cold, pelting downpour.

The setting sun spread its rainbow rays across the sifting clouds that remained from the passing tempest. Bob and Boudine, still wore their oilskin ponchos, as they continued further south and into the night.

===

Early morning in Deadwood brought Calamity Jane into Lucretia Marchbanks' Grand Central Hotel restaurant. "You look like you needs some fresh brewed coffee there, Miss Jane."

"More like a gallon there, Aunt Lou," Calamity said, as she eased herself into a chair at a small table next to a window.

"Bad night?" Lucretia asked, as she deposited a mug of coffee in front of Jane.

"Ain't they all?" Jane uttered with a sarcastic chuckle.

"Got some fluffy pancakes goin' or fried eggs'n'grits with bacon if'n that sounds better."

"Sounds better. Listen, Aunt Lou, you heard anythin' from Otis Thigpen yet?"

Aunt Lou hesitated a moment, then said, "No-no I ain't and he better have some story if'n he do show up."

"Well, if'n you do, tell'im to look me up, willya?"

"You know that fella Cyrus James what sometimes helps out at Mount Moriah Cemetery and Boot Hill?" Aunt Lou asked Calamity.

"Seen'im about, here'n'there. Why?"

"He's also been lookin' for Otis. Says all the gravediggin's been fallin' on him, since he disappeared. Says they wants'im to go out to Sheriff O'Banyon's old place and dig up his dead wife and move'er somewhere's else. Seems the place is bein' sold and the buyers don't want no bodies buried there."

Calamity Jane stiffened a bit, then uttered, "Really..."

Soon after, Calamity Jane pushed her horse at a fast pace on the trail north toward Belle Forche.

Otis lugged a large wooden pail of chicken dung over to the fertilizer pile next to the Pickering plowed under vegetable garden and dumped it. Nathan came out from the path to Bob's homestead. "Say there, Otis."

"Yessir?"

"I been thinkin', Otis," Nathan said, as they met up, "if'n Bob has to bring his ailin' mother here, he wouldn't have a place for her to reside, 'cept the schooner and that's already full-up. I was thinkin' here, since I have all the tools and some extra time, why'n't you an' me stake out a cabin over to where Bob was talkin' 'bout doin' such. Might be able to get it up 'fore they return. Won't be a big one, but least they'd have a roof over their heads come winter. Figure we got at least three-four weeks."

Otis thought for a moment, then said, "That be a fine idea."

It was afternoon, by the time Calamity Jane reined her horse to a halt in front of the Pickering's. She dismounted and, as she cinched the reins to the hitching rail, Abigail came out onto the porch. "Well, as I live an' breathe, Miss Jane! What brings you out all this way?"

"Well, first of all, how's that miracle boy of yours doin'?"

"Fine and dandy thanks to you. In fact, I think he's makin' a slower recovery than he needs to. Somethin' to do with book learnin' and chores, I'm thinkin'," Abigail said with a chuckle.

"The t'other thing is I need to speak to Bob and Sally Mae, and Otis too..."

"Oh, they both be gone. Headin' south to Fort Randall. Seems Bob's mother was taken ill and near died."

Calamity took a breath.

"But Otis is here. He be workin' with Nathan over at Bob's homestead. Just follow that path over yonder."

Just then, Sarah came charging out of the cabin. "Can I go with'er? Can I?!"

"No, young lady, you and I got all that dough kneadin' to finish."

"Next time there, Sarah." Jane said and headed toward the pathway.

===

It was near dusk as Bob and Boudine were ordered by one of two Fort Randall Sentries to, "Halt!"

Bob said, "Robert Duncan. Here to see Sergeant Major Bartholomew. I believe he may have brought my ailin' mother here to..."

The second sentry spoke up. "Yessir, Mister Duncan. I met you awhile back when we escorted you and your mother back to her homestead after the Lakota trouble. Private Dolan, sir."

Bob nodded to the private, "This here's Sally Mae Boudine. She be a friend of mine and my mother. Come to see if she's here abouts."

Private Dolan nodded to the other sentry and they both pulled the log gate open. "She's being cared for in the Sergeant Major's quarters, third house down from the main headquarters building."

Bob touched the brim of his *Boss of the Plains* hat and said, "Thank you, Private. Good to see you again."

As they entered the fort, the first sentry said to Bob, "That was a pisser of a storm t'other day." He then abruptly turned beet red and apologized to Boudine, "Oh, ma'am, I'm sorry! I didn't mean to..."

Boudine eased his embarrassment with, "Yup. Sure was a pisser of a storm there soldier. Sure was a pisser."

Completely wrapped in a heavy military blanket, Millie Mae Duncan sat in a rocking chair right in front of a roaring fireplace fire. Alone in the spartan but exceptionally clean and orderly military quarters of Sergeant Major Bartholomew, she did not hear Private Dolan open the front door.

The private spoke softly, "Miss Duncan. It's me, Private Dolan, ma'am. There's someone here to see you."

Millie Mae moved slightly within the wrapped blanket. "Yes?" she uttered.

Bob eased in past Dolan and placed his hand on her bent over shoulder. "It's me, Mother. It's Bob."

Without speaking, Millie Mae eased her small hand through an opening in the blanket fold and covered Bob's hand with hers.

===

Dawn was about to break over Sheriff O'Banyon's home. Next to Otis's parked coffin wagon, Calamity Jane and Otis shoveled more dirt away from the shallow grave of the sheriff's dead wife. "This ain't gonna be a pretty sight there, Miss Jane."

"I seen worse in my time, Otis," she uttered and kept digging.

"Still worrisome that O'Banyon still be buried under the name of Slye up on Boot Hill. They see that he was shot three times like Miss Boudine used to do in her shootin' act might not sit well with Sheriff Bullock."

"Then we got more work to do there, Otis."

"Where're we gonna bury'er?" Otis asked.

"Where Mother Nature will find'er and take care of business." Calamity answered. *"Ya-know, Otis, bet'cha didn't know they was never married together. T'was a winnin' bet payment to the sheriff by Al Swearengen she was..."*

"Yes, Ma'am, I did knowed that."

===

Sergeant Major Bartholomew sat huddled with Bob and Boudine at a small table away from Millie Mae, still wrapped in a blanket in front of the fireplace.

Speaking softly, Bartholomew was saying, "She had the fever somethin' fierce. We've been doin' the best we can. When she couldn't keep anything down our cook, Jasper Spence, came up with something called Confederate Hospital Soup that she could take without…"

"What the hell's that?" Boudine half whispered.

"Something the Rebs came up with during the war. Seems all they had. But it worked. Two pieces of burnt toast in hot water and fed as a broth. She was able to keep it down. Got'er on regular beef soup now and she seems to be getting a little stronger by the…"

"I can hear ye over here," came Millie Mae's soft voice from beneath her wrapped blanket. "I be leavin' here sooner than y'all think."

Bob set a wicker cage with Buzzer, Millie Mae's cat inside, into her wagon with as many of her personal things, from her sod house, that could fit and also have space for her to rest and sleep on the trek back to Belle Fourche. Stubs the dog fidgeted nervously around the goings on. "That's about it then, Mother.

Can't fit no more. The Major said he'll tend to the goats and such back at the fort for you."

"You mean, Jasper Spence will be cookin' up chicken soup and goat stew for the troops is what you're sayin'," Millie Mae muttered.

Bob didn't answer as he mounted his horse. Boudine tied the length of rope from around her horse's neck to the back of the wagon and climbed up onto the driver's box beside Millie Mae. As she started to slap the reins onto the rump of Millie Mae's horse to get started, Millie Mae held up her hand. She gave her homestead a quiet look-around and let her life's memories flood back one last time.

"Sometimes just sayin' it won't do it. But, doin' it will more than just say it.
Let's go then."

===

Otis hoisted a cleaned-up log rafter support to Nathan atop the nearly finished roof of the small cabin they've been constructing, since Bob and Boudine departed.

"How long now since they left?" Otis asked.

"Been near on four weeks give or take. Remember, it be 'bout six-hundred miles with the turnaround."

Just then, an out of breath Abigail came bustling from the pathway through the woods up to them. "Nathan! Otis! There's the Sheriff Seth Bullock come to the house!"

Seth Bullock appeared from behind Abigail and stopped a distance apart, with his hand next to his holstered six-gun.

"Hello, Otis."

Otis did not respond.

"As I remember, you were going to meet me at the sheriff's office to turn in your badge and collect what you were owed," Bullock said.

Otis took a deep breath, gathered his resolve, then retorted with, "Well, I seen things different. Ain't no way I go back to swampin' an' catchin' rats for Mister Swearengen or no one else no more!"

"Well, Otis, be that as it may, you up and leaving Deadwood without saying anything did leave me and also Miss Marchbanks with some questions about..."

"'Bout nothin'! I ain't goin' back there again for no reason! Ain't no law about leavin' Deadwood!"

A bit frustrated, Bullock cleared his throat but stayed calm. "There's a fella name of Cyrus James, who I understand worked with you up on Boot Hill. Said he thinks he saw you leaving the back way from there yesterday night. Said he's sure it was you and..."

Otis blurted out, "He's a drunken fool. By mid-mornin' he be 'bout as much help as a dead fly on a cow-flop. By noon, he be face down where he was last standin'."

Nathan stepped forward. "If I may, Sheriff, Otis here is part of our family now. And, as you know, if'n he didn't give his old badge to my son, Ben, we wouldn't be havin' this conversation. Also, I'm a pretty good judge of character. For, if'n I wasn't, I'd be starin' down into an empty gold siftin' pan 'stead of buildin' up this crop raisin' homestead you seem so interested in. Now, I believe you have wasted enough of our time here." He then said to Abigail, "Would you please take Sheriff Bullock here back to his horse and see that he has water and whatever else he needs for his ride back to Deadwood."

Bullock raised his hand and said to Otis, "Mister James was sent out to O'Banyon's home to retrieve his wife's coffin."

"T'weren't his wife an' there weren't no coffin she was buried in."

"I see. But what I was saying is that Mister James came back and told me the grave was empty."

Otis stiffened a bit, then uttered, "Prob'ly varments got to'er."

===

"We gotta do somethin' here, Slye. She's burnin' up and babblin' about things," Boudine said to Bob, as she reached down from her perch next to him on the driver's box, to where Millie Mae was laying beneath some blankets on the wagon bed and felt her head.

Bob reined the horse to a stop. Stubs the dog was curled up at Millie's feet and began to whine. Bob jumped down from the driver's box and leaned over his mother.

"Mother?" he said softly and felt her head. "Damn," he breathed.

"What're we gonna do?" Boudine asked Bob.

"When I got the fever one winter, she packed me in snow to bring the fever down. Looks to be we're comin' up on that cold creek outside of Scooptown we come across. Maybe, half day's ride."

At the creek, Bob had taken a blanket and soaked it in the cold water. Boudine was at the wagon, taking the dry blankets off

Millie Mae. Bob brought the wet, cold blanket up to them and they began to cover her with it. Millie Mae let out a gasp, but didn't move it away.

"This's colder than the balls on a brass monkey, Slye!"

"S'gotta be done!"

"We should push on," Boudine said. "Only 'bout a day's ride from here on in I'm thinkin'."

"It's all gone!" Millie Mae blurted out and tried to sit up.

"Easy, Mother," Bob said and pressed his hand on her shoulder to keep her down.

"That was all I had... I put my whole life into that place... and... and, now it's all broke up and gone forever." Millie Mae uttered with deep sobs. "What'd I ever do wrong? I never danced with the Devil! I was good to folks. I read my Bible…"

Bob took the wet blanket and headed for the creek. "I'll wet this up again and we'll head on 'til dark. Don't think travelin' at night be a good thing. You set there with'er and keep the blanket tucked in around'er."

"I ain't never seen her like this. She never cried about nothin'. She always told me to stick to it. Stick it out. Things're bound to get better."

"She ever had the fever like this?"

"Don't think so. Least not when I was around. Never said nothin'."

"Then she don't know what she's sayin' or thinkin'. I seen the fever take over people and scramble their head somethin' fierce. Probably, won't remember a thing once the fever leaves'er."

===

The finished little log cabin seemed to glow beneath the late morning sunlight that sifted down through the pines onto where Otis and Nathan, along with a much better Ben, stood admiring their handiwork. A small log bed frame. "Now, that be just the right size, I'm thinkin' there, Otis."

"Need two more, Pa," Ben piped up.

"S'right, but this'll do for Bob's mother 'til we get to the others. Let's get this into the cabin. Your Ma and Sarah are sewin' up the bedding and..."

The sound of Abigail's clattering meal triangle rippled through the woods. "What's this now? Ain't near mealtime," Nathan said, as he and Otis hefted the bed frame into the cabin.

Ben took off running. "I'll go see!"

Nathan and Otis walked from the woods to where Abigail and Sarah watched a wagon approach from a distance. Sarah ran to her father and exclaimed excitedly, "Pa! It's them! It's Bob and Boudine!"

"But, there ain't no one else." said Ben.

Nathan spoke up, "Just hold your britches, Son, there be three horses altogether and I do believe I see a dog pokin' its head out there."

As Bob guided the wagon up in front of the Pickering cabin, he made a hushing gesture and looked down at Millie Mae. "She's still sleepin'. Had a rough time with it all," he whispered. But the Pickering hound spotted Stubs the dog and Buzzer the big gray cat in the cage and started barking and scampering excitedly around the wagon.

"What's all the fuss?" Millie Mae said, as she eased herself up to a sitting position.

Bob looked stunned for a moment.

"Well don't just sit there, Son. Introduce me to your friends here."

Nathan stepped forward with his hand out. "Nathan Pickering, ma'am, and this here's my wife Abigail. Our daughter

Sarah there, and our son Ben, who's about to get our hound there to stop barkin', right Ben?"

"Right honored to meet y'all," Millie Mae said.

Still taken aback by the change in Millie Mae, Bob asked, "How're you feelin', Mother?"

"Much better thanks to that medicine Sally Mae give me last night. Much better indeed."

Bob shot Boudine a quick look of utter disapproval.

"You give'er that Chinese Medicine of yours? Are you goddamned crazy? She ain't never had nothin' more'n goat's milk or cow milk or plain water her entire life!"

"She kick the bucket?"

"What?!"

"She look like she's dyin' there, Slye?"

"No-but..."

"Well, there-ya go then."

Sarah stepped closer to the wagon. "My brother got shot right in his badge!"

Abigail said to Sarah, "Not now, Sarah. That'll all come later. Now I suggest you lead the way 'cross to Bob's homestead. I believe there's somethin' waitin' for them to see.

Sarah brightened and raced to the head of the pathway through the woods. "This way! Follow me!"

Sarah was already standing at the door to the new log cabin. Bob reined the horse and wagon up to the newly built hitching post that'd been set into the ground. As the Pickerings and Otis followed, Bob looked stunned, as well as Boudine. Taking in the sight, Millie Mae uttered, "What's all this then?"

Nathan clapped Otis on his shoulder. "Well, we thought it a good idea that y'all might want a roof over your heads during the coming winter months. Gets dang cold here and snows some at times."

Ben piped up, "I helped."

Nathan agreed, "You sure did. Now, it ain't the biggest cabin in the world, but it should do until spring."

Millie Mae, still seated in the wagon bed uttered, "My goodness... I don't have the words... I..."

Bob went to her, "You feelin' good enough to get down from there?"

Millie Mae brightened, "Surely do... I surely do!"

With that, Bob helped his mother down from the wagon. Millie Mae wavered a bit. "Woe-is-me. Bit shaky there, I'm afraid."

Bob held her arm firmly. "I've got'cha."

Sarah hurried over in front of Millie Mae. "What am I to call you?"

Abigail admonished her, "Sarah, your manners, please."

"But I can't call her *mother*, I already have one."

Millie Mae started gaining her balance and smiled at Sarah, "You're absolutely right, Sarah. You just call me Millie Mae is all that's needed."

"Why is your dog shiverin' so bad up there?"

Abigail said again, "Sarah, please."

Millie Mae looked at Stubs, still up on the full wagon, shivering to beat all. "Well, that's Stubs. We been together for I don't know how long. He ain't used to people and other dogs, but he's a kind one and I think he'll get used to it here in due time. Now that Buzzer cat is another thing. Have to put'er in this here cabin for a bit, 'til she gets out on'er own."

"Now, Sarah, you hush up and let Millie Mae take a look inside," Abigail ordered.

Sarah said, "I'll get the door." and scooted to the cabin door and opened it wide.

Standing in the open doorway, with the morning sun streaming in behind them, Millie Mae and Bob tried to take in the clean, new shelter. Although Millie Mae did her best not to give in to an overwhelming feeling that seemed to be overtaking her, she couldn't help dabbing at a tear welling in her eye. Sarah slid in around them and announced, "See the bed they built? Me and Ma been stitchin' up the bed makin's for-ya."

As Millie Mae stepped further into the cabin, Bob said softly to her, "I told you I was gonna be makin' somethin' good here one day."

Mille Mae didn't answer, just lightly patted his arm.

Abigail stepped in, "Now, I suggest that the men here start unloadin' Millie Mae's things and..."

Sarah jumped in with, "Can I help? Please?"

Abigail sighed deeply and said to her over-excited daughter, "Not now, young lady. You and me's going to go back and put a food table together for all these folks and then, maybe, you can help."

With most of Millie Mae's possessions moved into the cabin and Millie Mae now seated in her bedroom rocking chair, Bob looked around and said, "Lookin' better now."

"Indeed, it does," Millie Mae said, but rather weakly.

"Nathan spoke up," How're you feelin' there?"

"Well," Millie Mae replied, "rather tuckered, I'm afraid, but still thankful to y'all for all you've been doin' for me here."

"Oh, this is just the beginning. Now, we'll get that potbellied stove you brung with you put in first thing, then we'll see to it you have a wash sink built over'n that corner, I'm thinkin'."

Ben piped up with "And a privy so she can…"

Nathan instantly started to admonish Ben, but Millie Mae's hearty chuckle brought the others to a chorus of robust laughter.

Very quietly, Stubs the dog poked his head into the doorway and then, after a moment, went over to Millie Mae and laid his head gently onto her knee.

That night, Bob was in his bedroll in the prairie schooner next to Boudine.

After a moment, Bob spoke to her in low tones, "I'm gonna hav'ta get somethin' goin' real soon. I'm runnin' out of money. Gettin' down pretty low because of all these new doin's."

"What'chu wanna do 'bout it then?"

"Either go back and clean out that rattlesnake nest hidin' place of yourn or sit at the tables in Deadwood again."

Boudine was quiet for a moment, then, "Might be faster to hit a couple of stages. An' a lot easier."

"No... I promised myself that, once I got my mother moved off'n that dirt pile, I'd quit the robbin' business for good."

"Humph! Them's the kinda promises that's meant to be broken."

"Not by me..."

"Then, the tables it is then."

Suddenly, something hurled itself through the canvas canopy opening and landed between Bob and Boudine. "What the hell!" Bob reacted.

"Shite!" Boudine shouted, as she reached for her holstered gun lying nearby.

Then, it was the loud buzzing purr of Buzzer, Millie Mae's big gray mouser, that quickly allayed their fears, by showing off the large rat-kill she had just undertaken.

DEAL THE CARDS

NINE

"I don't think it'd be a good idea that we play cards at the same place," Bob said.

"Why not? We got a good way of not comin' up empty."

"I might still be known at Nuttal and Mann's and you might be too."

"Me? Might know me as a sixteen-year-old boy, but they don't know me," Said Boudine with more than a little defiance in her voice.

Bob said firmly, "Maybe you don't remember that woman, dressed like a man, with a man's haircut, what cleaned out those poker players a couple of nights a'fore Wild Bill was killed."

Boudine took this in.

Bob added, "And, maybe you don't remember those stages that were hit outside of Deadwood that everyone said were robbed by a woman."

Still defiant, Boudine said, "Well, Wild Bill ain't there no more and sure as hell, I don't look the same, or ain't you noticed?"

Bob looked at Boudine's longer, curly, auburn hair and the cleaner clothes she was wearing and, the fact that she was looking more womanly than before. "Still..."

"Still what?"

"We can't take chances that someone finds out we been workin' together. 'Specially, since I been takin' up roots in Belle Fourche. Also, there's your friend, Calamity Jane, and weren't you questioned by that Sheriff Seth Bullock there?"

"Only because of Jane shootin' out that saloon window. Nothin' about what I was doin'."

"But that's what I'm sayin'. You are known to them folks, so's we got to be more careful, that's all," Bob said.

Boudine thought about it for a moment, then said, "Alrighty then, we split up. You go to Nuttal and Mann's and I'll sit in at the Gem."

"You sure they's gonna cotton to a woman at the poker table?"

"They'd better if'n they knows what's good for'em."

A place at a poker table opened up at the Gem Theater and Gambling Hall. Boudine immediately took the open chair, sat down, took off her range hat and shook her curls rather noticeably. The men at the table did, indeed, take notice. One player, in particular, spoke up, "I don't play against no woman!"

Boudine smirked, sniffed and wiped her nose on her sleeve. "You mean, you don't lose against no woman."

The man gritted as the other men at the table chuckled, "I said..."

Boudine spoke over him, "Tell'ya what. If'n I don't win the first three hands dealt to me, I'll leave y'all to it, how's that?"

A seasoned drover spoke up, "Hell, I'll be glad to take yer money. Deal the cards."

===

Hearing dogs barking outside of her new cabin, Millie Mae shoved back covers on her new bed, got up and opened the door. There, outside, were both the Pickering's hound and Stubs tearing around in circles after each other and having a hell of a time!

Millie Mae walked out of the woods and across the yard to the Pickering cabin. Abigail called out from the chicken pen, "Millie Mae! Fresh eggs for breakfast. Help me gather, they been over workin' here."

In the cooking area of her cabin, Abigail answered the question Millie Mae had posed to her, "They must've left before daybreak. Otis said they headed into Deadwood for supplies. I reckon to stock you up with."

"Is it far?"

"Not bad as the crow flies. Less'n a day's ride round trip. We go in several times a year for salt, flour and such. Soon's you get your sea legs, we'll go on and show you the place. But I have'ta say, it really ain't no place for a good Christian woman to be hangin' around in, 'cept they do have what we need to fill out the necessaries here."

At Nuttal and Mann's, as he usually did, Bob let the first few hands go, before setting himself for some high pot wins. A carpetbagger spoke up, as Bob hauled in the winning chips. "You look kinda familiar, there. You played here before?"

Without hesitating, Bob answered his question, "Yessir, I did play at this very table some time back. Best I can recollect, t'was the night before Wild Bill Hickok was killed."

The carpetbagger cut the deck that Bob offered him. "I do... I do remember you. Did quite well as I recall."

"T'was a respectable evening," Bob said as he dealt out the cards to the players.

"Don't recall what you said you do, besides poker."

"Don't remember sayin' but I do have another line of work," Bob said, as the players discarded, and Bob dealt them cards.

"And what might that be, if I might ask?"

Bob looked at his hand and stood pat... "I write stories about the Western Frontier for magazines and books for publishers in the East."

The carpetbagger was taken aback. "Hell, you say. And, that writin' game pays good?"

"It pays 'til it don't."

"Humph... well, maybe someday you can make me famous."

"Maybe," Bob said, as he spread his cards face up on the table and let the players see his straight flush.

"That's five winnin' hands in a row there!" The player who disliked Boudine snapped, as he tossed his cards right at Boudine at the Gem poker table.

"Guess I get to stay at this table then," Boudine retorted, sniffed and gathered up the cards into an expert shuffle, then set the deck right in front of the player as a challenge.

"I think you're a goddamned cheat! What's your name anyway? I ain't never seen you around here a'fore."

She did not hesitate, "Name's Boudine and I don't need to cheat. I'm just a goddamned good player. You in or not?"

Over at the far end of the long bar, Calamity Jane went unnoticed by Boudine, as she watched the goings on with great interest.

At the table at Nuttal and Mann's, Bob folded his hand and passed the cards to the winner who shuffled the deck and was about to start the game when three quick loud shots rang out from a distance away.

A wrangler, standing in the opened doorway with a beer in his hand announced, "That came from over'ta the Gem!"

Without showing any alarm, Bob indicated that he was out of the game, by gathering in his chips and getting up from the table. "Gentlemen," he said, as he touched the brim of his *Boss of the Plains* hat and headed for the doorway, "Hope to see y'all again soon."

As Bob pushed through the onlookers and entered the Gem Gambling Hall, he could hear Sheriff Seth Bullock shouting for everyone to quiet down. "Everyone stay in your place until I say. No one leaves."

On the floor opposite where Boudine was seated. The angry player lay prone with three bullet wounds. One in the right shoulder. One in the left shoulder and one right between his eyes... *"King-Queen-Ace"*

Bob stood back, as Bullock ordered Boudine, "I want you to come with me over to the jail right now."

"What the hell for?! The sumbitch drew on me! I just kilt'im 'fore he kilt me!"

Calamity Jane walked over and said to Bullock, "She's sayin' the truth, Seth. I seen the whole thing."

Bullock reddened noticeably at Calamity's declaration. Then, he said to the others in the room, "Anyone here say different?"

A gambler at the table spoke up. "That's so. He done drew first, but she was winnin' way more'n anyone here and it looked pretty damned fishy if'n you ask me."

Boudine spat out, "That ain't no reason to pull a dang gun on me, goddammit!"

"Quiet down!" Bullock shouted. Then to Boudine he demanded, "Now, you get yourself over to the jail office and wait for me there."

"I'm takin' my winnin's with me," Boudine said loudly and started sweeping her chips off the table into her range hat.

"I'll go with'er," Calamity said to Bullock, who just nodded at her.

Bob headed unnoticed out the front door.

Two horse-drawn traveling show wagons lumbered along the rutted, piss-puddled street toward the Gem Theater in front of Calamity and Boudine who stopped to let it pass. Boudine, in particular, noticed the gaily painted figures of the scantily clad female dancers and the large, colorful portrait of the star of the troupe, the Irish singer Grace Doyle. "You seen that show a'fore?" Calamity asked Boudine.

"No," Boudine answered, then mumbled, as she followed Calamity along toward the jail, "heard of'er once."

Bob stepped up onto the boardwalk in front of the jailhouse office, where Boudine and Calamity Jane were waiting for Sheriff Bullock. "What the hell were you thinkin' there, Boudine? One shot would'a done it."

"What the hell was I supposed to do let'im shoot me, for chrissakes?"

"You didn't have'ta shoot'im with your *King-Queen-Ace* there, Boudine. Might's well put a damned sign on'ya," Bob retorted, "Now you got'cha'self a little predicament here."

"He won't do nothin'," Calamity said to him. "That fella's been askin' for trouble for some time now. Was bound to get his sooner or later. It's just that Seth and Al Swearengen have been at each other since Seth was appointed sheriff."

"That so?"

"Yeah, Al has been gnawing on Seth for not keepin' the peace around the Gem an' Seth's been sayin' that it's Al's fault there's been so many dustups lately over there."

"You there!" a man called out to Bob, as they turned toward the sheriff's office door.

Bob didn't answer, but certainly recognized the portly man as the one-and-the-same Judge Raintree, who signed and stamped his hanging paper the morning that Sheriff O'Banyon led him out to the hanging tree.

"You look familiar there. I know you?"

"Don't think so," Bob said quietly.

"Yeah-yeah, I know you from somewhere."

"I only play cards at Number 10 Nuttal and Mann's, you play there?"

"No," Raintree answered, getting a bit irritated. "I never forget a face."

"Who might you be, then?" Bob asked, not the least bit flustered.

"Judge Raintree."

Calamity Jane spoke up, "Oh, you be the Hangin' Judge what used to do ol' Jack O'Banyon's dirty work for'im," she said with a very sarcastic chuckle.

Raintree turned livid. "You can't talk to me like that, woman!"

"Fuck you! I hear tell you ain't even a real judge an' you ain't supposed to be 'round here no more."

"What's all this now?" Sheriff Bullock said, as he strode along the boardwalk to the sheriff's office. "What the hell're you doing here, Raintree?"

"I ain't been paid for the last hangin' signin' I did for O'Banyon. I came to collect."

"How much?"

"Twenty dollars gold."

"That's a pretty fancy sum there, Raintree. Especially to someone who might not even be a real judge."

"That's what I said," Calamity chimed in with.

"You stay out of this!" Raintree barked, then said, "I ain't leavin' 'till I'm made even."

Bullock reached into his pocket and came up with a gold piece and handed it to Raintree, who immediately bit into it to test for a counterfeit. "Now, make yourself scarce around here, if you know what's good for you. The rest of you into my office here," Bullock ordered as he opened the office door.

As Bob passed by, Raintree hissed at him, "I know you. I seen you before."

Bob did not respond as he followed the rest into the sheriff's office and closed the door behind him.

Inside, Bob noticed that little had changed since he was sentenced to death in front of the same desk that Bullock stepped behind. The case of O'Banyon's guns was gone, the lingering stench of human waste from the hallway to the jail cells was the same.

"First off, this situation isn't over yet. Miss Boudine, I want you to remain in Deadwood overnight. I still have more people who saw what happened to talk to.

"Am I under arrest?" Boudine demanded.

"Not yet and maybe not ever, the way the stories are going. But I want all the details in before I let you go. Also, that man you shot was fairly important in this town and... "

Calamity interrupted, "Important to who? He was just one of Al Swearengen's ruffians."

"That's enough, Jane!" Bullock shouted. Then to Boudine, "Be here nine o'clock sharp."

"You can stay with me at the Gem," Calamity said to Boudine.

"No, she can't. I don't want her anywhere near the Gem. You hear me?"

"You can put up over t'the Grand. I'll tell Aunt Lou," said Bob.

Bullock looked at Bob for a second, then said, "You're the one who put down that bank robber's horse I shot the other day."

"Yessir."

"Thank you for that. Very bad shot on my part, I'm afraid. What's your name again?"

"Bob Duncan."

"Right-right... you're the one who owns the homestead next to the Pickering place."

"Yessir."

"And you're friends with these two here?"

Bob hesitated for a moment, then said, "Well, more of a friend to Boudine here. I just recently met Miss Jane."

Bullock muttered to himself, then to Boudine he said, "I would like to hear more of your own story. Seems you might be more than just a *horse trainer*."

Bob and Boudine huddled at a small table in Lucretia Marchbank's restaurant. Night was accumulating outside, and the distant rumbling of a thunderstorm was roiling toward Deadwood.

Bob said to Boudine in hushed tones, "Look, that judge you saw before came all too close for comfort."

Boudine said, "Bullock said he ain't a real judge. 'Sides he was drunk."

"Don't make no difference. He was the one who signed and stamped my hangin' paper for O'Banyon."

Boudine leaned in closer. "But you're dead and buried. The Bandit Bob Slye is in a box up there on Boot Hill."

"No... that be Sheriff Jack O'Banyon who's dead an' buried up on Boot Hill."

"That ain't what the marker says."

Bob went silent for a long moment, then uttered, "Lessen they open the box."

Lucretia Marchbanks came through the door of the hallway to the Grand Central Hotel and said to Bob and Boudine, "Only but one room left. Good thing you two are friends," she said with a sly grin. "Now, I'll dish y'all up some vittles to tide you over." Then, right to Boudine she said, "And don't you worry none 'bout what happened. Words comin' back that you had every right to shoot that old coot. Had it comin' to'im s'what's bein' said."

Just then, a drunken Mexican wild-eyed cowboy came bursting through the front door brandishing a six-shooter in every direction and shouting wildly in Spanish, "Acabo de disparar a una Indio y quiero disparar un poco mas!"

Bob instantly went for his holstered Peacemaker. Just as quickly, Aunt Lou waved him off and strode right to the drunken cowboy. In one motion, she slapped the gun from his hand and pulled her meat-cutting knife from its sheath on her apron belt and set the sharp edge right next to his jugular vein. Then, spewing rapid-fire Spanish, she shoved the man toward the front door, "Sal de Deadwood y no vuelvas nunca!" With that, she pushed the drunk hard right out the door flat on his back onto the wooden walkway. As Aunt Lou turned back into the room and shoved her meat knife into its sheath, the patrons in the restaurant started clapping and whistling their approval.

Lucretia grinned at them all and walked over to Bob and Boudine. Boudine spoke up. "That was really somethin'."

"Well, people like me get someplace by doin' things and last… or don't do nothin' and don't last."

Later, outside on the dimly lit walkway in front of the Grand Central Hotel, a steady rain was falling. Some rolling thunder and flashes of distant lightning brightened the receding storm clouds. Boudine started to open the hotel door, then noticed that Bob was looking off up the street. "You comin'?" she asked.

"In a while… got somethin' to take care of first."

Boudine hardened a bit, "Well, get done with'er quick then."

"What?"

"You heard me. Get over what you have'ta get over with that Irish singer over there at the Gem. But don't linger too long or I might just come over there and show'er my *King-Queen-Ace*."

With that, Boudine went into the hotel, leaving Bob standing in the dark, in the rain.

Although their horses had been put up at a livery, the decorated traveling troupe wagons were still parked outside the Gem in the muck and rain puddles. Bob wandered quietly up to the lead wagon. The one with the voluptuous Grace Doyle's mural painted on the side. He saw that there was a low flickering light coming from behind a small, curtained window. He hesitated for a long moment, then lightly knocked on the closed wagon door. No one answered. He knocked a bit harder. A raspy voice, with a distinct Irish brogue called out, "Who's there?"

Bob exhaled a sigh, then uttered, "It's Robert Duncan, ma'am."

"Who?" came an irritated rasp.

"Robert Duncan, ma'am. We met some time ago and..."

"Go away," came the rasp again.

"Um... you gave me the mustache and the white greasepaint for my horse."

There was silence from inside. Then, Bob heard movement and saw the door handle turn and open the door slightly. He could see a shadowed face peering out at him. "Come closer," the raspy Irish voice demanded.

Bob stepped closer. He could see that it was Grace Doyle staring back at him. Slowly, Grace pushed the door open and eased back into a chair inside the wagon. "Come in, Robert Duncan."

Bob hesitated then gingerly stepped up into the dimly lit wagon and closed the door. As he sat in another chair opposite her, Grace continued, "Or, should I say, Bandit Bob Slye?"

Bob began to focus on the person opposite him in the glow of a single oil lamp set on a small round doily-laced table next to her. "That is who you are, isn't it?"

Bob cleared his throat. "He was hung out on a hangin' tree some time ago."

"Mmmm..." Grace uttered and took up a packet of three-for-five-cents cheroots and dragged out one of the dark hand-rolled smokes with her tongue. As she lit up with a sulfur head match, she said, "And, here he sits right in front of me. A miracle..." She then sucked in a gulp of cheroot smoke and began a deep series of coughs, until she was able to speak again. "You know there, *Robert Duncan*, I liked you enough from our little time together at the old Gem Theater, to follow the exploits of this certain bandit in the newspapers that I'd pick up in the different stops where we played. I rather enjoyed seeing the wanted poster likenesses of that fellow with that mustache I gave to you and the description of a roan horse with a white star on its forehead.

Funny, they never mentioned that the star was some of my very own white greasepaint."

She sucked in more cheroot smoke and broke into another coughing spasm. Bob noticed that her heavily made-up face wasn't as round and pink as he'd remembered. The oil lamp flared up for a moment. Grace reached over and turned the wick down a bit. He saw that her cheeks were more hollow and, even though she was only a few years older than Bob, her skin had a sallow look and seemed to sag more than a woman her age should. "You sayin' you ain't one and the same there, Bob?"

Bob was silent for a moment, then said quietly, but firmly, "The Bandit Bob Slye is dead."

Grace sat back and exhaled a billow of cheroot smoke and tried to stifle her cough by reaching for a brown medicine bottle and taking a healthy sip. "Laudanum. Cures what's ailin'ya."

As she re-corked the bottle, Bob noticed a slight shaking in her hands. She gave him a big grin. Bob could not help seeing that the bright, white-toothed smile he remembered had disappeared into a smoke-stained shadow. Her once laughing eyes seemed dull and distant. Grace saw that he was staring at her and said in a low, Irish tinged voice, "You know, Bob, I taught ye well back then. I can see that in you here. So, it makes me feel glad and proud that we met up again, now." She broke into a long coughing spasm and took another slug of Laudanum. Grace regained her voice and said. "Now, it's time for you to skedaddle on and go about whatever it is you do now. There ain't nothin' more I can teach you, Robert, that you ain't already learned. But always remember, I taught you what I knew then with love."

Bob stood in the darkened hallway outside the room in the Grand Central Hotel for a moment. The sight of the tear in Grace's eye, as he left her wagon, still in his mind. Finally, he opened the door and went inside.

In the darkness, Boudine said to him, "You alright now?"

"Yes."

"Good."

"A boy like you – I know you ain't a boy no more – but a boy like you only comes by once in a lifetime and deserves to be remembered. You were that boy to me, that's why I followed your exploits as best I could in the newspapers. That's how I know you got a woman in your life. Another bandit, for sure. How do I know, you say? We rolled into Yankton the same day the train was robbed by a bandit with a mustache, a horse with a white star on its forehead and a lady bandit with a lightning-fast draw, who was able to stop two American Express Agents in their tracks before

disappearing with carpetbags full of loot. I also read in the Press Democrat that a certain bandit said he wanted to repent and gave instructions as to where all his plunder could be found Jesus, I sure hoped that stupid sumbitch wasn't you!"

Bob woke with a start! He looked around the small daylight lit hotel room and saw that Boudine wasn't there. "Shite!" he uttered and threw the blankets back.

As Bob hurriedly stepped from the rain-soaked muck up onto the boardwalk in front of the jail office, Boudine came out followed by Calamity Jane. "I'm sorry I slept through...I..."

"Don't make no matter. We can go."

Calamity said, "She's clean as a whistle, 'cept she can't go 'round the Gem poker tables no more."

"Damned shame too. I would'a liked to've cleaned out some more of them suckers."

Calamity said to Boudine, "Look, Seth ain't a bad sort, but he has'ta try an' keep this place from blowin' up. He let you off after you told'im 'bout bein' with the Bill Cody shows an' workin' with me an' Wild Bill. So, a word to the wise..."

Boudine grinned a little. "Like not shootin' out saloon windows?"

Calamity chuckled, "Shite, Sally Mae, get your ass outta here!"

===

"How much your winnin's come to?" Boudine asked Bob, as they rode back toward Belle Fourche at a leisurely pace.

"'Nough to get a start on puttin' together a cabin. But, not near enough to do what has to be done. Just have'ta get a move on 'fore the snow hits."

"I done pretty good."

They rode on quietly passed where the three rivers merged when Boudine said, "There's more..."

"More what?"

"More of what Bullock had to say."

Bob reined in his horse and stopped. Boudine did as well and turned her horse to face Bob. "Didn't seem like much at the time, but he seemed curious about that there judge. Asked a few questions about what you do for a livin' and about how we become friends."

"I already told'im what I do."

"I know, I told'im the same thing, that you do writin' 'bout the West an' stuff."

"What else?" Bob asked.

"Nothin' really. Said he and his partner might be comin' out here to talk to Nathan and you 'bout some buildin' thing they're thinkin' of doin' 'round Belle Fourche. "

"That's it?"

"Yup."

Bob chirked his roan forward. Boudine did the same. "Don't feel right," Bob uttered, as they picked up the pace.

===

"Boudine says that Sheriff Bullock said him and his partner, Sol Star, may be comin' out this way to talk to us 'bout some buildin' they plan on doin' here'bouts."

At the head of the dining table in the Pickering cabin, Nathan passed a bowl of squash to the others. "I spoke with Mister Star, when Bullock first tried to talk to me about slicing off some of our homestead here. Shifty eyes that one. Their kind never stops."

Millie Mae, rather quietly, spoke up, "They just can't take away a homestead, can thay?"

Otis, who almost never spoke during a meal, added quite abruptly, "Them that's got money think they can do anything they wants."

His utterance caused a pause in the conversation, then Bob said to Millie Mae, very forcefully, "I don't want you to worry none, Mother. They don't know who they'd be comin' up against, ifin' they try."

All eyes were on Bob for a long moment, as what he said sank in.

Millie Mae broke the silence with, "Well greed begets greed, and nothin' happens 'til it happens."

As Bob and Boudine settled into their bedrolls in the prairie schooner for the night, Boudine said, "I'm thinkin' we'd better go on to the hidin' place and retrieve our loot. Looks like we're gonna need it."

The first frost appeared on the skinned logs, piled next to the log frames of the four-room cabin that Bob and Otis had erected, in a cleared area, not a far distance from Millie Mae's small cabin. "Might have'ta get these walls and roof done up sooner than later. I smell the flurries not far away."

"We'll do it in time, Mister Duncan. Don't you worry none."

"For the last time, Otis, stop callin' me *Mister*. The name's Bob."

Otis set his large iron sledgehammer head on the ground and put both hands firmly on the handle top. "There's some that deserves to be called, *Sir* and *Mister* and thems that don't. You deserves to be called *Mister* and that's it."

"Where'd you ever hear that, Otis?"

"Aunt Lou."

"Oh, well, then if she said so, I guess it's so. Have you found a spot to build your cabin yet?"

"Lots to do here, but I'll get to it. Maybe, come spring. The barn suits me fine for now."

I might be needin' to borrow your wagon for a bit, next couple of days. Got some things to fetch back here 'fore the feeeze sets in."

"Sure thing. You need anythin' else, just say."

"Grappling hook and a rope."

"Got that too. Used it to lower all them coffins into their ditches. All 'cept for O'Banyon's. Just kicked his over into the hole. Landed upside down s'I recall."

Bob reined in Otis's coffin wagon, as Millie Mae crossed in front of it, heading to the Pickering cabin.

'Mornin' there, Son! You're up bright an' early," Millie Mae greeted.

"Might say the same for you there, Mother."

"I be helpin' with the youngun's Bible readin' so's Abigail has a little time for herself. You do remember our Bible readin' growin' up, Son?"

"I surely do, Mother, I surely do. Um, Boudin's in there puttin' together some travelin' food for us. Tell'er to get a rustle on so's we can get started."

"Where're y'all headed?" Millie Mae asked curiously.

"Gon' to get some of Boudine's particulars she left down Scooptown way 'fore the winter sets in. Ain't all that far as the crow flies. Two-three days at the most."

"Oh, good!" she exclaimed as she hurriedly reached into her pant pocket and pulled out a sealed mailing envelope and handed it to Bob, "If'n y'all could kindly post this on yer way that'd be most helpful."

Bob looked at the address. Millie Mae said, "'Tis to Mister Bartholomew. He be waitin' on word of my well bein'. Want to let'im know how such good things are happenin' here." Bob put the envelope into his shirt. "Now, I'll go on in and fetch Sally Mae and you take good care, hear?"

"Yes, ma'am," he said with a dutiful smile.

SNAKES

TEN

Wisps of dust twirled in little twisters across the rugged trail where Bob and Boudine drove Otis's coffin wagon. A large, dried ball of sagebrush bounced in front of them and caused the horse to shy a bit. Bob reined it in. Boudine spotted a lone rider approaching from a distance and said, "Damn, don't need no roustabouts nosin' around us."

A scrawny, wizened, down-and-out stranger, riding a boney horse, passed by. He gave Bob and Boudine a silent, squinted, sidelong look and kept going.

Boudine remarked suspiciously, "You see that look he give us?"

"What about it?"

"Don't feel right. He's heftin' a ton of fleas, that one."

"Just a saddle-tramp traveler s'all."

"They's always *just a traveler* 'fore they shoot you in the back."

With the coffin wagon parked nearby, Boudine approached the abandoned well and tentatively looked down into it. "Stuffs still there. Fetch me the grapple hook'n'rope there," Boudine said to Bob. As Bob brought her the hook and rope, he said, "You be careful there, Boudine. We don't need no snake bites."

Boudine eased the grapple hook and rope down into the well and hooked one of the tied-up sacks. Immediately, the sounds of rattlesnakes erupted from within the dark well. "Oh, Jesus!" Boudine exclaimed, "It's covered with'em! Get back! I'm gonna bring'er up an' flip it your way. Shoot the suckers!"

With that, Bob drew his Peacemaker and readied himself. Boudine announced, "Here she comes." Boudine jerked the hooked sack up and out with several good-sized rattlers clinging to it. The sack landed several feet away from Bob who dispatched the rattlers with three quick shots.

"Hey, good shootin' there, Slye. Like shootin' snakes in a barrel."

As they continued to haul the sacks of their loot up and out of the well, Bob's shooting echoed off across the hills and through the woods.

"Stay watchful there, Slye. Last one comin' up." Boudine said, as she flipped the grappled sack out of the well up into the air and onto the ground with a thump. Several snakes started to skitter away. Bob aimed quickly and shot two with two precise shots. A third rattler raced toward Boudine, coiled and struck, its poisonous fangs right though her pant leg.

"Shite! Got me!"

Bob ran to her, grabbed the rattler by its tail, whirled it and bashed its head against the well wall. Just then, the same grizzled stranger who passed them earlier appeared from the trees, reined up, pulled his six-shooter, and pointed it at them. "Well, lookie here. Looks like Christmas come early for me."

"Oh, you shouldn't'a done that." In a flash, Boudine whipped the Peacemaker from Bob's hand and fired off three rapid shots. One in the man's right shoulder, one in his left shoulder and one dead center between his eyes – *"King-Queen-Ace"*

The surprised look in the dead man's eyes traveled with him out of his saddle onto the ground with a thud. "Pull'em over'n dump'im in the well." Boudine ordered. "Then get out that cuttin' knife and cut me an X on the bite and start suckin'. "

As Bob dragged the dead bandit over and into the snake-filled well, Boudine muttered, "Damned waste of good lead."

"My bet is we take this wagon through another way over to where Otis hid that coffin and let him hide this for us. We don't need no curiosity comin' from the family," Boudine said. *"Be full on night by the time we get there anyway."*

"How're you feelin'?" Bob asked.

"Better. Not as good as before I got bit." Boudine sniffed.

"You use that Chinese medicine of yours?"

"S'none of your beeswax... but, yeah."

"Let Abigail have a look. She's good with wounds and such."

"Think you must've sucked most of the venom out."

"How do you know?"

"Still here, ain't I?"

===

The Pickerings were all going about their early morning chores, when Bob and Boudine appeared on the pathway from Bob's homestead. Bob led the dead bandit's horse. Boudine walked with a bit of a limp. Seeing Abigail leave the chicken coop with a basket of eggs, Bob called to her, "Mornin', Nathan about?"

"Well, mornin' there. He and the younguns went to the river with the water buckets. Should be back in a jiffy."

Bob led the horse to the hitching rail and wrapped its reins around it. Abigail approached, looked at the horse curiously but said only, "Well, looks like you made your trip without any hiccups."

Bob said, "Well, not so fairly. Boudine here..."

Boudine spoke up, "Got hit by a rattler."

Abigail reacted. Took in a deep breath, "Oh, my! We'll have'ta see..."

"Feelin' pretty good, so far. Bob here cut an X and sucked out the venom. It's mostly the cut that's bothersome."

"Alright-alright! Get yourself in with me and we'll see to it."

As Boudine followed after Abigail, Bob said to her, "I'll wait for Nathan. Got to 'splain this horse."

After listening to Bob tell him how he came to bring the horse back with them, Nathan paused. As he studied the horse, with noticeable concern showing on his face he said, "Sounds quite a similar situation with the other horse you give to us back on the trail to here some time ago."

"'Bout the same."

"Road agent?"

"Thief. Tried to rob us."

Nathan looked at the horse. "This all that's left then?"

Bob nodded and added, "No brand. Seemed not right to just leave it. Not the horse's fault."

After another pause, Nathan laid his hand on the horse and patted it. "Seems a bit scrawny. In need of some good handlin', I'm thinkin'."

"Extra mount for the young'uns," Bob said.

THE FLURRIES

ELEVEN

Gusts of wind, mixed with fallen leaves and light snowflakes washed over Bob, as he hammered iron nails into the split and hewn plank that Otis held in place, on the last opening in the roof of the four room cabin they had built on Bob's homestead. "This should do it there Otis," Bob announced. "With any luck, this should hold back the winter."

They stepped gingerly toward the ladder up against the cabin eve overhang. Otis said, "I did say, we'd get it done in time."

"Good thing. My hands are 'bout to freeze off."

"Bob! Otis!" Ben shouted, as he came barreling in from the woods, "Pa says to come quick. There's a stranger rode up to our house!"

With Ben leading the way, Bob and Otis strode up to where Nathan and Abigail stood apart from a tough looking man wearing a black wool full-length winter coat and range hat. The serious expression on Nathan's face told them that the man, standing, holding the reins to his horse, might not be there as a friend.

Nathan spoke up, "This fella here says he speaks for Seth Bullock and Sol Star. Says he wants to offer us an arrangement for a goodly slice of both our homesteads. Says that they's going to start building a new town here-abouts come spring and wants to purchase the rights to the river."

Bob paused and stared directly into the man's eyes. "Who might you be then?"

"Name's Lester Hurd. I represent Mister Bullock and Mister Star."

"What's *represent* mean?" Bob asked tersely.

"I work for their company, and they've asked me to make both of you gentleman a generous offer for..."

Bob interrupted, "Why'n't they here themselves?"

Hurd gritted a bit and answered with, "They're very busy men, sir."

Bob's eyes squinted. "Really... well, I suggest that you get back on your mount there and go back to Deadwood and tell them, that's too busy, that we here are far too busy to waste time talkin' to someone who ain't them."

Hurd stared at Bob and said, "I wouldn't recommend that, sir."

"Why's that?"

"Just that, I would not recommend that."

Bob rested his hand on the handle of his ever-present holstered Peacemaker.
"Are we to take that as a threat, Mister Hurd?"

Hurd hardened even more, "You can take it any way you wish, sir."

"Well, I believe I can speak for both Mister Pickering here and myself. As legal owners of each of these homesteads, you are trespassing and if'n you don't get your ass into that saddle and beat a hasty retreat out of here, Mister Bullock and Mister Star might not have you to call on anymore."

Hurd looked from Bob to Nathan. Neither spoke. The Pickering hound, who had been watching from the porch, sensed the tense situation and began a low growl. Stubs, Millie Mae's dog, who was right next to the hound, joined in.

Hurd slowly turned, stepped up into a stirrup and set himself into his saddle. As he reined his horse around, he said, "You're going to regret this."

Nathan spoke and said, "And I can assure you, Mister Hurd, if'n we ever see the likes of you here and about our property, we will clear you a path to Hades."

With that, Hurd jammed his spurs into his horse's flanks and galloped off in the opposite direction.

All were silent for a long moment, until Abigail said with a rather sturdy smile, "Well, I do declare. Bad egg that one."

Without going into anything at all, Bob asked Nathan to show him the boundaries of his homestead and help him determine the boundaries of his own parcel. "I'm thinkin' we should try to figure out what their aim is with wanting the rights to the river."

Nathan spoke rather calmly, "My thinkin' is that Seth Bullock already knows my answer, so's he sent his henchman to put some fear into us. If'n they do, indeed, intend to start buildin' a town hereabouts, they will need access to the river for delivery boats and barges, which means roads right through our lands and full ownership of our riverbanks. Which means more saloons, gambling and those other places of pleasure. Which brings all the trouble already got more than enough of in Deadwood and other places."

As they walked back toward the Pickering cabin, Nathan asked Bob, "You ain't said nothin' much there, Bob."

"Thinkin'..."

"Yup, it is somethin' to ponder about."

Bob stopped. "I'll be takin' Boudine and Otis into Deadwood early tomorrow." He did not continue with his thoughts.

Nathan asked hesitantly, "Pondering something?"

"Yes... pondering something. Thank you for helpin' get a good picture of what we have here, Nathan." With that, Bob headed for the path to his homestead.

Otis was finishing up building a veranda onto Millie Mae's small cabin. Bob walked up to him. "Looks good there, Otis."

"Yup, nice place to set a rocker now for the missus."

"Is Boudine about?"

"Over your place, I reckon."

Bob's voice turned serious, "Follow me, Otis."

Inside Bob's new cabin, there was a tenseness in the air. Boudine addressed Bob, "I tol' you I won't never be goin' back to Deadwood. So, what's this all about then?"

"Look, I think I have a way to fend off Seth Bullock and his like from tryin' to take over our land rights here, but it's got to be done fast, or it'll be too late."

===

The three riders approached the crowded, muddy main street of Deadwood, with the dawn fully exposed behind them. Bob led them directly to the small Land Office and dismounted. Without speaking, he opened the door for Boudine and Otis to enter. "Mornin'," Bob said to the clerk at the counter.

"Mornin'," the rather thin and boney man wearing a white business shirt with black arm garters said. "Can I help you?"

Bob spoke, "These folks are here to make claims for two full one-hundred-sixty-acre homesteads."

"Well, that's what we're here for. Now, whereabouts are these claims for?"

"Over in Belle Fourche territory. Right next to mine that I already claimed sometime back."

The clerk stiffened noticeably.

"The price is still eighteen dollars, I suspect, ain't it?"

Nervously, the clerk stammered, "Yes-No! No, it's three-hundred dollars now."

"What?!" Boudine blurted out, "You joshin' me?"

"Just when did the price change then?" Bob demanded.

The clerk stammered, as beads of sweat appeared on his forehead and upper lip. He turned and called back into the back room, "Margaret. Will you please go over to the diner and see if that *special* coffee I ordered is ready."

A tiny, youngish woman, with nervous eyes poked her head through the doorway to the back room. "Now, please," the clerk demanded. The woman disappeared and a door was heard opening and closing.

"You didn't answer my question there."

"The-the fee structure changed without notice."

"Who changed it?"

Nervously, the clerk attempted to answer, but his words became more scrambled, "I... it... just changed... that's it, it just changed."

"Bullshit!" Boudine spit out.

Bob said, "Did the United States Government change the fee? Or was it changed by someone in this town. Someone by the name of Seth Bullock, by chance?"

Otis spoke up, "Don't think that there woman's goin' to pick up no special coffee."

Bob agreed, "No she ain't, Otis, no she ain't." He turned to Boudine, "Set yourself up beside the door there." Boudine did just that. Flattened herself against the wall, drew her pistol and waited. Bob pulled his Peacemaker from its holster and set it on the counter with the barrel pointed directly at the clerk's middle. "Sure hope it don't come to this. What's your name, anyway?"

"O... Owen..." the clerk stammered.

"Okay, Owen, now reach for two homestead papers and write in the fee of eighteen dollars on each of them. Can you do that for these folks?"

Owen froze. Bob rested his hand on his Peacemaker. Owen blanched and reached into a drawer behind the counter. "Make sure that's all you come up with there, Owen."

His hands shaking, Owen set out two homestead forms on the counter. "Now, write in the eighteen-dollar fee there, Owen."

"But..."

"No *buts* there, Owen." Bob said calmly, as he moved his Peacemaker toward Owen. "Just write in the fee... NOW!"

Owen jumped and took out an ink bottle and writing pen. "Go ahead," Bob said easily.

With a very shaky hand, Owen dipped the pen in the ink and wrote the $18 figure in the space provided on both forms. "Now, you sign your name and stamp the form... DO IT!"

Again, Owen jumped and pulled out a government stamp and ink pad and quickly signed both forms and stamped them with the government seal.

Behind him, Otis announced from his position at the office window, "Someone's comin' in a hurry."

Bob reached for his Peacemaker and holstered it, leaned against the counter, and waited.

Lester Hurd came bursting into the office. "What the hell's goin' on here?"

Bob smiled and said, "Well, Mister Hurd, Mister Owen here is fillin' out two homestead claims for these folks here, that's all."

Hurd drew his gun and brandished it at both Bob and Otis, "The hell he is. Get your asses outta here and outta this town!" Hurd growled. His expression quickly changed as he felt the barrel of Boudine's six-shooter pressed behind his ear and the click of the hammer cocked back.

"Drop it or I drop you," she said with a knowing sense of authority.

"Fuck you! You won't shoot me!"

"Oh, well, that's not what I'm known for, but if'n you wanna chance it, be my guest."

Bob said to Hurd, "Set that piece on the counter here, Mister Hurd. Nice an' easy."

Hurd started to slowly put his gun on the counter, but made a sudden move that he shouldn't have. Because the whip-fast and accurately aimed boot that Boudine sent directly up from behind into the center of his precious bollocks, sent the larger man right to the floor in a howl of excruciating pain. "You fuckin' bitch!" Hurd screamed.

"Yup, that's me," Boudine replied, with a bit of a chuckle.

Bob stepped back from the counter and stood over the groaning Hurd. To Otis and Boudine, he said, "Now you two step over here and help Mister Owen fill out the rest of these forms, then pay the man the eighteen dollars fee each and we'll get goin'. Bob then said to Hurd, "You might want to tell Seth Bullock that this kind of treatment ain't going to sit well with the folks around Belle Fourche."

Otis stood in the doorway of the Grand Central Hotel restaurant and waited until Lucretia Marchbanks finished serving up breakfast to a table of four. As she turned back toward the kitchen, she sensed someone in the doorway and said, "Just grab a seat anywhere." Otis didn't move. Aunt Lou looked up. Her breath stopped in her throat. "Oh-my-God," she whispered, "it's you..."

"Sorry, Aunt Lou, I can't stay. Just wanted you to know things is gotten a lot better and are goin' good with me of late. Was taken in by a farm family out Belle Fourche way. Think you met the Pickerings when their son Ben was hurt awhile back. Good folks. Been workin' for my keep and for Mister Bob. They do pay me some when they can, which I been savin'. That's how I was able to pay the fee for the homestead paper I just bought at the Land Office. Now, you can go ahead with your plan to open a business place of your own that you been savin' for all these years."

"Oh, Otis... this is so much to..."

Otis said quickly, "Now, don't you worry none, Aunt Lou. I'll be back real soon to 'splain everythin'. Things is changin' real fast."

CHANGE IN THE WIND

TWELVE

Bob was up early on a crisp fall morning, chopping firewood on a stump near the completed cabin. As he swung his axe down onto a log and split it in two, Boudine came charging out of the cabin and ran around to the back. Bob stopped, as he heard her retch and groan. Then, he heard her retch a second time. "Goddammit!" Bob heard her curse. He put his axe down and started toward where she had gone. He stopped as Boudine emerged and headed back inside.

"What's wrong?" Bob asked.

"Hell, if I know! Must'a been somethin' I 'et," she tossed back and went inside, closing the door behind her.

Bob stood there for a moment, then went back to chopping firewood.

===

"Well, where's Sally Mae then?" Abigail asked as she set a large bowl of stew and loaves of freshly made bread on the dining table for lunch.

Bob spoke up, "Says she's feelin' a bit peaked today. Restin'."

"Well, I'll look in on'er and take'er some of this warm chicken stew. It usually does the trick." With that the bowl of hot stew was passed around to the others to ladle out.

Bob asked Nathan, "Anymore word from Bullock 'bout his plans for buildin' a town in Belle Fourche?"

"Not an inkling. But them kind're always looking to tear down and build up somewheres. Just have'ta keep an eye out."

"Someone's comin'," Ben announced and jumped up from the table to open the front door.

Abigail asked, "Who is it, Ben?"

"It's that Calamity Jane lady."

Bob, Nathan, Otis and Calamity Jane sat in chairs on the Pickering front porch. Jane took a healthy drag on a cheroot as Nathan smoked a long-stemmed tobacco pipe and said, "So, here we are again. Mister Bullock sends us someone else to speak with us and not himself is that it, Miss Jane?"

"Well, he's quite busy with all the sheriffin' and buildin' his new hotel there in Deadwood. And he's real sorry 'bout that fella Hurd gettin' beyond hisself. That t'weren't his job at all."

"Be that as it may, I was always taught that orders always come from the top; so, no offence to you, Miss Jane, but I don't think there be anyone above Mister Bullock in this situation."

Jane sighed and sucked on her cheroot, letting a puff of smoke curl into the afternoon air. She then added, "I know that Seth don't want trouble between you folks and him. He just hopes that y'all will hear him out."

Nathan said, "Well, if the man was in earshot, might help."

Abigail and Sarah came out onto the porch. Sarah carried a napkin wrapped hunk of bread. Abigail held a tin of warm stew. "Goin' over to see 'bout Sally Mae then. Miss Jane, you're sure you ain't hungry?"

"No, ma'am, I'm fine, thank you. What's the matter with Boudine?"

Bob answered her, "She upchucked this mornin'. Said she was feelin' a bit peaked."

Abigail and Sarah stepped off the porch and headed for the pathway through the woods, followed by the Pickering hound and Stubs. "That ain't like her to be laid up. I'll have a look-see after we finish here," Jane said to the others.

"You're welcome to stay over. We have room now," Bob said to Jane.

"Might just take you up on that. Gettin' dark earlier nowadays."

Nathan tapped the ashes from his pipe and stood. "Miss Jane, I'm thinkin' there ain't nothin' more to speak of on this, without Mister Bullock present. I think that's the message that should go back to 'im... Bob? Otis? Y'all agree?"

Bob and Otis nodded in agreement. Nathan added, "And, that Mister Hurd better not come within spittin' distance of any of us. Although, I understand Miss Boudine already give him the boot," he said with a chuckle and stepped off the porch.

Inside Bob and Boudine's new cabin, there was a knock on the door. "Come in," Boudine called out, as she sat with Abigail and Sarah at the small eating table that Otis had fashioned for them. Calamity pushed the door open and looked in. "What the hell're you doin' here, Jane?"

"Damn, Boudine, you don't look the worse for wear. What's ailin'ya?"

"Nothin' special. Nothin' that this here chicken stew can't take care of. Hey, don't just stand there with the door open, your lettin' all the heat from the heatin' stove out."

Later, Boudine and Jane sat alone on log-built chairs near the large potbellied stove in the corner of the front room. "Well, damn, you're doin' good for yourself here, Sally Mae. Long ways from holdin' up stages."

"Shite, Jane! Will you stop with that stuff. T'ain't funny."

"I hear'd tell you walloped ol' Lester Hurd right in the bollocks. Good for you. That sumbitch deserves anything bad that happens to'im. I keep tellin' Seth he's bad news, but he says he needs a man like'im to help keep things level in Deadwood. Maybe so, maybe not. So, anyway, you're a homestead owner of your own now."

"Yup."

"What the hell're you gonna do with one-hundred-and-sixty-acres?"

"Hell, if I know. But we'll figure somethin' out. Bob's plannin' on buildin' a tradin' post down on the river maybe come spring. Says we got to start clearin'."

"What're y'all gonna be tradin' there, Boudine?" Jane asked a bit cynically.

Boudine paused a bit, then answered Calamity with, "This'n'that."

Jane paused, then looked at Boudine for a long moment... "I have'ta say, you've come a long way from bein' that sixteen-year-old boy in Cody's shows. A long way, indeedy."

Boudine started to say something, but suddenly blanched and put her hand to her mouth. She bolted out the door and around to the back, where Calamity heard her loudly retch and cuss and retch again.

Calamity came out to see what was wrong and met Boudine coming back.

"What the hell's this all about, Boudine?"

Boudine wiped her mouth on her sleeve and said, "Don't know. Just a tummy bug's'all."

"How long's this been goin' on now?"

"Few days. Kinda creeps up and lets go."

"You takin' that Chinese medicine of yours?"

"Yeah. Don't seem to help."

"Since I'm staying the night, I'll put my horse up in the barn. I got some Laudanum with me. You can try some. See if it helps."

Calamity woke from a sound sleep, in the small bare bedroom where she slept under her bedroll, on a single log bed that Bob had constructed. She listened as she heard Boudine outside retching and cussing loudly. She also heard Bob talking to her and got off the bed and went outside.

"I'm alright, dammit Bob! I told'ja, just a tummy bug!"
"And I told you that all that Chinese medicine's gonna be the death of you. You have'ta stop usin' that stuff."
Boudine uttered caustically, "Bullshit!" and walked toward the front of the cabin where she ran into Calamity.
"You're comin' with me."
"Hell, you say," bleated Boudine, as she stepped around Jane. Jane took her firmly by the arm and said, under no uncertain terms, "Yeah, I say, Boudine! I say!"

With both Calamity Jane and Boudine mounted up under a chilly, early morning cloud cover, Bob stood close and said, "I'd better come along."
"No need," Calamity said. "I been workin' at Doc Babcock's for more'n a month now. He's a good man and knows his medicine. He'll be able to tell what's goin' on here. Ain't no use for you bein' a nuisance. Anythin' wrong, I'll see'er back. If'n

it ain't nothin', you'll be seein'er by nightfall." With that, Calamity chirked her horse forward. Boudine said to Bob, "I ain't never been to a doctor a'fore. Somethin' new."

Boudine touched her spurs lightly to her horse and followed Calamity at an easy trot. Sarah ran out of their house and shouted to Bob, "Where're they goin'?"

"Goin' into Deadwood for a bit."

"Awww." Sarah said with overdone disappointment, "I wanna go too."

"Oh, what's all this, young lady?" Abigail asked from the front door, "You haven't finished your breakfast here."

Sarah hustled back into the cabin. Bob turned toward the pathway back to his homestead, just as his mother came out of the henhouse with a full basket of eggs. "Mornin', Son. I hear someone ride off?"

"Boudine went into Deadwood with Jane."

"Oh, prattle. I would've asked her to check at the Wells Fargo Office for any letter back to me from Mister Bartholomew."

"I'll be headin' in soon for more buildin' supplies. I'll check with the agent."

Millie Mae sensed there was something disturbing in Bob's voice. "Everythin' all right?" she asked.

Bob paused and then said, "Hope so. Boudin's been out of sorts of late. Been upchuckin' near every day. Calamity's takin' her to see her doctor."

"Oh-my-goodness." Millie Mae started to say something else but didn't. "She'll be fine. Don't you fret. She's real pioneer stock, that one. She'll be fine. Now, whyn't you take these eggs to Abigail. Told'er I'd go to her root cellar and gather some turnips and taters for her makin's."

===

"So, you're a friend of this scallywag here?" Doc Babcock asked Boudine in front of Calamity Jane in his home office.

"Yessir."

"Well, you better help keep her powder dry, or she'll keep you runnin' that's for sure," he advised good-naturedly. "Now set yourself up on this examinin' table and we'll see what's goin' on here. Upchuckin' you say?"

"Yessir..."

"A lot?"

"Near every day for 'bout a week."

"Mornin' or night?"

"Mornin' mostly."

"Okay, now I'm going to ask you to open your shirt a bit, so's I can have a listen."

"Listen to what?!" Boudine asked with some alarm.

"Oh, your heart for one thing and your breathing for another. You ever been to a doctor before?"

"Nossir, not a once."

"Well, I can assure you none of this will hurt and I am certainly not going to get fresh with you, 'less I want to get Jane here all over me," he chuckled. With that, Doc Babcock went to an instrument cabinet and took out a stethoscope hearing trumpet and brought it over to Boudine.

"What the hell's that?" she uttered.

"So, I see your friend here's taught you to cuss alright."

Calamity chimed in. "It's called a stethoscope. It's to hear better what's goin' on in there. Now open up your shirt so's he can have a listen."

Reluctantly, Boudine unbuttoned her shirt a little. Doc Babcock very gently put the trumpet stethoscope against her chest and listened through the other end. He then gently moved the instrument around and listened. "Mmmm..." he uttered.

"What?!" Boudine asked aloud.

Doc Babcock stepped back and said, "You're still ticking."

"I could'a told'ja that."

"Boudine. Stop it," Jane scolded.

"Now, if you'll open your shirt just over your tummy, I'd like to take another listen."

Boudine looked at Jane with widening eyes. Jane nodded at her to do it. With her shirt opened slightly over her stomach, Doc Babcock gently listened around her stomach area for a few moments, then stood back, put the stethoscope in the cabinet and turned to Boudine. He paused, took a breath, then said, "Well..."

Boudine stood with Calamity Jane on the boardwalk outside the doctor's home office. A large caravan of oxen-pulled prairie schooners surged through the piss-damp muck. With drivers shouting and snapping whips, the dog-tired passengers failed to hear Boudine exclaim to Calamity Jane, "What the hell'm I gonna do with a baby?!"

Riding back along the trail toward Belle Fourche, Boudine's mind was as far away as far could be, when Lester Hurd spurred his horse out from behind a thicket and cut her off. His gun was drawn and pointed right at her middle. "Well now, you little pig bucket, you're about to find out what it's really like to come up against Lester Hurd. Get off that horse. NOW!"

Hurd didn't get to hear an answer from Boudine or the crack of the rifle that sent the lead slug through his forehead that blew out the back of his skull, sending his brain spattering along with it. As he toppled from his horse, Boudine turned and saw Calamity Jane calmly trotting over to her from where she had been watching from a clump of trees. She reined up beside Boudine and shoved her rifle into its scabbard.

"Thanks," Boudine said.

"Saw that heap of coyote shite take off after you from the Gem. Figured he might have somethin' else in mind than sayin', *Howdy.*"

Boudine indicated Jane's rifle, "What happened to your Kentucky Percussion rifle. That there looks like a Winchester."

"Winchester '76 Centennial that Wild Bill give to me. Damn good one. Still got the Kentucky, but this one sends a .45-75 right where you aim it."

"I give one to Bob for his birthday some time back."

"Alright, there, Sally Mae, you skedaddle on now, I'll clear out this mess. This never happened and we was never here."

Boudine hesitated. Jane said, "Skat!"

Boudine turned her horse back in the direction of Belle Fourche.

===

A three-quarter moon shined down on Millie Mae's cabin. Sitting in the quiet, in the rocking chair, on the front porch, the moon's light outlined Boudine. After a few moments, the front door opened, and Millie Mae appeared in her nightclothes. "Well, I could feel you out here, Sally Mae. You need someone to talk to now. Come on inside where it's warm and we'll get to it."

Millie Mae placed a small log into the heating stove, then set a lighted lantern onto her small eating table. As she settled into a log chair across from Boudine and let Buzzer her cat snuggle into her lap she said, "There... now take that sorrowful look off your face. No need for that."

Boudine attempted to speak but had trouble with her words... "I... I..."

"You tell Bob yet?"

Boudine looked surprised. "Tell'im what?"

"That you're with child."

"But I... how'd you know?"

"Well, I almost did say somethin' 'fore y'all left, but I figured it best for you to hear from someone else."

"But..."

"Why else would a strong, healthy woman like yourself be upchuckin' in the mornin'? Only one reason comes to mind."

Boudine took a deep breath and tried hard not to let the tears well in her eyes. "I... how'm I going to do this? I ain't never really been around any..."

Millie Mae reached out and put her hand on Boudine's. "Mother Nature and the Good Lord have a way of workin' together and teachin' what you need to know. Besides, you have all of us here to help you along."

Boudine swallowed hard.

"Have you told Bob yet?" she repeated.

Boudine shook her head *No*...

"Well, don't let it go too far 'fore it gets to be somethin' else. Keepin' secrets ain't always a good thing. Putting it right out there gets it over'n'done with."

With dawn just breaking over the homesteads, Bob and Boudine stood quietly silhouetted at the riverbank. After a long moment, Bob reached out and gathered Boudine into him.

DRAWING THE LINE

THIRTEEN

Nathan sat on his horse outside Bob's cabin with a shotgun lying across his lap. "Bob!" Nathan called out. After a moment, Bob opened the door and came outside. "We got ourselves a problem. I don't usually carry a gun, but this might be different."

Bob and Nathan rode slowly through the woods between their homesteads. Nathan informed Bob of his concern. "This mornin', I was checkin' to see where I might start clearin' another field. Heard voices up yonder and sounds of poundin' and diggin'. Went closer and spotted quite a few men with diggin' tools and what looks to be surveyin' instruments. All wearin' guns and lookin' like they mean business. Don't know if we're in for trouble, don't know if we ain't."

Bob and Nathan rode slowly through the heavily wooded area until they came to the edge of an expanse of a rather flat field. They stopped just inside the trees to watch a group of six men working with surveyor scopes and markers that were being pounded into the ground. A family of quail burst from the nearby underbrush and flew into the air, startling their horses. The surveyors were too far away to hear or see them. As Bob steadied his horse, he said to Nathan, "What do you think?"

"I think what I know. They're well over the homestead line."

"Breaking the law."

"Breaking our boundary law for sure."

"Don't think they're lookin' for a shootin' fight," Bob observed.

"I ain't neither, but this scattergun of mine is loaded up just in case."

"So's my Peacemaker and Winchester."

"Think we should ease on over and have us a talk." With that, Nathan reined his horse out onto the field. Bob followed. As the two neared the group of surveyors, the men stopped working and waited, eyeing them suspiciously. Bob saw that two of them had rested their hands on their six-shooters.

Bob urged his roan out ahead of Nathan and stopped several yards from the surveyors. He directed his remark at the two men, as he himself, rested his hand on his holstered gun. "Hope you gentlemen don't intend to use them weapons," he said with a confident smile.

"Not unless you do," came a rather nervous answer.

Nathan reined up next to Bob and eased his shotgun into the crook of his arm with the chamber broken. "Name's Nathan Pickering and you're trespassing on my homestead here."

The men all looked at each other and said nothing until the lead surveyor, working with the scope, raised his hand. "Might I approach?" he asked seriously.

"Surely can," Nathan answered.

The surveyor walked the several yards up to Nathan and Bob. "We've been tasked to survey this land to make sure the boundaries are exact and not just walked off as such."

"Seth Bullock send you?" Nathan asked rather tersely.

"I do work for Mister Bullock's company presently."

Nathan settled back in his saddle and took a breath, then said. "Mister Bullock and I have already had several words about all this. He knows my feelin's all too well, to just set out here without any warning that y'all were comin'."

The surveyor started to comment, Nathan spoke over him. Bob kept a sharp eye on the others. "I find this intrusion onto my land rather ungentlemanly to be sure. And, quite ungodly in nature."

Again, the surveyor attempted to speak. Nathan held up his hand and indicated, "See them three tall pines over yonder? The ones 'bout fifty-sixty yards from where y'all are drivin' them markers?"

The surveyor turned to look...

"In them trees is a post that me and my son drove into the ground to mark a stretch of the border we walked off near two years ago. The boundary goes right along with the official Land Office paper I paid for and got signed and stamped."

Bob shouted and halfway drew out his Peacemaker, "DON'T DO IT! Put'er back if'n you don't want a third eye!"

Startled, both Nathan and the surveyor looked toward the group of men and saw one of them slowly drop his six-shooter back into his holster.

Nathan gritted and asked, "That be a surveyor?"

Nervously, the surveyor answered, "Nossir, he's one of the guards Mister Bullock sent along with us. Seems his main man up and disappeared yesterday. Ain't seen hide-nor-hair of'im. Horse wandered back into town with blood on it."

"Who might that be?"

"Tough hombre name of Lester Hurd."

"Think they'll be back?" Bob asked.

"Probably. Hopefully, Bullock is enough of a businessman and less of a bully to want to discuss this man-to-man."

Bob was quiet.

"You know Bob, I been noodlin' somethin'. Together, we all got us six-hundred-forty acres stretched out side-by-side along the river. Without our cooperation, there ain't no access to it. If'n they do want to build a town, there be a few main things they's gonna need. Pathways to the river. Wood for buildin' and food. We got access to all three. See where I'm aimin'?"

"Mmm..."

"Now, I been noodlin' some more. Might go ahead and set up a proper lumber mill on the river. We got more'n enough pines to build ten towns. Got more'n enough good growin' land to feed everyone and then some. Got the rights to gettin' to the river. I'd say, if Bullock wants our cooperation, then he'll have to deal with us on a business basis. He'll balk, sure as there's a Hades, but in the end, he seems a practical man."

Bob was quiet, then uttered, "We'll see."

Nathan changed the subject and tentatively asked Bob, "Might I ask you somethin'?"

"Yup..."

"Ah... Miss Boudine... she feelin' better?"

Bob was quiet, then said, "Better, but still a bit peaked."

"Tummy upset?"

"Some."

"Mmmm..." Nathan mused.

After a moment, Bob volunteered quietly, "She told me."

"Uh-hum... good. Good to hear."

COMES THE WINTER STORMS

FOURTEEN

Bundled in a heavy coat against the winter chill of a blustery early morning, Bob finished stacking more firewood onto the pile he'd built up on Millie Mae's porch. Millie Mae swept off the last streaks of the night's light snowfall dusting.

Millie Mae asked rather quietly, "How's Sally Mae doin'?"

Bob could hear every other question his mother really wanted to ask in her one question.

Bob set the last logs onto the pile and turned to leave. "She's doin'," he answered flatly, then asked, "I be headin' into Deadwood. Back by nightfall. Anythin' you need?"

This caught Millie Mae off guard, "I... ah... just... could you check for a letter from Mister Bartholomew, in case he wrote?"

"Sure, s'that all then?"

Millie Mae stepped to the edge of the porch and rather nervously said, "I would've asked Sally Mae, but she didn't seem to want to talk much..."

Bob stopped and looked at his mother with a puzzled expression. "How's that?"

"Well, she was off in a hustle real early. Didn't even say *good mornin'*."

"Told me she was goin' to help Abigail," Bob said with some surprise.

"Heard'er ride off from the barn. Don't think she saw Abigail t'all."

Bob stood silently for a moment, then turned and walked toward his cabin.

===

A gray dreariness hovered over the cold, muddy main street of Deadwood. The usual hustle and bustle of the hard-charging residents and transient travelers had been reduced by the cold to a trickle. Boudine guided her horse up the nearly deserted street toward Doc Babcock's home office.

Boudine quickly opened and closed the front door to Doc Babcock's front waiting room. She waited a moment. "Be there in a minute. Set yourself down," she heard Calamity Jane's voice call out from the back-room surgery.

Boudine began to pace in the small room. She looked at the framed medical credentials on the wall and paced again. From a side table, she picked up a copy of a days old *Black Hills Pioneer* newspaper and gave it a glance. Something caught her eye and she quickly folded up the paper and stuffed it inside her winter coat, just as Calamity Jane came out of the surgery. "What the hell're you doin' out here, Sally Mae?"

"Gotta talk to you 'bout somethin'."

"You ride all the way here through this shite weather? Must be terrible important." Boudine's look said it all. "Okay-okay. We just hadda take off some frozen toes of an old drunk. Doc's finishin' up. Go on over'ta Nuttal and Mann's an' wait for me. Won't be long." Calamity disappeared into the surgery and closed the door.

Boudine stood on the Doc's front porch. Gusts of snow-dust whipped in and about. She watched a skinny, wrinkled old prospector, well on a path with no end, quietly trying to slip her rifle out if its scabbard. Slowly, and rather casually, Boudine drew her six-shooter and stepped to the edge of the front porch. She aimed her gun at the thief and pulled the hammer back with a sharp click. The old man didn't seem at all perplexed, as he continued to go after the rifle. Boudine stepped a bit closer and said, "Here's what I ain't gonna do to you. I ain't gonna shoot off your left shoulder, then I ain't gonna blow off your right shoulder, then I ain't gonna put a bullet right through your forehead, givin' you a third eye. That's 'cause you're all of a sudden gonna get real smart and piss off right now. If'n you think this gal won't do what she says, you might step up there on Boot Hill and take a gander of some'a them rottin' wood grave markers. If you like, I can get one for your mangy little ass."

    The thief stopped, stared, then shoved the rifle back into the scabbard. Boudine reached into her pants pocket and took out a small coin. "Here," she said, "this'll warm y'all up for the day." The old thief tentatively took the coin. "Good choice. Consider this your lucky day. Now, scat!"

    Calamity Jane ordered herself a whiskey and another backup for Boudine, at the long bar in Nuttal and Mann's Number 10 Saloon. Only a few diehard gamblers played at the tables. The bartender set out the drinks, then went over to a large potbellied stove, stoked the fire and added some firewood.

Calamity unwrapped the scarf she had around her neck and set it on the bar.

"Okay, Boudine, let's have it."

Boudine hesitated, then asked, "You workin' for the Doc full time now?"

"Yeah. Got a lot goin' with the pox comin' on 'round here."

Boudine took a sip of whiskey and fiddled with her glass. "Ain't you 'fraid of gettin' it?"

Calamity gave Boudine a hard look, then said abruptly, "Look here, Sally Mae, you din't come all this way in the freezin' snow to chitchat about me. Now, get to it, or I'm leavin'."

Boudine reddened then spit it out and indicated her stomach, "I want this to go away. I want you to get me somethin' to make it go away. I know them workin' girls around town and over at the Gem do it all the time."

Calamity did not expect this. She took a slow sip of whiskey, set the glass down and flatly said to Boudine, "What 'bout Bob? You talked to him 'bout this?"

Boudine shook her head, "S'my business."

Calamity didn't hold back, "Are you full-up crazy?! Jesus Christ, Boudine, that fella of yourn might be quiet, but he's one loaded gun when he has to be. I'd think twice about goin' against'im. That kid you're carryin' in there is half his."

Boudine didn't say anything. Just stared blankly at Jane for a long moment…beating back the tears that welled in her eyes.

"Oh. don't go givin' me that cryin' shite! All the time we was workin' the shows together, I ain't never seen you cry once. An' I'll bet all my rifles and six-shooters you didn't cry when that bastard Jesse James threw you down in the dirt and jumped your bones, did you?"

Boudine hardened and shook her head, *No*.

"Damned straight you didn't. But I'll tell'ya what. I'll make you a deal. You want outta ol' Bob an' all this, then, hell, I'll take the sumbitch off'n your hands. He's a good looker an' a good shooter. Right up my alley! Then I'll get you a job with Swearengen at his Gem Theater, hoppin' from room to room and dodgin' rats. Real ones and big fat hairy naked ones with stinkin' sweat drippin' off'n'em. How's that sound?"

Boudine went completely silent.

Finally, Calamity took her drink, tossed it back, and set herself to leave. "I think that fella standin' in the doorway over yonder might wanna talk to you."

Startled, Boudine looked around and saw Bob silhouetted just inside the front door.

===

With darkness folding in around them, Bob and Boudine approached the outer boundaries of their homesteads. Bob reined up. "You ain't hardly said nothin' since we started back, Boudine."

Boudine reined her horse around to face Bob. After a moment, she said, barely above a whisper, "I'm scared... I don't think I've ever been so scared a'fore, but I'm real scared."

Bob sat in his saddle for a moment, looking at Boudine. Then he quietly dismounted and offered his hand to her. Boudine shied away for a minute, until he took her hand and tugged her into dismounting. Without saying a word, Bob took Boudine in his arms and kissed her long and deep, as some new snow started lightly dusting their shadows.

CRACK IN THE ICE

FIFTEEN

Bob told Nathan, "I run into Bullock and Sol Star in Deadwood. They's opened their new hardware store. Both said they want to talk 'bout usin' some of our homestead lands for buildin' the new town they're plannin'. Said they'd talk money."

Nathan said, "How much they talkin' 'bout?"

"Didn't go no further. 'Told'em I don't speak for all of us. They want to talk about money and land, they have to speak to you, me, Boudine and Otis all at once."

"Good," Nathan said, "We might be gettin' somewhere. Could be a crack in the ice.

Except for Bob's own early morning footprints and those of some small critters, the night before had left an untouched blanket of white snow on and about Bob's cabin. Otis emerged from the woods on his way to the Pickering's. He stopped and listened to the sounds of someone moaning in distress coming from inside the cabin. He realized it was Boudine and hurried to the front door and lightly knocked.

"Miss Boudine?" he asked quietly. No one answered, but her moaning continued. Otis tapped on the door again. Again, no answer. He then turned and ran off toward the Pickering's.

Otis and Abigail hurried through the snow up to the cabin. They listened and heard Boudine's cries of distress.

In the fog of her dream, Boudine could see clearly that a man was being lashed to a pole by several other men. The man had been stripped naked and was pleading for "mercy" but to no avail. Two men proceeded to paint hot pine tar onto the chest and genitals of the stricken male, who screamed in pain. Another man held onto a child and a rather timid woman and forced them to watch the torturous goings on. The woman's frightened tears ran down her cheeks. The little girl's expression did not show any compassion or fear, nor were there any tears flowing from her eyes.

'Easy there, Sally Mae... easy there... s'only me here now. Nothin' to fear. Open your eyes and we'll be done with whatever it is that's botherin' you." Abigail said, as she sat on the bed beside Boudine wrapped in her blankets.

Boudine's eyes fluttered open. She looked around and gathered herself. "Abigail?..."

"There'ya go now. That was some bad dream you was havin' there, Sally Mae."

Boudine sat up, took a deep breath and shook the cobwebs from her head.
"Must'a been…"

"Well, I still got some hot coffee left in the pot. Let's go fetch it 'fore the menfolk get back."

Abigail poured a cup of hot coffee into a tin cup and set it in front of Boudine at the dining table. Sarah and Ben sat cross-legged, next to the warmth of the fireplace, reading from their lesson books. As Abigail sat at the table, she said to Boudine, "If'n you ever want to talk about somethin' botherin' you, I'm a good listener."

"Ain't nothin' much to say."

"I've had one or two bad dreams myself. Usually, just my imagination runnin' away with me."

Sarah piped up, "I dreamt that the Devil was chasin' me once."

Abigail scolded lightheartedly, "Well, look who's listenin' in over there."

"Well, I did."

Ben took the opportunity to stick his tongue out at his sister.

"Mom! Ben stuck his tongue out at me!"

Ben said, "Did not!"

"Did too."

"Not."

"Too."

"Alright, that's enough. I'm gonna be testin' you on your lessons and you'd better get'em right if you know what's good for you."

Nathan pushed through the door, letting in a rush of snowy air. "Fresh venison tonight," he announced, as Bob came in carrying a pail of freshly cut meat. He set the pail on the kitchen counter and glanced at Boudine.

Sarah announced, "Sally Mae had a nightmare and Ma fixed it."

Bob and Boudine walked along the snowy path toward their cabin. After a long silence, Bob asked, "What was you dreamin' about?"

"Nothin'."

"Must'a been somethin', Otis said you were moanin' real loud, so he went and fetched Abigail."

"T'weren't nothin'."

Bob started getting irritated. "So, you ain't going to tell me?"

"S'my business," she flipped back.

"That's what you always say, if'n you don't wanna talk about somethin'."

Boudine stopped in her tracks and faced Bob. "How many things you have you don't wanna tell me then, Slye? Plenty, that's for dang sure!"

Bob gritted, then challenged, "What do you want to know?"

Boudine stared at him for a long moment, then said slowly, "Well... so far I know you was a stage robber and a gambler, and you once worked in a cattle yard killin' steers."

"You forgot that I never killed no one."

Boudine didn't let it go. "So far you ain't. But you come real close of late. S'only a matter of time."

"We'll see about that. What about you? You don't seem to pull back from killin' someone."

"Only when I have to and that ain't gonna stop. Anythin' else you need to know?"

A snow gust whipped in, but didn't stop the two from going at it. "All I know is you were a sharpshooter in the Buffalo Bill Cody shows and was let go. I know you were a stage robber 'fore we met up and a train robber because we done that one together. And I know you take too much Chinese Medicine than you should and..."

"Not no more," Boudine said rather quietly.

Bob stopped for a moment, then asked her, "Why's that?"

Boudine wiped away some windblown snow from her face, then turned back toward their cabin. "Calamity's Doc said it weren't good for what's goin' on inside me."

They walked along in silence for a minute or two until Bob said, "I also don't know nothin' about how you was raised."

"Me neither, 'bout you."

"The hell you say, Boudine. You met my mother back at her little homestead. You saw that little old soddy I was reared in. You know 'bout me helpin' out at Fort Randall. You were there when we saved her Lakota friend from dyin'. And, now Millie Mae lives within spittin' distance of the cabin. So, don't go sayin' you don't know nothin' 'bout me there, Boudine. You know plenty. An' you want to know more about me, then just go over to'er cabin and ask'er."

"Ain't all that easy," Boudine uttered.

"Ain't that easy for me neither. But we got a new reason to ask questions now, don't we."

Boudine said quietly as they approached the cabin, "Don't think I want to."

===

Itinerate roving evangelist, Isaiah Macpherson, known as The Preacher, broke from his ferocious, booming, religious haranguing sermon, to the small crowd of curious onlookers who loosely gathered around his pulpit and traveling wagon. Suddenly, the flowing-haired, bearded preacher, dressed all in black, stopped. He had spotted something, or someone, at the outer ring of onlookers. His eyes widened dramatically. He stood straight up and focused his full attention on what he'd seen that broke his sermon in midsentence. The assemblage followed his gaze to a rather thin, gaunt woman seated on the ground, holding a young, emaciated crippled girl in her lap.

"The Lord has brought your little girl here to me to be healed!" Isaiah bellowed. "Bring her to me! Help her!" He ordered. "Bring her to me now! Make way! I must heal this fragile thing today!"

Several men bent down and helped the woman and the crippled girl to their feet and supported them, as they stumbled forward through the opening in the gathering. The little girl's legs were each clamped tight with metal and wood braces. From hips to ankles. Lashed in place with leather straps. She stumbled several times and had to be helped back up and almost dragged to the feet of The Preacher.

"God is here!" The Preacher boomed. "The Lord has given me the strength to heal this unfortunate human being. Our Merciful Lord will help me cure her of all of her ills. She will walk again… I say, SHE WILL WALK AGAIN!" he bellowed.

Others in the group began to, "Praise-the-Lord!" The frail woman held tightly to the crippled little girl and began to cry openly. Tears streamed from her hollow eyes. "Praise-the-Lord!" "Praise-the Lord!"

The Preacher threw up his hand and demanded, "Quiet!" The onlookers hushed as one. The Preacher stepped down from his wagon pulpit and stood right before the terrified little girl. The Preacher's voice became as smooth as ruffled silk, "Are you her mother?" he addressed the woman supporting the little girl. She nodded a tearful 'Yes'. "Did you bring her here to be cured by the Lord through me?" Again, the woman nodded tearfully. The onlookers hunkered in closer. The Preacher ran his long thin boney fingers through his thick, lion's mane hair. He stared at the little girl and extended his hands over the top of her head, gripping her small skull in his grasp. He closed his eyes and demanded, "Take these bindings from her legs."

Immediately, two men started unstrapping the crude braces from her thin white legs. As they pulled them away, the little girl's bruised limbs buckled, and she immediately collapsed to the ground. The onlookers groaned *in unison. "Pick'er up! Hold her! Support her! I will heal her!" The men obediently took her under each arm and raised her up to The Preacher. Again, he placed his hands tightly over the crown of her head...*

"Lord! I call on your mercy to cure this little creature through me. Use me Lord! Use me Lord!" he pleaded. The onlookers tightened around them. The Preacher screamed, "Heal! Heal! Heal! Now, Lord! Now, Lord!" The Preacher began to violently shake the child's head from side-to-side, backwards and forwards. He screamed louder, HEAL! HEAL! HEAL!...

Boudine moaned in her sleep beside Bob, then screamed aloud and sat bolt upright, holding her head in both hands.

The early morning light filled the cabin. Boudine sat at the small dining table near the kitchen potbellied stove. A blanket pulled around her shoulders. She sipped coffee from a tin cup. Bob opened the grilled iron door of the stove and fed the fire inside with another log. He then poured himself more coffee and sat at the table. After a moment, he asked, "Then, where did your name of Boudine come from?"

She stayed quiet for a moment, then said, "I never took the name of Macpherson, because I weren't ever sure who the hell he was. He weren't a real preacher. He was a surefire fake through-an'-through. All that shite with leg braces was all part of it. He kept me an' my mother starvin' so we'd look like we was sick. He kept all the money what was collected and give us nothin'. And, if we complained, he beat us bad with a wood paddle 'til we cried. But I never did. He hated that, so he beat me more."

"But your name is Boudine, right?"

"S'only name I ever let be me."

There was a scratching at the door, Bob got up and let in both Stubs and Buzzer the cat, who immediately went to their favorite places near the stove and curled up for a nap. "I suppose you're gonna make me tell you everythin'," Boudine said.

Bob sat at the table and sipped his coffee. "I ain't gonna make you tell me anythin' you don't want to."

Boudine chuckled to herself.

"What's so funny?"

"Be only funny to me."

"What?"

"Seems The Preacher was dippin' his wick in some of his lady follower's candlesticks and dipped one time too many. Seems some of the men folks didn't take kindly to it all and took it upon themselves to put his candle out. Tarred'n'feathered'im and hung'im feet first over a bonfire."

"You see all that?"

Boudine hesitated, then said somberly, "Some. They knew we wasn't part of it. One of'em, name of Francis Boudine, took a fancy to Mother. His wife had passed and they started likin' each other. He was a coach driver for a freight company and was real nice to both of us. Treated me like his own daughter. So, when he up an' married my mother, I took his name of Boudine.

"Where are they now?"

"They hitched onto a wagon train headin' off to Utah, because of all the religious folks there. T'weren't at all for me. Not after all that preacher shite I been through."

"So, you left to be on your own?"

"Didn't you?"

Bob stopped, drank some coffee, then said quietly, "Guess so."

"Still think you should be tellin' all this to Millie Mae then?"

Bob hesitated before he answered with, "Don't think I want to."

"Well, there'ya go then."

===

Bob, Nathan, Boudine and Otis stood on the snow-covered riverbank opposite the pathway to the Pickering's. Nathan pointed to an area upstream a bit and explained his plan. "Spoke with the owners of a sawmill over there in Lead. They got a good business goin', cuttin' pine boards from trees, but they can't handle any more. Told'em my plan to build one here. Said they'd help me with settin' a paddle wheel in the river and advice on buildin' the mill. What with Bullock and Star plannin' a town, they're gonna need planks and beams of good pine an' we got more'n enough for ten towns right here on all four of our homesteads." Nathan stopped and waited for a reaction. Bob nodded, as he took in the plan. So did Boudine. It was Otis who held back. He started to sniffle. All eyes turned to him. His eyes began to crinkle at the sides; but, as hard as he tried, he could not hold back his tears. Boudine put her hand on his sleeve and said softly, "What'sa matter there, Otis?"

Otis whispered, "Nothin'." But then. he just could not hold it in and tearfully blurted out, "S'been a long time comin'. S'been a long time comin'."

Bob encouraged him. "S'okay, Otis. S'all changed now."

Nathan backed him up, "Bob's right there, Otis. Your life's now startin' on a new path an' we're all a family now."

Boudine looked at Otis's face, "Is that a smile comin' on there, Otis?"

Otis did break out into a rather big tearful smile.

"Well, there'ya go then," Boudine declared, letting herself offer a bit of a smile. "Looks like we'd better get crackin'!"

"Are you gonna have a baby?" Sarah abruptly asked Boudine at the Pickering lunch table. Mille Mae helped set out some mashed potatoes, biscuits and gravy from the kitchen. Nathan, Bob and Otis took their seats.

"Well, are'ya?" Sarah insisted.

"Sarah! Hold your tongue there, girl," Abigail admonished as she set down a plate of sliced pheasant.

"But I gotta know."

"You stop that right now."

Boudine spoke up quietly, "So I'm told."

"Is it a boy or a girl?"

"Oh, Lordy-Lordy," a frustrated Abigial sighed.

"Only the Lord knows for sure, Sarah," Millie Mae offered.

Nathan interjected, "I think now's a good time to say a bit of thanks for this wonderful meal both of our mothers here put out for all of us." With that, they all folded their hands in prayer. All except for Boudine.

As the group began serving and eating, Nathan said, "Where's Ben? He don't know what he's missin'."

Sarah answered. "Said he'd be right along. Sunny, my goat, ain't been feelin' so good. Didn't want to eat, so Ben said he'd sit with'im a bit."

Nathan offered up, "Might be a good idea to start selectin' trees and measurin' up where we want these new buildings to be built. Probably be best to have a pathway goin' right from the mill to the new town boundaries, once they're laid out."

Bob raised his hand a bit. "I been wonderin'..."

Nathan acknowledged Bob... "Bob?"

"Well, I been noodlin' somethin'. Since part of this new town will fall on part of our homesteads and a lot of the lumber will be cut from our pine forest here and abouts, I been thinkin' that a town council should be set up and that at least the homestead owners should be on that council, so's we all have a say in what goes on here."

Nathan's eyes widened and he slapped his hand on the table. "Yes, Bob! You have made a wonderful point here!"

"It's not that Bullock and Star are gonna cheat us, but they's been in business together for quite a time and we ain't," Bob added.

Just then, Ben came into the cabin and hurried over to Nathan and whispered in his ear. Nathan's expression changed to one of a serious nature. Without explanation, he rose from his chair and followed Ben. As they headed for the door, Nathan motioned to Sarah, "Sarah, come with us." Sarah gulped and got up from the table and followed her brother and father outside, closing the door behind them.

No one spoke. Abigail finally sighed, wiped her mouth with her napkin and said quietly, "She raised that little critter from a tiny newborn. Followed her everywhere, it did."

"'Into each life some rain must fall,'" Millie Mae offered softly.

"Yes," Abigail said.

Then, they all heard Sarah's howl of sheer grief come piercing through from the goat house.

===

A light snow had fallen on the small wooden cross that Sarah and Ben had placed on Sunny the goat's grave set out near the goat pen. Bob and Boudine walked from the pathway to the river, carrying pails of water. They stopped for a moment and looked at the small grave, then moved on.

"We're gonna start diggin' wells come spring. One near us that will be used by Millie Mae and Otis as well. The Pickerings will have their's near to their place. Might even have a pipe leadin' to the kitchen, so says Nathan."

None of this seemed of interest to Boudine.

"You alright, Boudine?"

"Retched two times this mornin'."

"How long do you think it's been?"

"Since what's been?"

Bob went silent for a moment, then asked, "Since this was all started."

Boudine looked around at the snow-laden pine boughs before she answered. "'Bout a month I suspect. Maybe more. Why?"

"Just wonderin'."

Boudine glanced at Bob, then asked, "Somethin' on your mind?"

"Just wonderin' about all that loot we brought in and hid."

"What about it?"

"What're we gonna do with it?"

Boudine bristled, "What d'you mean, what're we gonna do with it? Turn it into money, that's what we're gonna do with it." Boudine said flatly.

They stopped at Millie Mae's cabin and dropped off one of the pails of water, then continued on until they were out of earshot.

"So, what're you thinkin' then?" Boudine asked, already anticipating hearing something she wouldn't like.

Bob said, "Don't think we'll be needin' any of it."

They had reached their cabin. Boudine stopped abruptly and faced Bob dead-on. "What?!" she exclaimed. "Are you full-up crazy? What're you gonna do, give it all back? Them folks is all long gone with the wind."

"How're you plannin' on turnin' it into money? People in Deadwood know us now. We start lookin' up them that takes stolen stuff, they don't keep secrets so good." Bob heaved a sigh and said, "Let's talk about this another time." He picked up the water pail and headed for the door.

Boudine stopped him. "No. We gonna talk 'bout this now. You tellin' me that after all we been through with goin' to the Wind Cave and almost gettin' run down by a thousand stampedin' buffalo, then pullin' it outta the snake well and me gettin' snakebit?... What about me savin' your life with the *King-Queen-Ace* shot through O'Banyon?! That weren't nothin' or'd'you forget already?"

"No, I didn't forget about any of it. But we're landowners now. We got no need for stolen loot. We don't have to rob stages or..."

Boudine's frustration boiled over, "Hell, Slye, why'n't we just let all go! Just load it all up in a wagon and take it into Deadwood and dump it right on Sheriff Bullock's jailhouse steps? How's that sound, Bandit Bob Slye?" With that, Boudine turned and went into the cabin and slammed the door behind her. Bob looked up at the gray winter sky and shook his head. Suddenly, Boudine jerked open the door, ran around to the rear of the cabin and retched.

Bob waited until she came back around and followed her inside.

"I'm gonna lay down until this shite passes." As she headed into the bedroom, she gestured to Bob and said, "I forgot, I brung you that there newspaper from Deadwood. S'over there on the shelf." With that, Boudine went into the bedroom and closed the door.

Bob picked up the folded copy of the *Black Hills Pioneer* and opened it to the front page. His breath caught for a moment, as he read one of the headlines:

THE POPULAR IRISH SINGER, GRACE DOYLE, HAS DIED.

While traveling to her show's next stops in Lead and Sturgis, the popular Irish balladeer, Grace Doyle, passed away yesterday of consumption. As per a letter a member of her troupe made available, she wishes to be buried at Mt. Mariah Cemetery in Deadwood, where she had purchased a plot. No services have been announced.

Bob read the rest of the notice and set the paper on the eating table. He then stepped to the front window and stared quietly at the light snow falling outside. He stood there for a long moment, then turned away, picked up the newspaper from the table, folded it and deposited it in the potbellied stove. He then went to the closed bedroom door and knocked lightly.

===

At the river, two battered canoes slipped silently over the water and scuffed up onto the riverbank next to the Pickering's tied off fishing and logging raft. Three rather rough looking young men gingerly stepped out onto the bank and pulled the canoes ashore. They were all wearing soiled clothes and holstered six-shooters, with one carrying an old model Springfield Breech Loading rifle.

Sarah brushed her teeth at the kitchen sink. "Where's Pa?" she burbled to Abigail, who was flipping a ball of bread dough in a bath of sifted flour.

"Went off to Lead to meet the owners of the sawmill there. Gonna help your Pa and the rest build one on the river."

"When's they comin' back?"

" 'For nightfall, I suspect. Why? You need somethin'?"

Sarah rinsed her mouth with a cup of water and spat into the sink. "Oh, just wonderin' if'n we could go into Deadwood and see 'bout gettin' a new goat."

"Now, you know very well that come spring, nature will accomplish that very thing with the goats that we have here. Who knows, you could end up with more'n one newborn. Maybe, two."

"Maybe, three!" Sarah exclaimed.

Bob headed away from Millie Mae's cabin, through the woods, carrying two water buckets to be filled for the day. Taking a shortcut, instead of the regular pathway, he walked through the snow and snow-covered brush, then suddenly stopped short. Off in the distance, through the snow-covered pines, he spotted the shadowed figures of the three men sneaking along the Pickering pathway toward their house. Bob quietly set the buckets down and reached for his Peacemaker, only it wasn't there. *"Shite!"* he thought. He'd gotten into the habit of not wearing it, unless something called for it.

Bob watched, undetected, as the shadowy figures carrying empty rucksacks, moved slowly along the path. He quietly crouched, turned back and hurried away toward his cabin.

Bob was in a flat-out run as he reached his cabin and burst through the door. He grabbed his holstered Peacemaker and strapped it on, as he turned to run back toward the Pickering's.

"What's going on?!" Boudine, wrapped in a blanket, exclaimed with alarm from the bedroom door.

"Bad lookin' intruders headin' to the Pickering's. Nathan and Ben ain't there." With that, he ran outside with his gun drawn.

"Ma!" Sarah said, backing away from the front window.

"What is it, Dear?"

"There's three bad lookin' men headed this way with guns!"

With a quick sense of calm, Abigail set down the dough and quietly said to Sarah, "Alright, you know what to do."

Sarah immediately dashed into the main bedroom. Abigail followed and closed and bolted the door from the inside and set a thick length of wood into the iron catches on either side of the door. Sarah quickly and quietly closed the wood panels over the bedroom window and set the iron hook to lock them. Then they kept very quiet and listened. Abigail reached into the closet and took out the loaded shotgun, kept there for emergencies. Sarah, as she was trained to do, opened a drawer in the bureau against the wall, reached in and took out a six-shooter, checked to see if it was loaded and cocked the hammer. Their breathing was heavy, but not fearful. They waited. Hearing the front door squeak open, they listened.

"Ain't no one here," said one of the strangers.

"Just take whatever you can an' fill them rucksacks," said another.

Abigail and Sarah were dead silent, until someone tried to open the bedroom door. Abigail put her hand to her mouth to hush. "This'n's locked," said a raspy voice.

"Kick'er in," said another.

Abigail and Sarah aimed their guns right at the door. A loud bang rattled the heavy wooden planks, but it didn't budge. Again, a heavy kick rattled the door. "Shoot the goddamned lock off."

There was a loud gunshot from outside. One of the men shouted, "I'm hit! Jesus Christ! I been shot!"

Another very loud gunshot came from beside the house. "The next load from this here LeMat Revolver shotgun load is for whoever don't walk outta there with their hands stretched above their heads." Abigail and Sarah heard Boudine shout.

"I can tell you, she means business, gentlemen." Bob called to the bandits inside, "I recommend you set your guns down on the floor in there or we'll be conducting a funeral right soon."

The Pickering hound and Stubs joined Bob and Boudine outside with loud barking. Sensing danger, they scampered around and around the cabin.

"I got me eight cap'n'ball loads left in this here LeMat for y'all and I'm just itchin' to fire off this here 20-gauge birdshot load and blow one of your belly buttons all the way to Camp Sturgis," Boudine shouted.

Dead silence came from inside the cabin, as the dogs picked up their pace, encircling the cabin with their loud barking. "Dogs is gettin' restless out here," Boudine said, "an' so'm I. Gonna count to ten and, if'n we don't see you fellas come through that door, we're all comin' in after'ya."

Bob glanced at Boudine, who shrugged and gave him a cocksure grin. "One!..."

The front door slowly opened, and a bare hand came out, then an arm, then a rather young man with a scruffy beard and a load of worry and fear on his dirty face.

Bob aimed his pistol right at the man's chest. "Get on the ground. Now!" Bob commanded. Then shouted out, "Hope you other two are as smart as your friend here, 'cause if you ain't, we're good at diggin' ditches for dead bodies."

"Or, just dumpin' y'all in the river an' lettin' the catfish an' river snakes pick at yer bones."

Bob shot Boudine a look and rolled his eyes a bit.

Another hand came out of the open door and then another. Two disheveled young men stepped out onto the porch. One had ahold of his left arm. As the two dogs yelped and growled at them, the two started to get down on the ground. Then the wounded one broke into a run toward the pathway to the river. But, not for long, as Otis came out from behind a snow-laden tree, carrying a shotgun and blocked his way. "Get on back'ere!" Otis ordered.

A NEED FOR LAW

SIXTEEN

As the afternoon sun lowered over the Black Hills, Otis reined in his coffin wagon in front of the Deadwood Jail. The three young bandits were shackled together with wrist and leg irons that Otis just happened to have in his possession.

Bob dismounted from his roan and tied off the reins on the hitching post, just as Sheriff Seth Bullock stepped out of the jail office.

"Well, what have we here?" he said, rather amazed at the sight.

Otis answered with a new sense of purpose about him. "Thems tried to rob the Pickering house, but things didn't go too good."

"They have canoes?"

"Yessir. Two. They're back at the Pickering landing."

"Just the ones we've been lookin' for, gentlemen. They've been giving folks along the river a bad time lately." Then, to Otis he said, "Appreciate it if you would go over and tell Aunt Lou we'll be havin' three here for dinner and breakfast until further notice."

Otis stepped down from the wagon. "Yessir."

Bullock took a closer look at the dirty young bandits. "Hand and leg irons?"

Otis stopped and said flatly, "Come with the wagon."

They exchanged a quiet look, then Bullock said, "Good thing."

"One of'em's wounded there," Otis said as he headed toward the Grand Central Hotel. "Cat scratch."

===

Sheriff Bullock was seated with Bob and Otis at a table near the kitchen in the Grand Central restaurant, away from the other customers that Aunt Lou was attending to. "Who gave that wounded fella the 'cat scratch' as you put it, Otis?"

Bob spoke up, "That would be Boudine. Lucky for him she didn't follow-up or he might've ended up with three eyes. She's that good a shot."

"A main attraction, I understand, at Bill Cody's Wild West shows awhile back."

"'Til she was gettin' too good and showin' up Wild Bill Hickok and Calamity Jane. Had to let'er go," Bob said.

Bullock sat back in his chair and nodded, then said to Bob, "Understand you yourself are quite a shot, Mister Duncan."

Otis flinched a bit and took a sip of coffee.

"So, I've heard," Bob answered without any hint of meaning otherwise.

Bullock said, "I never got the chance to meet Wild Bill myself."

"You would've liked him," Bob offered, trying to figure out just where the conversation was going.

"Most likely," Bullock said, as he leaned forward on the table and took a slow breath. "But... there is one story about you and him that..."

Bob cut him off. "Wait. Stories about me and Wild Bill? There ain't no stories about me an' Wild Bill Hickok. We only met the one time."

"Well..." Bullock cleared his throat. Otis pretended not to listen but wasn't very good at it. Bullock continued, "One was overheard when you was last seen with'im. Says you told him you never killed anyone. True?"

Bob was silent for a moment. Otis waited. So did Bullock. "True," Bob said quietly.

"And, according to the story, Hickok asked if anyone ever drew down on you. True?"

Bob's expression didn't change. "True."

No one seemed to notice that Aunt Lou was nearby, pretending to be preoccupied with her work.

"And... you never killed anyone?"

"True."

"And the story goes that you said, 'I'm still standin'...'"

Bob sighed a little, then said straight out, "True."

Bullock smiled a bit sarcastically, then said, "Pretty hard to believe."

Bob took on the challenge with, "Not for me."

"And, not for me neither!" piped up Aunt Lou. "I heard it right from the horse's mouth just a'fore that bastard, Broken Nose McCall, kilt him."

They all looked up at Aunt Lou as she winked at Bob and headed into the kitchen.

There was silence for a bit, until Bullock said to Bob, "You know, we could use a good deputy marshal around here, Bob."

Bob didn't expect to hear that, but answered with, "Word has it there's a marshal on the way here."

"You mean, Marshal Wyatt Earp out of Tombstone and his brother Morgan? Well, they did show up. Took a look around and said they didn't want any part of it. I believe Wyatt went on to California. Not sure about his brother. So… there it is. There is a need, if you're interested."

===

Boudine turned from warming herself at the potbellied stove in shocked disbelief at what Bob had just told her. "You? Marshal of Deadwood! Are you joshin' me, Slye?"

"No."

She stepped away from the stove and faced Bob who was seated at the small dining table next to the kitchen area. As she spoke of his rather incredible announcement, a sarcastic smirk appeared on her face. "But you're a gambler and a stage robber. You're the Bandit Bob Slye for crissakes!"

"No more," he answered quietly.

Boudine's expression changed. "You ain't foolin' are'ya."

"No. Bullock asked me to think about it."

"Who else knows 'bout this?"

Bob took a breath, "Otis and Aunt Lou."

Boudine took a moment, then said, "You ain't gonna do it."

Bob clasped his hands together on the table. "Not in Deadwood."

"Damn!" Boudine exclaimed. "I thought you was serious."

Bob sat back in his chair and spread his fingers apart in the table.

"What?" Boudine asked. "What're you thinkin'?"

After a moment, Bob said, "I am serious. Maybe, in the new town that's bein'

built."

Boudine stood for a moment, trying to take all this in. "Calamity know 'bout this?"

"Don't know. She weren't around. 'Sides, she's your friend not mine." Bob sat back in his chair.

Boudine's expression changed again to one of near desperation. She glanced anxiously around the small room; as if looking for a place to hide. She unconsciously put her hands on her belly and sat in a chair at the table. Almost to herself, she said, "This is all nigh on to crazy."

"What is?" Bob asked, rather sternly.

The glint of moisture appeared in Boudine's eyes. "All of this," she said and nearly started coughing. Her lips began to quiver. She started to pant in short breaths.

"You cryin' there, Boudine?"

"No! I ain't cryin'!" she snapped, as she ran the back of her hands over her eyes and abruptly got up from the table.

"Don't remember you ever cryin' a'fore..."

Boudine glared at Bob, "I said I ain't cryin' goddammit!" She then quickly covered her face with her hands and broke into body shaking sobs. Bob quickly got up and helped her back into a chair.

"What the hell, Boudine? What'sa'matter?"

She pulled her hands away from her face and slapped them hard on the table. Then, between sobs, she blurted out, "My pants don't fit. My gunbelt's ridin' high messin' with my quick draw. And... and... Oh, shite!" she suddenly came out with, jumped up and charged outside and around the back, where Bob could hear her retching. Bob saw something move at the edge of the opened door. First Stubs, then the Pickering hound, then Buzzer the cat peaked in to see what the commotion was all about.

Quicker than an unswatted fly, Sarah excitedly told everyone at the dinner table about how she was able to fend off the river bandits. "...and then I slammed the window doors shut and locked'em. Then I got out the loaded pistol just like Pa taught me to. Then me and Ma pointed our guns right at the door and waited for the robbers to get in."

"Were you scared?" Brother Ben asked.

"Nope. I was not scared one bit. Was I Ma?"

"Well, maybe we were both a little bit scared there, Sarah."

"Well, I wasn't scared at all. I had my gun all cocked and ready. Anyone come through that door was a dead man!"

No one at the table spoke. Then Otis asked softly, "You ever kilt anyone a'fore?"

"Oh-my-goodness," Abigail uttered, taken aback by the question. But, Nathan held up his hand.

"That's a good question there, Otis. Gettin' to the point of what I was about to ask you, Sarah." He stopped for a moment, as everyone waited for what he would say next. "What if the robber did come through the door, Sarah?"

"I would'a shot'im!"

"That's right and, I'm sure your Ma would've shot anyone else who tried to get in. But that's not my point here... nor Otis's

I suspect. What about after? What about killin' another human being? That's what I mean. Because, once you've taken a person's life, you can never give it back. So, Daughter, that's somethin' you should ponder. You did the right thing in this situation. But every situation is different. You have to make sure you are right. No mistakes… because you have to live with the deed the rest of your life."

Boudine sat silently, as she listened and looked down at her hands folded in her lap. Bob did not comment. Nathan said to Ben, "That goes for you too, Son."

"Yessir."

Bob toyed with his food for a moment, then asked Millie Mae. "Mother?"

"Yes, Son?"

"I near forgot, I got you your letter from Sergeant Bartholomew. Everythin' alright?"

Millie Mae was quiet for a second.

Bob quickly apologized, "I'm sorry. If'n you..."

Millie Mae held up her hand and put on a smile. "S'all right. Just a little hiccup is all."

Abigail tried to pick up the conversation with an offering to help Boudine.

"Now, Sally Mae... I just want you to know that, while you're comin' along there, I've saved all of my clothes from when I was gettin' ready to have these two rascals. So, as you find the need, just say so and I'll fit you up good," she said sincerely.

Boudine's face reddened. Bob looked perplexed. Sarah exclaimed, "I ain't a rascal!"

Boudine eased up from the table as she said, "Sorry... ain't feelin' so good." She then opened the front door and stepped outside into the dark, cold night.

Abigail flushed, "Oh-my-goodness. I hope I didn't make her sorrowful."

Bob did his best to ease the situation. "S'alright. She's been not quite herself of late." He got up from the table. "I'll go'an see to'er."

When Bob left, Millie Mae spoke up. "She'll be right as rain after a bit. Just takes some gettin' used to 's'all."

In a stall in the Pickering barn, Nathan worked a horse's hoof with a hoof knife, cleaning it. Bob held the horse's halter and patted its neck to keep the animal relaxed. "Otis was there and heard it all and I've told Boudine."

"That'd be a pretty bold move on your part there, Bob."

"Yes, it would. But my place is here with y'all. 'Sides a Marshal Wyatt Earp, out of Tombstone, and his brother already were asked to take the job and said they weren't interested. I don't see no good in it for me, 'cept endin' up on Boot Hill. There really ain't no law in Deadwood. Place is pretty much run by Al Swearengen and his band around the Gem Theater. I think Seth Bullock only took the job to protect his businesses at his end of town."

"So, you told'im 'No'?"

"Not yet. I will next time I go to Deadwood. But, I'm thinkin' that it might be somethin' I could do for this new town. It's gonna need the law. There will be saloons and gamblin' and ladys' businesses. Not near as much as in Deadwood, but them businesses do bring in some rambunctious folks from time to time who have to be dealt with."

Nathan let down the horse's hoof and stood facing Bob. "Well, if we hold out for places on a town council and hold out for the marshal's job, then we might just be helpin' to build a respectable new town from the bottom up. Also, I'm going to suggest strongly that a church or two be included, as well as a proper schoolhouse."

"Yep-yep," Bob said, as he left the stall.

"What does Sally Mae think about all this?" Nathan said as he closed the stall door.

"Well, she's pretty cranky about everythin' nowadays."

"Then you tell'er, when she gets the fidgets, to go on and have a talk with my Abigail. She's a wonder at scrapin' away the barnacles that come about durin' these times."

THEY KEEP COMIN'

SEVENTEEN

The winter sun peeked through the snow-covered pine boughs as Bob carried an armload of chopped wood into the cabin. Boudine was looking at the sideboard he had built and set against the wall in what would become the kitchen area. He put the wood into a wood box next to the potbellied stove.

"What d'you think?" he asked Boudine.

"'Bout what?"

"'Bout that kitchen workin' table? I figure that should be the kitchen and come the thaw, I'll be addin' another room, maybe two, off'n the bedroom and me and Otis will be cuttin' a hole in that other wall and buildin' a rock fireplace and chimney."

Boudine absently put her hand on her belly, which had become noticeable.

"You expect me to do all the cookin' here?"

Bob cleared his throat and set a log into the stove. "Well... we can't keep dependin' on Abigail all the time for our meals now can we."

"Only thing I knows how to cook is a skinned rabbit and a pheasant on a campfire spit."

"Plenty of time to learn now," Bob replied a bit too seriously.

"You said you was goin' into Deadwood this mornin'."

"Yep."

"I'm goin' too."

===

"Ain't talkin' much today."

Boudine didn't answer. Bob kept Otis's coffin wagon headed toward Deadwood at an easy pace. Seated beside Bob, Boudine was dressed in her usual clothes with her six-shooter holstered and ready, although a bit tighter than usual. She finally spoke, "I already told'ya I ain't one for cookin' and cleanin' and chasin' kids around... I know I told you that."

"Yes, you did. That you did. More'n once. An' I told you, more'n once, that I was not goin' to stay robbin' stages. Only 'til I could get my mother off'n that dirt pile of a homestead."

"So that's it then."

"That's it. I done what I said I'd do."

Boudine stared off at the passing trees.

"Didn't you believe me?" Bob asked.

"Yeah… I suppose…but…"

"But, what?"

"Guess I never thought the day would come."

"Did'ja think we'd just go on robbin' stages and trains forever?"

Boudine didn't answer right away, then said. "Guess I never give it much thought."

On up ahead, the early morning stage from Deadwood came around the bend. Bob touched his *Boss of the Plains* hat with a two-fingered salute as it passed by.

Boudine chuckled sarcastically, "We could'a had that one."

"Could'a been killed doin' it too."

"Hell, not me!"

Bob sighed, "No, most likely not you."

"You didn't say why you're goin' into Deadwood today."

"Abigail and Nathan gave me a list of needs and I have to mail my mother's letter."

"She never talks about that Army fella of hers. He still comin' round?"

"Don't know. Says there was a hiccup of some sort."

"That's it?"

"When she answers like that... that's it. Learned that a long time ago. She wants you to know somethin' she'll tell'ya."

Bob reined the horse and wagon up in front of a feed and grain store.
"Gonna load up some feed for the Pickering animals. Won't be long."

Boudine stepped down off the wagon and adjusted her gun belt.

"Don't think you'll be needin' that," Bob said.

"It's Deadwood. 'Sides, I see you wearin' your Peacemaker there, Slye."

Bob nodded. "It's Deadwood."

"I'm goin' to find Jane. Got some things I wanna ask her." She saw the immediate concern on Bob's face and said flatly, "No, I ain't gettin' no Chinese medicine or any other medicine stuff."

Bob nodded. "I'm goin' on to the Wells Fargo to mail the letter and then to the hardware store."

"Where else?"

"What d'you mean, where else?"

"Just what I said. You think I don't know you didn't come all this way for chicken and horse feed."

Bob waffled a bit, then answered her quietly, so no passersby could hear. "Told Bullock I'd give'im an answer 'bout the marshal's job."

Boudine's face darkened. "Still the same thinkin'?"

"Yep."

Boudine nodded and started up the boardwalk. Bob watched after her for a moment, then went into the feed store.

Seth Bullock settled into his chair behind the desk in the sheriff's office and gestured to Bob to pull up a chair. "I'm sorry to hear this, Bob. We really need someone who can handle himself. There's not many trustworthy souls to choose from around here."

"I'm sure there're better choices than me," Bob said flatly.

Bullock almost let out a knowing chuckle, as he chewed on Bob's comment about himself. "Most everyone who comes to this Western Frontier brings a bag full of their past with them… including me. My goodness, the Earp's certainly do so with what's comin' in from Tombstone, Arizona. So, what I mean is, it's more important to this town what someone can bring to it now."

Bob let out a bit of a sigh and said, "I talked it over with Nathan and Otis and Boudine. They all agreed that it's the best for us right now. We got a heap of work to do to get ready for y'all come spring."

Bullock said reluctantly, "I understand-I understand. Guess if Wyatt Earp wouldn't take the job, I shouldn't have expected you to."

Bob leaned forward in the chair and said, very matter-of-factly, "We do have a proposition to present to you."

"I see." Bullock said apprehensively, "And what might that be?"

Bob explained the idea of setting up a town council and also that he would consider a lawman's job in the new town. "Also, Nathan insists on a couple of churches and a proper schoolhouse."

Without any change of expression, Bullock began tapping his fingers on the desk. He looked right at Bob for a long moment, then said. "Bob... I personally don't see anything wrong with these suggestions. I do have to run them by my partner Sol

Star, but I think in actuality, they might just be right for the new town."

Bullock stood. Bob too. Bullock offered his hand. They shook. "I appreciate you coming here to speak to me directly, Bob."

Bob touched the brim of his hat and started to leave but hesitated. "One more thing. Me and Boudine were walkin' off her new homestead claim and came upon what looks to be some bags of stolen goods hidden about. Looks to have been there for quite some time." Bullock shrugged. "If'n you want me to load it up and bring it on in to..."

Bullock held up his hand. "Haven't got the time nor the hardiness for that. Most likely, anyone involved have already passed on through. Consider an old Scottish phrase, *Possession is eleven points in the law, and they say they are but twelve.*' Or, better yet, *finders keepers.*"

"Just wanted to say hello, 'fore we headed back. See if everything's alright with you," Bob said to Aunt Lou from the doorway of her restaurant.

"What? No time for my plum puddin'? Shame on you, Bob Duncan!" Lucretia Marchbanks teased.

Bob chuckled. "Next time for sure, Aunt Lou."

"How's my Otis there, Bob? Doin' okay, is he?"

"More than okay, Aunt Lou. More than okay." With that, Bob tipped his hat with a big smile and left.

Bob walked along the boardwalk to where he'd left the loaded-up horse and wagon. With the afternoon light beginning to fade into the hovering cold gray sky, he started to unwrap the tied reins from the hitching rail. A gruff voice called out from the middle of the filthy snow and mud filled street. "Hey! Bob Slye! You lyin' bag of horseshit!"

Bob looked to where he saw a bedraggled, drunk Justice Raintree waving a rolled-up piece of paper. "I got'cha now Bandit Bob Slye. I got me the fuckin' hangin' paper signed by me and Sheriff O'Banyon." He shook the scrolled paper and shouted, "This time I brought the goddamned proof, Bob Slye!"

Raintree then drunkenly fumbled for his six-shooter and drew down on Bob. A decision that he would never know was the right one or the wrong one.

"Hey, you there!" Boudine shouted out to Raintree from across the street. The few stragglers who were still braving the stinging cold, saw a fight coming and turned tail. "Drop the damned gun 'fore you get…" Boudine didn't get a chance to finish. Raintree weaved in her direction and pointed his gun at her and got off a shot that went wild. He should not have done that. In the split second, after he'd pulled the trigger, the blur of Boudine's draw and her fan-fired shots ripped into both his shoulder joints that exploded them into two blood and bone splattered masses that someone like Raintree would never expect.

Bob knew what would come next and shouted at Boudine to, "Stop! Don't do it!"

In that moment between pulling the trigger, that would have blown a hole clear though Raintree's brain and out the back of his head, Boudine stopped. Raintree sank to his knees.

The bullet that blew a hole in his forehead and shattered the back of his skull did not come from Boudine's pistol. Both she and Bob saw a man come out of the shadows as he holstered his gun. It was Bullock. He walked silently up to where Raintree had keeled over face first into the excrement-filled snow and freezing muck.

===

Bob guided the supply filled wagon along the trail back toward the homesteads.

"Why'd you make me stop there, Slye?"

"'Cause, we don't need no more killin'. 'Sides you don't want that *King-Queen-Ace* act of yours catchin' up with you."

As the wagon rumbled along, Boudine thought about what Bob had said. "Bullock seemed kind of pleased to be rid of Raintree."

"Think he was at that... Shite! Damn!" Bob suddenly uttered and reined in the horse and wagon.

"What?" Boudine asked. Alarmed.

"The damned paper! He had the signed hangin' paper! Bullock sees that and..."

Boudine reached into her pocket and withdrew a crumpled up dirty wet ball of paper. "You mean this?" she said with a smirk.

"You haven't said nothin' about Jane."

"Nothin' to say."

"Ain't that why you were so all-fired up about goin' into Deadwood?"

"I seen'er."

"Everythin' okay 'tween you an' her?"

"Mostly."

Bob didn't respond.

"...She asked me what I was doin' for Thanksgivin'."

"Okay. Somethin' wrong with that?"

"No, it ain't okay!" Boudine snapped.

"Why's that?"

Boudine paused for a long moment, then answered, "I ain't never had a Thanksgivin'."

"Never?"

"My sumbitch father didn't allow it. Said it took away from the Lord's message. Whatever the hell that meant!"

Bob didn't comment.

"How'bout you?"

"Yes, my mother made sure we celebrated the holidays. T'was pretty near simple, but we managed. Sometimes we'd pack up and visit another homestead family or Fort Randall would invite us to Thanksgivin' dinner. Sometimes I'd hunt a turkey or two and Millie Mae would ask her Lakota friends in."

"What about Christmas?"

"You didn't celebrate Christmas neither?"

"Oh, sure we did," Boudine said with a mawkish laugh. "If'n you could call prayin' all day and all night and carryin' around a heavy wooden Jesus cross on your back with a crown of thorns prickin' your scalp so's the blood would run down your face."

"But that'd be Easter."

"*Made no difference to him. His loony followers loved seein' the shows he put on.*"

"*Jesus...*"

"*Yeah... Jesus is right.*"

Bob did not or could not respond. Then, he asked, "What was in that bundle you brought back with you?"

"*Bigger pants.*"

===

The moon slipped in and out of the snow clouds that gathered over the Pickering barn. Bob and Boudine came out and Bob closed the barn door. Boudine carried a paper and string wrapped package. Under a grayish night sky, they headed toward their cabin.

"You mean you never celebrated Thanksgiving or Christmas?"

"No... not really..."

"But you was long gone from your family for a few years."

"Just another day in the year, that's all."

"What'd you do, then?"

"Had myself a drink or two and slept wherever I was stayin' at the time."

"Jesus..." Bob muttered.

"Yup, there he is again... I mean, I was asked to come over to someone's place for eats a few times, but I never went. Easier that way. What the hell was I gonna talk about anyway. How my mother was a weakling, and my father loved beatin' the shite outta me? Hell, that'd make for good celebratin' talk now, wouldn't it?"

Bob didn't speak again until they were near the cabin. He stopped and said to Boudine, "Well, things are about to change this time. You'll be celebratin' both Thanksgiving and Christmas with these good folks here."

"But I seen that people bring food and stuff. What the hell am I supposed to bring?" Boudine asked with a slightly bitter edge.

"Boudine, I just seen that your shootin' hands are still as good as ever."

"What the hell's that supposed to mean?"

"Bring the turkey."

===

Abigail and Millie Mae bustled about in the kitchen making sure all the Thnaksgiving dinner fixings were coming along. Abigail called out for Boudine who sat near the fireplace and watched Sarah and Ben spin string tops on the floor. "Sally Mae, come on over here. I'll show you how to stuff this bird."

Boudine reluctantly got up from the chair she was seated in and went over to where Abigail was getting the turkey stuffing ready. "You ever done this a'fore?"

"No."

"Well, I'm gonna teach you."

Bob and Nathan came in from outside. "Whew! It's colder than Hades out there!" Nathan said.

"Hades ain't cold, Pa. It's hot." Sarah corrected as Ben laughed.

Nathan hung his winter coat on a hook by the door and laughed with them. "You are one hundred percent right. Of course, I've never actually been there, so I can't be sure of that."

"You're just bein' a silly-head, Pa!"

Bob asked to anyone who might know, "Anyone seen Otis? He don't seem to be about anywhere."

Nathan said, as he headed toward the fireplace to warm up, "Said early this mornin' that he might be bringin' us all a surprise today. Left before daybreak."

Both the Pickering hound and Stubs were curled up on the braided rug that covered the space in front of the fireplace. Stubs raised his head to listen. The hound did the same and began to bark. They both got up and headed for the front door, tails wagging cautiously. "You boys hush now." Abigail said to them.

There was a light knock on the door. Sarah sprang to her feet. "I'll get it!" Sarah opened the door to reveal Otis and someone else bundled up against the cold. He stepped in and presented his surprise guest. "Y'all, I brung the best cook in the world to help with the dinner."

With that, the bundled-up guest said, "I brung y'all a batch of my famous Plum Puddin'!"

Boudine watched quietly as everyone at the Thanksgiving table folded their hands as Nathan said Grace. "Dear Lord thank you for your patience and for watching over everyone at this table and for giving us the strength and fortitude to continue on with our earthly endeavors. In the name of our Lord and Savior Jesus Christ, Amen."

Everyone uttered a worshipful, *Amen,* except for Boudine...

"Well now, we are so blessed to have such a bountiful meal set before us. I personally cannot wait for that famous Plum Pudding that our newest friend, Miss Marchbanks, was kind enough to bring to this Thanksgiving table."

"The name's *Aunt Lou* and I will accept nothin' but," she said to all with her bright eyes and smile.

Nathan lifted his cup of apple cider, "To Aunt Lou!"

With the table cleared, Aunt Lou delivered her large bowl of Plum Pudding to the table. Abigail and Sarah set out the dessert dishes. "Who's takin' care of your restaurant, Aunt Lou?" Sarah asked.

"Well. I close twice a year. On Thanksgiving and Christmas," she said, as she spooned out the pudding onto the dishes. "But I do have some news. I've been offered a position over in Lead at the Golden Gate Mine. Want me to set things up for the miners there and I said, I'd take it as long as I have the last word on how things is run."

"But, what about the restaurant?" Sarah persisted.

"Oh, questions-questions-questions... I declare." Abigail broached.

Aunt Lou chuckled, "Oh now, that's how I learned everythin' I know. Questions-questions-questions." Then, as she sat at the table, "I started trainin' a young lady who come all the way west, all by her lonesome. Kinda like me. I needed someone. She asked for a job. I think she might be of Italian extraction. I tasted her tomato sauce and the bread she baked and hired her on the spot. 'Course it'll take some time a'fore she tames my Plum Puddin'."

"What's her name?" Sarah asked.

"Mary Theresa and she's cute as a button, ain't that right, Otis?" Otis reddened. "See there! I do believe my boy there has already taken a shine to her."

Otis blushed and shook his head.

"Aunt Lou?" Sarah asked rather hesitantly.

"Yes, dear…"

"Are you… I mean…"

Millie Mae suggested to Sarah, "A question not asked, is an answer not given."

"Go ahead," Aunt Lou encouraged.

"Are you Otis's mother?"

Otis blinked. Abigail reddened and held her breath. Nathan sighed.

"Well…" Aunt Lou said.

"I mean you're a…"

"A colored lady?" Aunt Lou said nicely.

"Um... you said, 'my boy'..."

Aunt Lou chuckled, "Well, ain't you one for the ages. You see, I ain't really his mother, but at the time, he had none of his own. I took one look at that scared, scrawny little kid and said, 'He's worth savin'. So, me an' some of the workin' ladies in town took him under our wings and taught'im to read, write and count, so's he could get along by hisself. An' seems like he's doin' pretty good. Ain't that right, Otis?"

Otis nodded.

"He saved my brother's life." Sarah announced. "He got shot right in the deputy's badge Otis gave him."

"He surely did... I know we don't look much alike, but I still think of him as my son."

Millie Mae retrieved her coat and scarf on the rack by the door and said, "I'm goin' outside for a bit and get me a breath of fresh air."

A light, steady snow fell over the shadows cast by the lamplight that glowed through the cabin windows. Nathan's soft fiddle sent out the popular tune, *Home On The Range*.

The moon shown over the new fallen snow. Millie Mae had walked a distance from the house and was standing silently on the pathway to her cabin. She was very quiet. Unmoving. Staring off at something or *someone*. The moon's light gleamed around her. The image of Ogaleesha seemed to shimmer in front of her, just a short distance away.

SNOW DRIFTS

EIGHTEEN

Inside the cold barn, steam rose from his horse's back. Bob stood in the stall and brushed the roan down. Otis came in and walked over to the opened stall gate.

"Mornin', Otis," Bob said.

"Mornin'."

"Need somethin'?"

Otis hemmed and hawed for a bit, then said, "I... I won't be about for Christmas."

"Oh?"

"Goin' to spend it with Aunt Lou in Deadwood."

"Well, you'd best tell Abigail, so's she knows how much fixin's to make."

Otis looked away and sighed.

"You want me to tell'er?" Bob asked.

"Be best. She gets so sad lookin' if'n everyone isn't about for her special fixin's."

"I'll do that. So, I hope I'm not talkin' out'a school here, Otis, but I hear tell that Aunt Lou brung you up as a youngster. That true?"

Otis looked away, then answered Bob. "She did that, with some of the workin' ladies. T'was more her than them 'tho. Taught me to read and write and count money."

"So's you could fend for yourself."

"Yessir."

"And, you done just that."

"Well, pretty much I guess."

"Pretty much there, Mister Thigpen, pretty much indeed. Given what others have gone through in these parts, I'd say Aunt Lou really done right by you."

Otis paused for a moment, then brightened, straightened up and turned toward the barn door.

"Where're you off too?"

"I'm goin' to tell Miss Abigail myself."

===

Ben and Sarah ran through the snow to Bob's cabin and pounded on the door. "Come on out!" they shouted together, "We're goin' to pick out the Christmas tree!"

Nathan and Abigail waited nearby with their hound and Stubs.

Sarah stopped short amongst a cropping of young fir trees. "Here it is! This is the one!" she shouted.

Nathan, who held onto his axe, walked over to where Sarah was presenting *her* tree. He chuckled and said to her, "Now, you know that your mother always gets to pick out our Christmas tree."

"But this one's perfect, Pa."

Abigail, followed by Ben, Bob and Boudine waded through the snow drifts to view the tree.

"Lookit this one, Ma, it's perfect."

Abigail made a point of standing back, as she studied the tree. She then slowly circled the tree, further examining it. "Well... I'm not sure," she said very slowly.   Nathan stifled a laugh.

"But, Ma, it's perfect!" Sarah then ran to Boudine and grabbed her hand. As she pulled her toward the tree, she said excitedly, "Ain't this perfect, Sally Mae?"

"Boudine looked around, then said, "They all look the same to me."

Abigail went to the tree and shook the snow from the boughs. Then said, "I do believe this is the *perfect* tree."

As Ben and Sarah pulled the felled Christmas tree across the snow. Bob suddenly stopped and drew his Peacemaker. "Everyone stop..." He advanced on some thick snow-covered bushes and shouted as loud as he could. He then fired two quick shots into the air. The hidden cougar spun out from behind the bushes, turned tail and raced away. The hound and Stubs chased and barked after the cougar for several yards, then turned back, having done their part.

With the new Christmas tree on its wooden stand in the Pickering cabin, set apart from the fireplace, Abigail handed out handmade decorations from a box. Bows of colored ribbons. Painted wooden stars and angels. Strings of dried berries and such. Both children and Nathan placed them on the green branches. Boudine and Bob watched quietly. The hound sniffed at Buzzer the cat, got a hissed warning, and backed off. Millie Mae came in from the kitchen and handed out cups of warm cider.

"Oh, that looks wonderful," she said.

Abigail held up a batch of white crocheted doily snowflakes with ties. "These were made by my Nathan's mother back across in Londonderry before she and Grandpa Pickering and the Bell cousins emigrated to America because of the horrible Potato Famine over there." She handed the snowflakes to Sarah who passed some to Nathan and Ben to put on the tree. "The Bell cousins headed on up Maine way and the Pickerings headed west, which was lucky for me."

"Me and Ben too!" Sarah added. Then she and Ben happily said in unison, *"Because, if I wasn't born here, none of you would be here."*

Sarah took one of the crocheted snowflakes to Boudine. "That's what Pa always says every Thanksgiving." She handed it to her. "Your turn, Sally Mae."

Boudine waved her offer off with a wane smile. "That's okay, you go ahead there, Sarah."

"You wear this 'til I say not to, understand girl! With that, Preacher Isaiah jammed a crown of thorns down onto his young daughter's head, causing the thorns to prick her scalp and forehead.

Members of Isaiah's flock watched, as his daughter, dressed in torn rags, dragged a heavy wood crucifix on her small shoulders from behind the Preacher's wagon. Her bedraggled mother, cloaked in a weathered blue shawl, followed behind. "Behold!" Isaiah bellowed from his pulpit.

In one hand he held his Bible high. With the other he swept a grand gesture toward the bleeding crown of thorns on Sally Mae's head. "She wears the thorns of Jesus and bleeds his blood in search for eternal salvation!"

"Ahhh!" Boudine uttered suddenly in the darkness. She rose up from her pillow and tried to focus.

"What's wrong?" Bob asked from beside her.

Boudine shook her head, "Nothin'... nothin's wrong."

"Dreamin' again?"

"Nothin's wrong!" she said sharply and buried herself in her blankets.

A MIDNIGHT CLEAR

NINETEEN

In his home office, Doc Babcock listened to Boudine's belly with his stethoscope trumpet for a long moment. He gently moved it around and listened intently. He then stepped back and contemplated on what he had heard.

"What?!" Boudine asked nervously.

"Once more," the doctor said quietly and listened with the stethoscope. Finally, without saying a word, he turned and put the stethoscope in the instrument cabinet behind him.

"What is it? What's wrong?!" Boudine demanded.

Doc Babcock said to her, "Nothing's wrong. Just a very strong heartbeat..."

At the bar in Nuttal and Mann's No.10 Saloon, Calamity stood next to Boudine and downed a shot of whiskey.

"A Bible?! That ain't no present for crissakes!" Boudine exclaimed.

"You sure you don't wanna drink?"

"No. Even the smell makes me sick."

"You said you wanted to get the Pickering kids a Christmas present. They bein' a religious family, they should have their own Bibles not just one for the family."

"I ain't gettin' them kids no Bible. That's a stupid idea."

Calamity led Boudine into Seth Bullock's and Sol Star's hardware store. Boudine stopped and looked at the abundance of items stacked full to overflowing on the shelves that lined the walls and all the barrels and bins of tools and other supplies. "Damn, look at all this shite. Do people really need all this stuff?" Calamity pushed Boudine forward and said, "Yeah, should be able to find somethin' here."

Cal, the Proprietor, came up. "Hello there, Calamity, ain't seen you in here in a dog's age, what can I do for you?"

"L'o, Cal. This here's my friend Boudine. She's lookin' for gifts for..."

Boudine interrupted, "A girl maybe twelve and a boy maybe ten."

Cal glanced around, then said, "Well, I'm sure we can accommodate the boy, but not so sure about the girl. Might want to go on up the street to the dry goods store. They have some nice frilly things there and..."

Boudine brushed by Cal. "No, this stuff'll do fine."

Just then, a familiar voice came from the front behind Calamity. "Well-well, look who's here. To what do we owe this visit?"

Both Calamity and Boudine stopped and looked at Seth Bullock standing in the doorway. Boudine wasted no time answering defiantly, "T'ain't what you think. I ain't here to talk about Belle Fourche without the others."

Bullock smiled and said, "Didn't think so at all."

"Good! What'chu got here for presents for the Pickering kids? And no Bibles!"

Bullock gave Calamity a quizzical look. "Never mind," she uttered to him.

Boudine set several paper-wrapped and string-tied packages into the wagon she'd parked at the boardwalk. She turned and said to Calamity, "Thanks. Ain't never been much for buyin' presents for anyone."

"Can I ask you a question there, Boudine?"

"Well, you're gonna anyway."

"S'right, I am."

Calamity hesitated.

"Well?"

"You ever thought about gettin' hitched up there with Bob? I mean, you're gonna have a..."

"No."

"Why not?"

"Don't need all the fuss. He's there. I'm there. That's all that needs to be." Then, a little irritated, Boudine asked, "Why're you askin' me this?"

"Well, looks like Deadwood got itself a Preacher name of Henry Weston Smith. Seems like a nice enough fella. Methodist, I think."

"Not interested. Gotta get back a'fore dark."

"Fine then. Tell the folks I said 'l'o." Then Calamity got a mischievous smirk on her face. She gestured to Boudine's gun belt. "Looks like your gun belt's ridin' a little high there, *Boudine*. Still think you can out draw me?"

Boudine's eyes narrowed. "Try me."

Calamity chuckled and turned and walked up the boardwalk. "Not today, Sally Mae. Not today."

Rather good naturedly, Boudine said after her, "Bitch..."

Calamity shot back, "You're right about that!"

Boudine checked the wagon's harnesses and the horse's bit and reins. She didn't notice the shadow of a man coming out of the dark alleyway between two buildings. Obviously very drunk, the man weaved forward. As Boudine lifted a leg to the step to get onto the wagon, the drunk suddenly lurched to her and, with one hand, roughly grabbed her right up under her privates. He locked his other arm around her neck and began to drag her across the boardwalk into the darkened alleyway. He should not have done that. Boudine jammed a boot down hard on the drunk's instep and spun out of his grip. From the darkness of the alley, came a pathetic scream. "Jesus Christ! You bit the end of my nose off!"

Boudine skittered out of the alley, spit out a piece of flesh and mounted the wagon. As she reined the horse and wagon around in a circle, she heard the drunk shout, "Goddamned bitch!"

Boudine shot back, "You're right about that!"

"Looks like you're gettin' into the Christmas Spirit there, Boudine," said Bob.

"*Ain't nothin' of the sort! Just a few things for Sarah'n'Ben, that's all.*"

Bob pulled a small well-used Canadian trapper's toboggan, with full water buckets loaded onto it, over the snow up from the river and headed along the path to Millie Mae's cabin.

"*I know you don't cotton to questions, but you ain't spoken much 'bout the letter you got from Sergeant Bartholomew.*"
"*Nothin' much to say 'til I hear from him again. Been ordered to stay on for a time. Don't know how long. Can just pray. That's all.*"

===

A roaring fire filled the firepit outside the Pickering house. The light from the flames glowed up into he night sky and flickered off of the snow-laden pine boughs. Bob, Boudine and Millie Mae stood all bundled up together in the warmth. Nathan stood with his family. He hummed a note, in a full base baritone, that Bob had never heard before. The family responded by joining in with perfect harmony on the Christmas Carol, *It Came Upon A Midnight Clear*. When they finished, Abigail began to sing a lilting *Silent Night, Holy Night,* as the flames bathed its light on the gatherings' faces.

===

A rather heavy snow fell over Deadwood. Otis came out of a dry goods store in the semi-darkness. He carried several paper-wrapped, string-tied packages under one arm.

"You dirty, lyin' piece of crap." came a voice from behind him. Otis stopped and turned toward the man standing in the dim light on the boardwalk. He immediately recognized the drunken gravedigger, Cyrus James.

"'Lo there, Cyrus."

Noticeably slurring his words, Cyrus weaved forward and confronted Otis. "You was the one who took them bodies outta them graves. I saw it was you on Boot Hill an' you c'ain't tell me no different."

"Whyn't you tell the sheriff then, Cyrus. Jail's right up the way there."

"I aw-ready tol'im. Said to be on my way."

"Good idea, I'd say."

"Jes' 'cause you got yourself a homestead, an' jes' 'cause you was brought up by that there coon, don't make you better'n me, you sumbitch!"

Cyrus came within a foot of Otis. "You finished there, Cyrus?"

"No, I ain't finished!"

"Yes, you are."

Without dropping his packages, Otis sent a hard, bone-snapping, rotten teeth shattering punch full-on into Cyrus's face that sent him to the boardwalk with a thud. Otis then stepped over the groaning Cyrus and muttered, "Merry Christmas."

As he walked away, there was a noticeable straightening of Otis's spine.

===

"Now, we're going to wait until the others get here before we start opening presents," Abigail told the children who were itching to get started.

"The sun's not even up yet you two. 'Sides it's snowing like Hades out there."

Sarah protested, "It don't snow in Hades, Pa!"

"Don't know for sure 'bout that," Nathan teased.

There was a knock at the door. Sarah hurried to open it. "Merry Christmas!" Millie Mae greeted, as she entered with Bob and Boudine and Stubs. Bob held Buzzer and set her down. The hound gave Buzzer a wide berth and hustled over to Stubs. Mille Mae and Boudine set several packages under the Christmas tree, then warmed themselves in front of the fireplace. "My, it's snowin' to beat the band this mornin'," Millie Mae announced. "Be gettin' lots of use for the shovels come the 'morrow."

Both Sarah and Ben sat on the braided rug next to the Christmas tree. Sarah took it upon herself to organize the distribution of the gifts. "This one don't have no name on it."

Boudine spoke up, "S'for your Ma and Pa."

"It's heavy." Sarah got up and brought the package to Abigail, seated next to Nathan.

"T'ain't much," Boudine shrugged.

"Open it, Ma! Open it!"

Abigail carefully undid the string and eased away the paper without tearing it. "Oh, my," she said, "we sure need this," as she unwrapped a large cloth sack of Arbuckle's coffee beans.

"Noticed you was runnin' low," Boudine said rather nervously.

"Well, you noticed right there, Sally Mae. Thank you very much. Very thoughtful indeed."

Bob saw the slight blush come onto Boudine's face.

Sarah retrieved another unnamed package and held it out to Boudine. "Who's this for?"

"Looks to be for Bob."

Sarah hurried it to Bob. "S'for you, Bob. Open it."

Bob glanced at Boudine, as he opened the package and took out three smaller boxes. "It's bullets! Boudine got Bob bullets." Sarah announced.

Boudine uttered to Bob, "Noticed you was gettin' low on 45-75s for your Winchester '76." Bob nodded to Boudine, rather amazed at her thinking. Boudine then indicated to Sarah, "See that package there. That's for Bob too."

Sarah dutifully retrieved the paper wrapped package and delivered it to Bob. Bob gave Boudine another glance, then opened it. "It's a coffee grinder," Sarah told the others.

"Now, you won't have'ta keep usin' Abigail's no more." Bob didn't say anything; being a bit overwhelmed by this seeming change in Boudine.

Sarah brought Boudine two unmarked packages. "Who are these for?"

Boudine pointed to each of them. "That one's yourn and that one's Ben's."

Without hesitation, Sarah and Ben tore open their packages. Sarah held up hers first. "Look Pa! My own skinnin' knife with a leather holder!"

"Me too!" Ben said, as he slipped the leather sheath onto his belt.

Abigail looked at Nathan, "Oh, my…" she said quietly.

Bob asked Nathan, "Can I get that…"

Nathan got up from his chair and headed for the bedroom. He returned with a large blanket covered bundle and set it in front of Boudine.

"What is it?" Sarah asked.

Bob said to Boudine rather quietly, "Take the cover off."

Boudine leaned closer and removed the blanket. "It's a baby's rocker bed! It's a baby's rocker bed!" Sarah said excitedly.

Boudine stared at the handsome handmade cradle-rocker in slight disbelief.

"Me and Otis made it when no one was lookin'," Bob said, watching her reaction.

Boudine gritted back any tears that might have started and reached out to touch the cradle. Buzzer the cat decided it might be just right for her and jumped up into it. Everyone laughed. Everyone but Boudine.

Abigail saw that Boudine was holding back her emotions and decided to change the subject. "Alright, you two. It's my turn to hand out some presents."

Just as she went over to pick out some gifts beneath the tree, Stubs suddenly jumped up and made a beeline for the front door. His tail wagged furiously, and his loud barking was not at all threatening. There was as gentle but firm knock on the door. Stubs began to jump up and down. Nathan said, "Must be Otis then."

"I'll get it," Sarah said and jumped to her feet. Nathan reached out and cautioned her to wait. He then went to the door and opened it slowly. A furious gust of wind and snow blew in. Then, a large, bundled up figure of a man stepped inside. The dark woolen coat and muffler covering his face were thick with snow and ice chunks that hit the floor. Millie Mae's eyes widened, as the man shakily removed his gloves and began to fumble and unwrap the thick muffler to reveal the full red beard of Sergeant Major William Harrison Bartholomew.

"Oh, my lord," Millie Mae breathed in shock.

Sergeant Major Bartholomew tried to speak, but his body gave out and he sank to the floor, completely exhausted.

Sarah was closing the door against the cold, but spotted something outside in the snowstorm and exclaimed, "There's a horse out there. Looks like it's dyin'!"

===

Bob led Bartholomew's worn out, stumbling horse into the barn and let it lay down. Boudine followed with a water pail and some rags. "I think, if we wipe'er down with this warm water, might be able to save'er."

"Be a miracle, I'm thinkin'."

Nathan pushed open the barn door and brought in an armload of horse blankets. "We keep these in the house to keep'em warm."

Boudine helped spread the horse blankets over the animal. Bob rubbed the horse down, trying his best to get the animal heated up.

Nathan said, "We got the Sergeant over in front of the fireplace. Abigail and your mother are tryin' to fill'im with chicken broth. C'ain't believe he come all the way from Fort Randle in this weather."

"He'll make it. Them soldiers there are tougher'n nails," Bob said.

Bartholomew sat shivering in a chair close to the fireplace wrapped in blankets. Millie Mae spooned warmed broth to him from a clay bowl. "This should stop the shivers soon enough."

Sarah watched everything and piped up, "Is he a real soldier, Millie Mae?"

"He certainly is. Indeed, he is."

"I ain't never met a real soldier a'fore."

"Well, as soon as he's better, I'm sure you can get'im to tell you and Ben some soldierin' stories."

"Maybe... maybe someday I can be a soldier," Sarah said softly.

Nathan came back in and quickly closed the door against the storm. "They just might save the Sergeant's horse there. Started movin' and tryin' to get up."

Millie Mae placed her hands on her chest and uttered, "Praise the Lord."

Bob let Bartholomew's horse stumble to its feet. He held onto its harness until he saw that the animal steadied itself and was more surefooted. The wind and snow howled outside, but the barn walls and roof were built strong and held tight. The other horses watched from the stalls. "Think she's gonna make it. Open that empty stall there," he indicated to Boudine.

Boudine started to unlatch the stall. Suddenly, she grabbed at her belly and uttered, "Shite!"

Bob stopped leading the horse to the stall. "What's the matter?" he asked with alarm.

Boudine straightened up and continued to open the gate. "Nothin'. Get'er in here."

Bob led the horse into the straw-covered stall, quickly adjusted the horse blanket and stepped back out. "What was that, Boudine?" he asked, as he shut the stall gate.

Again, Boudine uttered, "Damn!" and pressed her hands on her belly.

"What?" Bob asked anxiously.

"Somethin's kickin' the hell outta me in there!"

===

Lucretia Marchbanks sat at a table with Otis in her restaurant in the Grand Central Hotel. What sunlight that was able to slip though the gray clouds, that nearly covered all of Deadwood, did brighten the large window that looked out on the snow and muck drenched street. As she sipped her coffee, she looked at Otis with a rather puzzled expression but continued without explanation. "Them was very thoughtful gifts you brung last night, Otis."

"What's Christmas without gifts then?" he said with a bit of a smile. He pushed back his finished breakfast plate and stretched some.

Lucretia indicated the cloth wrap around his right hand, "You gonna tell me what happened to your hand?"

Otis chuckled, "Nope."

"Hear tell that drunken grave digger Cyrus got his nose bashed in outside the dry goods store last night."

Otis nodded, "That so?"

"Yup, got his nose splattered all over and broke off whatever rotten teeth he had left. Someone laid the bugger out flat."

Otis just uttered, "Humph..."

"Must've done or said somethin' real nasty to someone, I'd say."

Otis took a sip of coffee and said, "Must've..."

"Never liked that fella. Stunk to high heaven. Don't ever think he ever saw a bathtub in his life. Couldn't let'im eat in here."

Otis set his napkin down on the table. Lucretia asked him, "Stand up there, Otis."

Otis looked at Lucretia, a bit surprised.

"Go ahead. Stand up and let me have a look at'cha."

Otis did what she asked. Lucretia studied Otis for a moment, then said, "There. It's true."

"What's true?"

"You done look like you growed some."

Otis said quizzically, "Don't reckon."

"Then, it's the way you're standin' there. Makes you look taller. And..."

"And, what?"

"Your eyes."

Otis raised his hand toward his eyes. "What's the matter with'em?"

"Ain't nothin' the matter with'em 't all. Bright-eyed-and-bushy-tailed! You always had them awful sad lookin' eyes, an' I could never for the life of me get you to stand up straight. Now, look at'cha?"

Otis sat back down and thought for a moment, then reached out and took Lucretia's hands in his. "I... I always heard what you was sayin' there, Aunt Lou. Just never felt good about nothin' much a'fore." Otis began to choke up some, gathered himself and said softly, "You was always there when I fell down. Always had a good word... always looked at you as... my Ma."

Tears welled in Lucretia's dark brown eyes. "Now, look what'chu gone and done," she uttered, as some tears ran down her cheeks.

. Otis squeezed her hands and said quietly but firmly, "Merry Christmas."

===

"Could've been the death of you comin' here through all this weather, Bill," Millie Mae said.

"Wasn't like this when I left. Thought I could make it through," Bartholomew said.

"Kept lookin' for a letter at the Wells Fargo Office from you, but..."

"Didn't send one, Millie Mae. Wanted to surprise you for Christmas."

"Well, bless you, you sure did that."

"I have another surprise. I'm out. Finished with the Army as of end of November."

"Oh, my..."

"My last mission was a real barnburner. Almost put me in God's graveyard that one."

"Oh, my..." Millie Mae sighed.

"Hadn't been for your Lakota friend there..."

"Oglaleesha?"

"Yes. We were after a breakaway band of renegades. Got myself separated from my platoon and surrounded by some very angry Sioux warriors who were after my scalp for tryin' to run 'em back to the reservation. Wasn't for him, I might not be here to tell the story."

Millie Mae was quiet, not saying a word.

"You alright?"

"He..." She stopped.

"What is it? Millie Mae, you look..."

"He sent me word."

===

In the barn, Bob watched as Bartholomew led his horse out of the stall and studied her as he walked it around in a circle. "Want to thank you and your lady friend there for savin' this'ne's life. She just about tuckered out on the way here. Didn't think either of us would make it."

"She's a strong one."

"She is that. Saved my rear end many times over."

Bob nodded, but didn't add anything. Bartholomew stopped and patted the animal's nose. "How're things with you there, Bob, since our last conversation back at your mother's old homestead?"

Knowing there would have to be a talk with the Sergeant Major, Bob just sighed a bit and said, "Different."

"You still in the card playin' business?"

"Not so much. No."

Bartholomew glanced at Bob, then led his horse back toward the stall. "Well, that is *different,* I do have to say. Your mother said something about you havin' got yourself a homestead of sorts. If I might ask, what're you planning on doing with it?"

Bob took a moment, then answered, "Build a town." Bartholomew just stood there with a perplexed expression on his face. Bob intentionally let his words sink in, then said, "A lot's changed since we last spoke."

Bartholomew led his horse into the stall and closed the gate. He turned to Bob and said quietly, "Might take me a bit of time to get myself regulated to civilian life. Been in the regiments for most of my life. Not sure what I'll be useful at here abouts."

Bob headed toward the barn door. "Won't be for lack of things to do, I can tell you that. Are you separated from the Army for good?"

"Yes. Was supposed to be held over for a time, but my replacement came in early and the fact I was wounded last time out sort of sped things up."

Bob hesitated, then said, "Wounded?"

"Arrow in the left calf. Slowed me down some. Gettin' a lot better as the days go by. That Lakota friend of your mother's gave me some sort of mixture to put on it. Don't know where he comes up with his cures, but this'n seems to be workin'."

"Didn't notice you limpin'."

"It's the Injun medicine. Takes all the pain away. Can't feel a thing."

Bob reached for the barn door and swung it open. "Abigail'ill have breakfast ready. Doesn't like anyone bein' late."

Bartholomew hesitated, then asked, "Said before you never killed anyone. That still stand?"

Bob paused, then uttered, "Yep."

"Your sharpshooter lady friend, she ever killed anyone?"

The question didn't settle well with Bob, but he answered rather flatly, "If the need be."

Bartholomew didn't comment. Bob, a bit irritated, asked, "How'bout yourself?"

Bartholomew's expression darkened. He headed out the door. As he passed Bob, he uttered, "T'was my job."

===

"Well, looks like you got yourself a good rest-up there Sergeant Major." Nathan said to Bartholomew at the Pickering table.

Bartholomew held up his hand. "Please call me Bill."

Nathan addressed Bartholomew, "Well, sir, you earned your rank and then some. Got cousins up Maine way fought for the Union. Don't see or hear from'em much but always refer to'em by their rank. Feel it's an honor to do so."

Bartholomew sighed and nodded. Nathan said, "It's settled then, "Sergeant Major it is."

Millie Mae helped out a bit with, "Maybe, just *Sergeant* will do."

Nathan looked at Bartholomew for a response. He nodded and uttered, "That'd do fine."

"Alrighty then. Ben, please pass me the taters there."

Sarah said, "Why do we have'ta take down the Christmas tree, Pa?"

"Well, Christmas is over 'til next year. It's back to work for all of us. We got the rest of the winter to get through and we got to get things ready for the spring plantin'."

"Shucks," Sarah protested.

Dusk closed in as Bob and Boudine walked with Millie Mae, Sergeant, and Stubs along the snow path to her cabin. They stopped at Millie Mae's cabin door. "I'd love to have you two come on in but, the truth is, I'm plum tuckered out and the Sergeant here's got to get off that leg of his."

The Sergeant protested, "I'm fine."

"I'll be the judge of that, Bill." With that, Millie Mae, Sergeant and Stubs went inside.

The lit lantern shed light from the small table next to the kitchen. Bob stoked the wood stove and added another log. Boudine set herself into a chair and leaned her elbows on the table. Bob closed the stove's iron gate and said to Boudine, "Sure could use that fireplace. You was extra quiet all day. Somethin' wrong?"

"No."

"If you say so."

Boudine sat quietly for a few moments, then uttered, "It's just that..."

"Just what?" Bob noticed the glint of tears in her eyes and waited.

"It's just that... I ain't... I ain't never had a Christmas a'fore."

VIOLETS & SNOWDROPS

TWENTY

The winter snow had begun to shed its blankets and drifts and replace them with mud and tufts of green grass that had begun to push up through the four homesteads. Even though the nights were still frigid, there was the smell of spring in the air that was unmistakable. Sarah burst into the house with a fistful of flowers to a surprised Abigail at work in her kitchen. "Look, Ma. Flowers... I got flowers. Spring's comin'!"

"Oh, slow down and scrape that mud off'n them clodhoppers 'fore you come trackin' into the house." Sarah spun back out onto the porch and began running her boots over the iron mud scraper screwed to the floor. Abigail met her at the door. "Let's see what you have there."

"Violets and... I forgot what these others're called."

Abigail gently took the flowers from Sarah. "What a pretty bunch of posies. Let's see here, there's violets and these little white ones are *Snowdrops* and..."

Suddenly, Ben came charging from the path to the river, exclaiming as he ran, "It's comin'! It's comin'! Where's Pa?! Where's Pa?!"

"He's in the barn," Abigail called out, "What's wrong? What's comin'?"

Ben ran toward the barn shouting back to her, "Nothin's wrong. The boat's comin' in with the paddlewheel."

At the river, Nathan, Bob, Otis and Sergeant pulled on the ropes to help bring in the large river raft carrying the paddlewheel to be erected on the new sawmill that was under construction on the riverbank. Stubs and the hound barked orders as they ran back and forth at the water's edge. Both Ben and Sarah stood with Abigail and watched the excitement. Millie Mae walked slowly with Boudine from the pathway and joined Abigail. Boudine was now showing that her condition was well along. For a small woman, her belly now appeared to be quite large. Once the raft was secured, the workmen on the raft helped the other men carefully roll the paddlewheel onto shore and then guide it back into the water next to the mill, where it would eventually power the saws that would be installed inside.

Sarah said, "This must'a cost a bunch."

Abigail said, "Mister Bullock helped out there."

Ever the inquisitive, Sarah asked, "How come?"

"Well, he needs wood to build the town and we all got plenty of it."

"Pa said they're going to build a school and a church."

"Yes... yes they will."

"So, it's going to be a town like Deadwood with all them hooligans runnin' around?"

Abigail paused, then said, "My goodness, young lady, so many questions."

Boudine said quietly, "Think I'll head back to the cabin."

Millie Mae asked her, "You not feelin' good, Sally Mae?"

"Just a bit tuckered out. Lots'a kickin' goin' on inside."

"I'll walk back with you."

"No, y'all stay here an' watch the goin's on. Just gonna get me a catnap." Boudine turned back toward the pathway.

"You sure there, Sally Mae? It ain't a bother."

'No, y'all stay. I'll be fine."

As Boudine walked away, Millie Mae said to Abigail, "She's got herself a lively one that's for sure."

As Boudine reached the cabin, she suddenly hunched over and grabbed for the porch beam. "Damn!" she uttered and struggled to the door.

Once inside, Boudine, in some discomfort, staggered to the bedroom door and went in.

Bob came up from the riverbank to where the women and kids were watching. "This is really exciting, Bob!" Sarah exclaimed.

Bob said, "It is that. It is that." Then he asked, "Where's Boudine off to?"

Millie Mae said, "Little one started actin' up. Went off for a catnap."

Bob said, "Yeah, she ain't been able to get much sleep of late. Think the little guy can't wait to get out."

"Is it a boy? It's a boy ain't it?" Sarah blurted.

Abigail scolded. "Oh, hush your mouth there, Sarah."

"Don't really know, but..." Bob started to say.

"But you hope it's a boy and not a girl, right?" Sarah pressed.

Abigail admonished, "Now, that'll be enough, hear?"

Bob said. "Don't make no difference t'all."

"Good! 'Cause girls can handle guns an' knives just like boys can, right Bob?"

Bob shot Abigail a quick wink and said, "That's for sure, Sarah. That's for sure."

"Remember, I could'a shot that stupid donkey what broke into our house. Could'a shot'im right in the…"

Just then, Nathan let out a whistle for Bob. "Need 'nother hand here, Bob."

Bob turned and hustled back to work at the riverbank.

Millie Mae said to the others, "Think I'll go check on Sally Mae. I ain't of no use here."

Sarah said excitedly, "I'll go!"

Abigail said to Sarah, "You stay right here. Don't want you to go botherin' her."

"Ma, I'm twelve and I got my new skinnin' knife right here just in case." Sarah shot back huffily.

Millie Mae said to both Abigail and Sarah, "Tell you what, you go on ahead, Sarah and I'll catch up in a bit."

With that, Sarah made a beeline back up the path.

Abagail sighed and said to Millie Mae, "Thank you. Don't know what I'm to do with that girl. Sometimes I'm fit to be tied, I swear. She's becoming real stubborn of late."

"Just growin' up, s'all."

Ben was getting itchy and piped up, "Ma, I'm goin' down closer to Pa." Ben didn't wait for an answer and hurried away from the women.

Abigail uttered, "Well, he's growin' up too there."

Sarah stepped to the door of Bob and Boudine's cabin and tapped lightly. Not hearing anything, she slowly opened it and stepped inside.

Not seeing Boudine, Sarah went to the bedroom door and quietly opened it slightly and peeked in. She then pushed the door wide. Boudine wasn't there. Sarah backed away and headed for the front door but stopped short as Boudine abruptly came in from outside, startling them both.

"I... I come to see if'n you was alright," Sarah said.

"Just went to the privy."

"Oh... so, you don't need nothin' then?"

Boudine sat in a chair next to the small eating table. "No, nothin' 'cept maybe a little sleep might help."

Sarah saw a chance to ask some of the questions that had been building up inside of her. "Can I ask you somethin'?"

Boudine looked at Sarah for a brief moment, then said, "Shoot."

"Is havin' a baby like a goat havin' a baby goat?"

Boudine didn't expect the question and hesitated. "Ah... I... don't rightly know. I... I mean..."

Sarah pulled back the other chair and sat opposite Boudine. She was now all business. "I know all about how goats get babies and horses and cows and chickens. I just wanna know if it's the same with people."

Boudine had never been faced with this before and wasn't at all sure how to handle it. "I suppose… might want to ask your ma."

Sarah leaned forward and said earnestly. "She won't tell me nothin'. Already asked. Says it's in God's hands." Then, without stopping, she added, "Did you and Bob get together like the daddy goats and the mommy goats do in the spring?"

Boudine sighed. "Um…"

Just then, there was a soft knock on the door and Millie Mae peeked inside and saw the perplexed expression on Boudine's face. "Well, now," she said as she came in and closed the door, "looks like you two are havin' a real set-to here."

Sarah said defensively, "No we ain't. We was just talkin' 'bout how babies are made."

"Are you and Bob gonna get married a'fore the baby comes so's it'll have a proper ma and pa?"

===

Nathan and Bob finished tying off the paddlewheel in the place where it would be attached to the saw workings when the mill building was finished. Nathan stepped back onto the riverbank and said to the workmen who delivered the wheel and helped them, "Can't thank you boys enough. Gettin' that wheel here by raft 'stead of by wagon was a sure smart idea."

Bob stepped up beside Nathan who said, "Now, you gentlemen follow me up to the house, where my wife, Abigail, has already cooked up a hot meal for y'all and well deserved I must say."

The group started to troop toward the pathway. Nathan turned to Ben as they walked on, "Well, whudda'ya think there, Son?"

Ben grinned widely and said, "Can I work the saws?"

TROUBLE BREWIN'

TWENTY-ONE

"I want to go see the Doc in Deadwood. All this goin' on inside me don't feel right."

Bob reined the wagon around in front of the cabin where Boudine was waiting. Bob noticed that she had replaced her gun belt with a length of rope because of the size of her belly.

"You need to carry that thing?"

"I ain't never goin' near that town without it," she said flatly and started to haul herself up onto the driver's seat with some difficulty.

"Suit yerself," Bob said and snapped the reins over the horse's rump.

With Deadwood going full tilt, Bob maneuvered the wagon through the tangle and bustle of humanity and their draft animals; steered clear of a resting team of oxen and headed through the snowmelt muck and dung toward the doctor's office. A voice called out from the boardwalk, "Bob."

Bob looked around and saw Seth Bullock waving at him. "Come see me when you're done."

Bob touched two fingers to his hat, acknowledging Bullock, then slapped the reins and continued up the main street.

"What's he want?" Boudine asked.

"Probably somethin' 'bout how the sawmill's comin'."

"Lot'a people out here today... s'funny."

"What?"

"I never noticed the stink of this place a'fore. But now that we live over in Belle Fourche, I can really smell…

"Hey, you there!" someone shouted.

Both Boudine and Bob looked around as a slovenly man hurried through the mud toward them. Two other ne'er-do-wells were on either side of him. As the man circled in front of their wagon, he fumbled with his holstered gun and shouted at Boudine, "You! You're the bitch what bit off my nose!"

Both Bob and Boudine could see that the end of the man's nose was an ugly scabbed over stump. Boudine mumbled, "Shite…"

The man sloppily drew his pistol and started to point it at Boudine. "Say goodbye, bitch!"

Unfortunately, he was a might slow on the draw because, even in her present condition, Boudine was still able to fan off two shots. One in his left shoulder. One in his right. But just as she went for her *King-Queen-Ace* shot, Bullock shouted from the other side of the street, "Hold up there!"

As the man fell back into the muck, the other two, who were about to draw their guns, jammed them into their holsters, turned tail and ran as fast as they could up an alleyway out of sight.

Boudine holstered her six-shooter, and said to Bob, "Still think I should'a left my gun behind?"

Sheriff Bullock stood over the groaning man and said to both Boudine and Bob, "Saw the whole thing. You two get on your way, I'll take care of this. He's mean enough to steal the coins off a dead man's eyes. Be sending him off to prison over in Yankton. Better off without'im around here."

Bob nodded and slapped the reins. Bullock said to Boudine as they started away, "Maybe, I should offer you the sheriff job."

"Doc Babcock ain't here. We been dealin' with a bunch of pox that broke out down the road aways. He won't be back 'til tomorrow sometime," Calamity said in the doctor's house.

"Pox?" Boudine said.

"Smallpox. Tryin' to stop it from gettin' away."

"Sounds bad."

"It is, but Doc got ahold of somethin' called a vaccination that's supposed to be a cure," Calamity said, unconvincingly. "We'll see."

"D'you take the cure?"

"Hell no!" Calamity exclaimed. "I ain't gonna put that shite in me. Damned stuff gives you the fuckin' pox then you get better an' yer supposed to never get it again. Goddamned crazy, if'n you ask me. If I get it, I get it. That's it."

Boudine heaved a sigh and uttered, "Jesus."

Then, Calamity asked, "What was all that shootin' up the street there?"

"Nothin' a bullet din't fix."

Calamity saw Boudine's fixed expression and decided to let it drop. "What're you here for, Boudine? Where's Bob?"

"Bob's meetin' with Bullock 'bout the new town and stuff… I… I think somethin's goin' wrong inside me."

Bob said, "You know Aunt Lou would'a got us a room at the Grand Hotel so's you could see the Doc tomorrow."

"Nope. he's workin' with folks what got the pox. 'Sides Jane took a listen with the Doc's listenin' tube and felt 'round a bit. Said there din't sound like anythin' wrong. Said probably just getting' to be a big'un."

A bit alarmed, Bob said, "Calamity Jane ain't a doctor!"

"She's been workin' with Doc Babcock nigh on a year now. Learnin' medicine stuff. She's also my friend. She wouldn't lie to me."

After a moment, Bob said, "I had a bead on that varmint as well…"

"Good thing you din't get off a shot."

"Why?"

"Then you couldn't say you never killed no one."

===

Bob stood with Nathan just out of earshot from two newly hired hands who were adding timbers to the new sawmill by the river.

"I had a meet-up with Bullock yesterday. Was takin' Boudine to see the Doc and he asked for a sitdown."

"'Bout the town?"

"Yeah, a li'l bit, but more about some trouble that might be brewin'."

"What trouble?"

"Seems Swearengen, owner of the Gem, and some if his kind, got wind of the things we was askin' for in the new town."

"What kind of things?"

"'Bout askin' for churches and a school and only a small number of saloons, so's it won't turn into another Deadwood. Seems they's all against it and might be ready to put up a fuss. Also, they want seats on the new town council."

Nathan paused for a moment. His face clouded over. Then, he said, quite firmly, "Well, that dog won't hunt."

Bob walked through the short patch of woods between his place to where Otis was beginning to set up framing logs for his own cabin.

"Want to ask you somethin' there, Otis."

Otis steadied the log he was setting in a hole and stepped back. "Mm-um…"

"Them new fellas Nathan hired to work on the mill, you ever seen'em a'fore?"

"Nope. Said, they just showed up lookin' for work. Ain't never seen'em around. Seem to be doin' the job right."

"Keep an' eye on'em. Not sayin' somethin's wrong, but there's a few in Deadwood what don't like our plans for the new town. Al Swearengen bein' one of'em."

This stopped Otis for a moment. "That donkey's always been trouble."

"Bullock ain't too keen on what he's heard from him."

"What… he wants more saloons and whore houses 'stead of churches and schools?"

Bob looked at Otis and almost smiled. "Yup."

"I'll keep an ear out."

MISSING

TWENTY-TWO

Both Seth Bullock and his partner, Sol Star, headed up a meeting at the new town building site on the Belle Fourche homestead properties. Several attendees, including Bob, Nathan, Otis, and a very with child Boudine, listened to Bullock who had set up a small folding table and was laying out some draft plans.

"These will give you an idea of how we've laid out the town so far. Please understand that this is not the final draft, and we are here to start ironing out any objections or ideas that might come up."

With that, Bullock spread out the plans for all to see. They all gathered around for their first look. Nathan was first to speak up, "These here buildings here and here," he pointed out, "look to be on the main street. They been sorted to what'll be in'em?"

Bullock didn't hesitate to answer, "Those, as well as these, are where different businesses will be established."

"What kinda businesses?" Nathan asked with a hint of trepidation.

Bullock's partner, Sol Star, spoke up in his soft, almost hard to hear voice, "It depends on who applies for a spot."

Bob listened as Nathan continued, "Well, who's the judge of them businesses? Who makes sure they ain't the sort of businesses we don't want built here?"

The other three men standing there reacted with concern to what Nathan said. One of them, a very stern, well-dressed portly man in a derby hat and a gold watch chain said, "What difference does it make to what business takes a building?"

Nathan began to get antsy. Bob interjected, "It matters to us here. We own these four homesteads and are the ones gonna be supplyin' the lumber. Also, we don't see any churches or schools on these drawings."

Bullock jumped in, "There will be-There will be."

Nathan looked squarely at the portly man and said pointedly, "You settin' up a business here, sir?"

The man hesitated and noticeably flushed a bit, "Me and my partners are thinkin' on it."

"And, who might them partners be?" Boudine blurted out.

The man was immediately offended that a woman confronted him and gritted, "S'none of your business, ma'am."

"Oh, it surely is, mister! It damned well surely is!"

Otis piped up, "The lady asked you a question. Who be your partner there?"

Bullock tried to temper the situation, "Easy, this is just a first step here and…"

Otis pressed ahead, "Partner wouldn't be Al Swearengen, would it?"

The man reddened and gnashed his teeth as he said with some spittle, "I was told you and them might be trouble."

Nathan spoke up, "We told Mister Bullock here, from the first, that this here town ain't gonna be 'nother Deadwood and that's that."

Two of the other men attending the meeting shot a look between them that was not pleasant and showed that they had other ideas.

The portly man said, "Well, then, *Mister*, whatever your name is, we'll just have to see about all this."

With that, the man turned and walked away toward his horse drawn buggy. The other two shook their heads and walked off as well.

Bullock put his hands on the sheets of plans and lowered his head for a moment. Then he straightened up and said to the others, "It's just about business. Always starts off rough and then eventually smoothes out."

Nathan said, "Them's not about puttin' good businesses in this new town."

"Not if'n they's partners with Swearengen they ain't," Otis said.

Bullock began to roll up the plans and said, "They'll come around. Meanwhile, just keep going with the sawmill and Sol and me will keep going with our work. He then tried to change the subject by asking Boudine, "How're you getting by? Looks to be pretty soon there."

"Mm-hum," she muttered.

Bullock and Sol Star shook hands with the group and headed away.

===

Millie Mae was in Abigail's kitchen kneading dough in a wooden bread trough, while Abigail cut turnips into a bowl. Sarah came bustling in from outside with a wicker basket of fresh eggs.

"I'm done with my chores. I'm goin' down to the sawmill," she announced as she set the basket down in the kitchen and turned back toward the front door.

"Wait just a darned minute," Abigail said to her. "You still got your Bible readin' to do. That's why Millie Mae is here bein' good enough to help out."

Sarah opened the front door and said over her shoulder, "I will. I'll do it later. I have'ta see how the mill is comin' along." With that, she left, closing the door behind her.

Abigail heaved a sigh and leaned over the bowl she was using. Millie Mae said to her, "S'not like I'm goin' nowhere. The Lord is patient."

"Land o' Goshen, she just seems to think she needs to know everythin' 'bout everythin' these days."

Millie Mae smiled and said, "Well, curiosity didn't really kill the cat, you know."

Ben held a pointed wooden stake and mallet and watched his father pace off several yards away from the side of the cabin and stop. "Okay, bring the stake here. Think this should do it, Good Lord willin'."

Ben brought the stake and handed the mallet to him. Nathan took the stake, set the point on the ground, then started pounding it in. "Now, we start diggin' 'til we strike water. No more luggin' buckets up from the river."

Just then, Abigail's iron triangle rang out for lunch.

"Oh, good. Just in time. I'm famished," Nathan said good-naturedly. As Nathan and Ben turned toward the front of the cabin, Ben stopped and looked toward the path to the river. "What's that smoke comin' from the river?"

Nathan stopped and turned. He immediately saw a column of white smoke funneling up over the pines and shouted out, "Abigail, grab some buckets! We got us a fire at the sawmill! Ben, you run as fast as you can and get Bob, Otis and Sergeant. Grab more buckets in the barn." With that Nathan took off running toward the river as Ben charged off to get the others.

At the sawmill, Nathan shouted out directions to where the fire was burning on the wall of the small mill enclosure closest to the river. "More over here." he called out to Abigail and Millie Mae, who had set up a bucket brigade with Otis, Bob and Sergeant and were furiously filling and handing off buckets of water from the river.

Boudine hurried, as best she could from the pathway, carrying two more empty buckets.

Within a short period of time, they were able to throw enough water onto the fire to get it under control and finally put it out.

"Well," Nathan said, out of breath to the others, "don't look like as big a catastrophe as it might've been thanks to y'all. Few new boards here and there, it'll be good as new, I'm thinkin'."

"Mister Nathan?" asked Otis.

"Otis?"

"Where's them workers y'all hired. Don't seem to be around. The tent's gone and so's them horses and that small, covered wagon they come here in."

"Oh-my-God!" Abigail suddenly exclaimed in shock, "Where's Sarah?"

They all looked at each other as they realized what might have happened.

"Thought she was with you in the house," Nathan said to Abigail.

"No, she got her gander up and headed down here to see the work bein' done."

"Maybe she went back," Millie Mae said hopefully.

"She ain't there," Boudine said, "I went there first, a'fore I come down here."

Bob had gone over to where the two hired hands had their encampment. Sergeant hurried to him. "This where they camped?" he asked urgently.

"Yeah."

Sergeant immediately started using his Army tracking experience and said, "They headed off that way. See, there's the broken-down brush tracks."

Bob spun around and took off toward the path to the cabins. As he passed Nathan he shouted, "I'm goin' after them!"

Nathan, Sergeant and Otis quickly followed him.

===

Inside the small, covered wagon, Sarah was tied hand and foot with a gunnysack over her head. As the wagon bounced and jerked her around, she was able to shake the sack from her head. She then saw that the kidnappers had not taken her skinning knife from the sheath on her belt.

Bob pushed the roan harder and his horse responded. Further back, Nathan, Sergeant and Otis galloped their horses together over the rough path the kidnappers had taken.

As the trail turned more toward Deadwood, the covered wagon came into view. Bob pressed the roan and began to close the gap. Nathan, Sergeant and Otis spurred their mounts on. The kidnapper, who wasn't holding the reins, looked back and saw Bob gaining on them. He grabbed his rifle and took a shot in the direction of Bob, but it went wild, and he nearly bounced out of the wagon. Bob reined the roan behind the wagon, so they couldn't get a bead on him. He closed in even closer. Nathan saw what Bob was doing and drew the Confederate Sharps rifle from its scabbard, the one that Bob and Boudine had given him when they had first met the Pickering family in the rainstorm on the trail out of Deadwood. Bob could see into the back of the covered wagon that Sarah was furiously cutting the rope tied around her legs, holding her skinning knife with both of her tied hands. Bob also saw that the kidnapper with the rifle had turned to look into the wagon and was starting to climb down inside. He urged the roan closer, something his horse was used to and excited about from their stage robbing and bandit days.

Bob pulled his Winchester '76 Centennial rifle, that Boudine had secretly slipped into his scabbard as a surprise, days before he was shot and captured by the evil Sheriff Jack O'Banion. He sat straight up in the saddle, flicked the lever, chambered the 44-75 bullet, aimed and fired: sending the lead slug ripping through the kidnapper's shoulder. The kidnapper recoiled in shock and pain and stumbled back out through the canvas opening onto the driver's box. The wagon hit a rock and tossed the wounded kidnapper out onto the hard ground into a tumbling heap. He then tried to get up to run, but was quickly surrounded by Otis, Sergeant and Nathan, who slid out of his saddle holding his Sharps rifle. He stood right up to the shaken, wounded kidnapper and pointed the gun right at the man's forehead. "Why'd you do this? Why'd you take my daughter?" he demanded.

"I... I... "

Sergeant and Otis spun their horses around and took off after Bob and the wagon. Nathan cocked the hammer on the Sharps. "Say your piece or meet the Devil!" he barked.

The stricken kidnapper whined, "It was... it was them saloon owners what wants to build saloons and whorehouses in the new town. We was only supposed to scare you. We... we wouldn't've hurt the girl. We wouldn't've..."

"Was one of'em Al Swearengen?"

The kidnapper looked confused. "I... don't..."

"The owner of the Gem Theater in Deadwood. Was one of'em him? Al Swearengen?"

"I don't know. We was just given a bunch of money and told what to do s'all. Please. I swear!"

Nathan looked to where the wagon was still speeding away. He then lowered the Sharps rifle, spun it around and sent the rifle butt smashing into the kidnapper's forehead, sending him dropping to the ground. Out cold.

The kidnapper frantically drove the horses and wagon over the rutted open field. He turned and saw that Bob was in position to jump from the roan onto the back of the wagon. He quickly wrapped the reins around the wooden brake handle and drew his six-shooter. He started to come into the wagon, just as Bob jumped through the canvas opening in the back. As the wagon jumped about over the ruts and rocks, he tried to aim his gun at Bob and pulled the trigger, missing Bob by several feet. That was the end of his attempt. He suddenly felt the searing pain of Sarah's skinning knife punch deep just above his shoulder blade.

As the kidnapper fell into the wagon in a writhing, painful heap, Bob charged over him and bolted through the opening to the front driver's box.

The two horses pulling the wagon were now in a panicked runaway. The reins had flipped off the brake handle and were flying free. Bob gingerly stepped down between the galloping horses onto the rig and harnesses between them and reached for their bits. He jerked and pulled their heads around so they couldn't see where they were going. As the animals began to slow, Otis and Sergeant galloped up on either side of them and grabbed the reins up, finally stopping the winded horses.

With the wounded kidnappers fully bound up inside the wagon, Otis finished tying his horse's reins to the back and then climbed up onto the driver's box. Sarah was being hugged by Nathan. Bob said to Otis. "Want me to go along with-ya?"

"Nossir, it'll give me great pleasure to deliver these varmints to Sheriff Bullock."

Sergeant spoke up, "What's the penalty for kidnapping a child out here?"

Otis answered, "Don't know for sure, but hangin' ain't good enough." With that Otis slapped the reins over the horses and pulled away in the direction of Deadwood.

Bob and Sergeant lead the way as Nathan rode with Sarah sitting on his saddle in front of him.

"Are you mad at me, Pa?"

Nathan thought for a brief moment, then said quietly to his daughter, "Don't think I have to be. What happened happened and therein lies the lesson."

After a moment, Sarah said, "Ya-know them stupid donkeys didn't even take my skinnin' knife off'n me."

As they rode along, Sarah asked her father quietly, "Is the Lord gonna be mad at me for stabbin' that man?"

Nathan mulled her question over, then answered with, "Well… no, not likely. Sometimes the Lord does need a little help down here durin' certain situations."

COMES THE TIME

TWENTY-THREE

It was dark outside. The Pickerings, along with Bob, Boudine, Millie Mae and Sergeant had just sat down for the evening meal. All was quiet, as Nathan led the Grace, "Dear Lord, we have a special thank you for your watching over our Sarah, during a frightening time for her and everyone here. Thank you for helping us through something that no one should ever have to go through." He paused, then continued, "Sarah asked me if I was mad at her. I thought about that for a moment and knew I could be, if I'd wanted to be, but sometimes, the lesson is in what happened. I do believe that the situation was enough and being mad would not make things better. Dear Lord, please remember our dear friends Bob, Otis, and Sergeant whose bravery went way beyond the call. In the name of our Lord and Savior Jesus Christ. Amen."

Everyone repeated *Amen*. Except for Boudine.

As the food was being passed around, Abigail put an arm around Sarah and gave her a little hug. Sarah gave her a shy smile and looked down at her hands folded in her lap. Just then, a wagon could be heard approaching and stopping out front. After a moment, there was a light knock on the door. Ben jumped up and opened the door. Otis entered, taking off his hat. "Sorry I'm late."

Nathan rose. "Oh, you ain't late, my friend. Set yourself down. That a wagon I heard out there?"

Otis took his usual seat at the table. "Yessir. 'Tis the varmint's covered wagon and horses. Sheriff Bullock said to take it. Had no use for it. Said we might be able to use it at the mill."

Nathan sat back down. "Well, I'll be. We will use it for somethin' good now."

Sarah spoke up rather softly, "Otis… what's the Sheriff gonna do with those two?"

Everyone looked at Otis for an answer. "Well, Sheriff Bullock said, if'n it t'was up to him, they'd have a hangin' right there in Deadwood, but he'll be sendin'em off to Yankton to the marshal there. Same one who had the hangin' of Broken Nose McCall who murdered Wild Bill Hickok."

===

"You been writin' an awful lot lately in that notebook of yourn. Thought you'd given up that stuff," Boudine said from her chair nearby to Bob's on their cabin's front porch. The sun was slipping down from the late afternoon. Bob set his pencil inside the leather-bound notebook and wrapped the cover around it.

"Just some notes to remember, s'all."

"You always say that."

Bob got up from the chair and headed inside.

"Otis's headin' into Deadwood tomorrow to pick up the saw blades for the mill at Bullock's hardware store. Think I be goin' with'im. Look in on Calamity and the Doc," said Boudine.

Bob stopped in the doorway. "Maybe, I'll tag along. Got a thing or two to get done there."

Boudine looked out at a beautiful sunset spreading its fingers out over a spring sky and rubbed her much-expanded belly.

===

Otis brought the newly acquired covered wagon to a halt in front of Doc Babcock's home office. Boudine slowly and carefully started to step down off the wagon.

"Y'all need a hand there, Miss Boudine?" Otis offered.

"That'll be the day," Boudine chuckled, as she descended to the ground.

"I'll be 'round to fetch you in 'bout an hour. Goin' to stop in to see Aunt Lou after I pick up the saw blades. That be alright with you?"

Boudine looked at Otis with a smirk and said, "I can still walk for crissakes! I'll meet you at the restaurant."

"Suit yerself."

"I will," Boudine answered emphatically.

Doc Babcock listened a bit more to Boudine's belly with his ear horn stethoscope and then stepped back. He picked up a notebook and jotted a few notes in it. Boudine didn't like the look on his face.

"Somethin' wrong?" Boudine asked, as she buttoned up her large men's shirt.

"Not really. But…"

"But what?" Boudine interrupted.

"Well, Sally Mae, you're getting real close and we should set you up with a midwife real soon."

Boudine eased off the examining table and let out a whoosh of air.

"You alright there, Sally Mae? Need some water?"

"Nope." With that, Boudine thanked and paid the Doctor with a five-dollar gold piece. "Where's Calamity? Thought she'd be back by now?"

"Over at Mount Moriah Cemetery visitin' old Wild Bill."

"She do that a lot?"

Doc Babcock hesitated…

"Never mind. Just tell'er I was about." With that, Boudine left.

===

"Well, look who's here and look at you there," Aunt Lou said to Boudine as she happily greeted her and led her to a table in her Grand Central Hotel restaurant.

As Boudine sat gingerly down on the chair, Aunt Lou had pulled out for her, she said, "Doc says I'm gonna need to get me a midwife. You know of one?"

"So happens, you're talkin' to one right here," Aunt Lou said with pride. "Delivered more babies than I can count and none of'em got away from me. Not a one!"

Boudine looked up into Aunt Lou's bright face and heaved a noticeable sigh. Tears started to well in Boudine's eyes.

Aunt Lou saw her fear and put a gentle hand on Boudine's shoulder. "Now, you got nothin' to worry about. Soon's you're ready, I'll be right there. Now, I'm going to fetch you somethin' nice from the kitchen."

"Where's Otis? Said for me to meet him here."

"Said, he had somethin' to tend to. Said, he'd be back in a jiffy. That was ten jiffies ago."

As Aunt Lou headed for the kitchen, Boudine asked after her, "Did Bob stop by?"

"Matter of fact, he did. Had himself a package to mail at the Wells Fargo Office."

Boudine watched after Aunt Lou, and her new helper, Mary Theresa, who came from the back with a tub to start collecting the dirty dishes from the tables.

Boudine looked around at the unfamiliar faces of the customers and couldn't help but feel a bit lost. Something that a whippersnapper of a woman like her hardly ever felt.

Bob came into the restaurant and said to Boudine, "We better get a move on back 'fore dark. Where's Otis?"

"Can't say."

"Supposed to meet us here."

Just then a man burst through the doors shouting, "Fire! There's a big fire!"

He was bumped out of the way by Otis who came through behind him. He went right to Bob and Boudine. "We gotta go!"

Neither Boudine nor Bob moved, as they tried to comprehend what was happening.

"NOW!" Otis demanded. Then to Bob, "Get outta here, I'll get Miss Boudine onto the wagon."

Aunt Lou came bustling out of the kitchen, "What's happening? What's all the fuss?"

Otis helped Boudine up out of her chair and started hustling her toward the front door. As they left, he shouted back to Aunt Lou, "Gem Theater's burnin' down."

"They know what started the fire, Otis?" Boudine asked.
"Don't know."
"Looked like it might burn to the ground."
"Appears so."

===

The new saw blade whirled in place, as a stripped pine log was pushed along the guide path toward the sharp, spinning teeth. The screeching whine of raw wood being cut by steel split the air.

Ben, who was next to his father as he shoved the log forward, threw his hands into the air and shouted out, "It works! It works!" The rest of the group clapped and laughed with joy at the sight of the first board falling away from the log.

With the new sawmill up and running, Bob, Otis, Ben and Sarah, loaded the two wagons with the lumber that Nathan and Sergeant sent through the saw blade, and delivered it to where the workers from Deadwood would start building the first buildings of the new town of Belle Fourche, South Dakota.

Since the recent mysterious fire burned the Gem Theater right to the ground, along with the capturing and delivering of the two hired varmints, who kidnapped Sarah, to Sheriff Seth Bullock, none of the men who wanted to build the saloons and gambling halls in the new town came around. There would be a few saloons and brothels, because that's what the cattle drivers and gold miners demanded. However, they would be regulated by the new Town Council, where members like Nathan, Bob, Otis and Boudine, among others, would have a weighty say as to just where those businesses were located. Certainly not near a school or any of the several churches that were planned.

===

Abigail and Millie Mae had their hands full readying the noon meal in Abigail's kitchen. Sarah and Ben came in through the front door. "Sarah, please ring for lunch, we're just about ready and Ben you wash up."

"Yes, ma'am."

Sarah went back out onto the porch. As she took up the iron rod to ring the hanging iron triangle, she noticed Boudine coming from the pathway to her and Bob's cabin and suddenly stop, hold her expanded belly with both hands, and look down at the ground. "Oh, no…" she uttered with dismay.

Sarah called out to her, "What's wrong? Is something wrong, Sally Mae?"

Boudine looked up and said fearfully, "I… I watered myself and somethin's happening!"

"Ma!" Sarah shouted to her mother and ran off the porch to Boudine who looked ashen and seemed to be terrified."

Millie Mae and Abigail helped Boudine into the Pickering main bedroom and helped her lie down. Outside, Sarah furiously rang the triangle and shouted at Ben, "Go get Pa and Bob and Otis! Hurry."

Ben took off like a shot.

Otis drove the small, covered wagon hard into Deadwood and reined up in front of Aunt Lou's restaurant at the Grand Central Hotel.

"Oh God, I'm scared," Boudine said to Bob, who hovered nearby in the bedroom. Millie Mae used a damp cloth to comfort her and wipe away the perspiration that was running down her face.

"Now, you don't need to be fearful, Sally Mae. Both Abigail and me have done this before and…"

"Two times. My Ma's done this two times." Sarah said, trying, in her own way, to reassure Boudine.

"And…" Millie Mae continued, "the Lord will be right here with you."

Suddenly, Boudine hunched up, "Ahhh!" she blurted out. "It really hurts."

"Sarah fetch some more warm towels and you men skedaddle out of here." Abigail ordered.

Nathan took Ben by the arm and followed Sergeant out of the room. Bob seemed frozen in place. "That means you too, Bob. Shoo!" she said with a hand gesture toward the door.

Otis drove the two-horse covered wagon hard over the trail back toward Belle Fourche. Aunt Lou was right there beside him. So was

Calamity Jane who said, "They still don't know what started the fire at the Gem. Went up like a pile of dry kindling."

"All the girls got out, so I heard tell," Aunt Lou said.

"What'd'ya think, Otis? You hear anythin' 'bout how the fire started?" Calamity asked.

Otis gave the horses a slap with the reins and uttered, "Don't know. Don't care."

"Oh, God!" Boudine exclaimed as she hunched up with another pain attack.

"Comin' pretty regular now," Abigail said, "Could be soon."

"Ya-have-ta wait for Aunt Lou!" Boudine nearly screamed with another painful jolt.

Millie Mae said softly, "Lord mighten not wait. If he needs us we're right here."

In the kitchen, Bob paced nervously in front of Nathan, Sergeant and Ben, as Boudine's shouts cut through from the bedroom. "She'll be fine there, Bob. It's just the way with birthin'," Nathan tried to reassure.

"Don't sound so good. Don't sound so good 't'all."

Ben heard something outside and made a beeline for the front door and flung it open. "They're here. Otis is back."

"I brung you some Laudanum and some'a that Chinese medicine for the pain there, Sally Mae," Calamity said from where she stood at the end of the bed.

"No. Don't gimme none'a that shite. Ahhhhh!" she shrieked.

Aunt Lou, who was seated next to Boudine and was holding her hand in hers, quietly got up and started pulling back the blanket that was over Boudine.

"Comes the time," she said to the others." Then to Abigail, she said, "Little girl might not want'a see all this."

Sarah blurted out, "I ain't little and I'm stayin'."

Abigail nodded to Aunt Lou.

Then, as Aunt Lou and the women readied themselves, Boudine became hysterical and started shouting and screaming incoherently, "You did this to me, Bob Slye! You did this to me *Bandit* Bob Slye!"

The women all looked at each other for a brief moment, then focused on what was about to happen.

In the kitchen, Sergeant had heard what Boudine had screamed and looked at Bob with a quizzical look on his face. So did Nathan and Ben. However, Otis just looked down at his boots.

Bob then uttered in a hoarse whisper, "She's talkin' crazy."

Then, everything went quiet for a bit, until the sound of a baby being slapped on its bottom and taking its first breath and uttering its first cry came through the closed bedroom door. Bob, who had been holding his breath, heaved a sigh.

Suddenly, Sarah opened the bedroom door slightly and announced, "It's a boy! Just like I knew it would be." She then looked around behind her and uttered, "Uh-oh!" and quickly shut the door.

From the bedroom, came another slap and another cry.

After a moment, Sarah reappeared and announced in utter amazement, "It's a girl!" Again, she shut the door.

All the men looked to Bob, whose expression was complete bewilderment.

Suddenly, Sarah came out of the bedroom. "Need more towels," she said as she grabbed some from the kitchen cabinet and disappeared into the bedroom.

Nathan put his hand on Bob's arm, "Looks like you got'cha self a family now, Bob."

The incomprehension on Bob's face was interrupted by yet another slap and yet another baby's first cry.

"Lordy," Nathan expressed, "you are certainly bein' blessed here, Bob."

Sarah pushed open the bedroom door and exclaimed in a high-pitched announcement, "Another girl! She made three babies! A boy and two girls. Just like my goats." Again, the door shut.

Sergeant said to Bob, "You better sit down, son. You look like you're about to pass out." Bob did not object to Sergeant pulling out a chair for him to sit on.

===

Aunt Lou sat in a chair by the Pickering fireplace. "Otis'll be takin' me back to Deadwood first light. My job's done here, and I've got lots to do to get ready to make my move over to Lead."

"We're going to miss you, Aunt Lou," Abigail said.

"Oh, Lead ain't the end of the earth. I'll still be around. And, y'all can come by to catch up any time. 'Sides, with the new town bein' built here in Belle Fourche, I'll be that much closer to y'all."

"Shhh!" Sarah sounded out and put her finger to her mouth to hush, "Come here," she whispered from the bedroom door that was slightly ajar. Sarah looked in and said to Abigail, Millie Mae and Aunt Lou, as they quietly gathered behind her to peek in at Boudine. "She's prayin' there. Sally Mae's prayin'," Sarah said. And she was. An exhausted Boudine lay under blankets with her head on a large pillow. Her hands were clasped in front of her, and she was silently saying a private prayer. Her newborn babies were quietly swaddled in the baby rocker bed that Bob and Otis had built. As the women stepped away from the door, Millie Mae uttered under her breath, "Comes the time."

Millie Mae eased the babies out of their bed and settled them into Boudine's arms. Sarah was right there behind her. "What're you gonna call'em?" she asked out of the blue. Abigail heard her and popped into the doorway.

"Now, you scat out of here right now, young lady. That's enough bother for one day."

Boudine cradled the three little ones in her arms and smiled up at Sarah. "Oh, she ain't no bother. She's right and I do have names for these new critters."

"What?" Sarah exclaimed, "What're we supposed to call'em? We have'ta know."

Boudine sighed some, looked down at the babies' faces, then to Sarah she said, with all sincerity, "Maybe, King, Queen and Ace."

ALL THE NEW BEGINNINGS...

TWENTY-FOUR

Bob pulled a small wagon with side boards behind him and stopped at Millie Mae's cabin. He let out a sharp whistle and his mother came outside. "Look what Otis come up with from Deadwood. Just right for pullin' the babies around."

"Oh, that's perfect. Would'a loved one to've pulled you around back then," she chuckled.

Bob started away, then turned back and said, "Ah…"

"Yes?" Millie Mae said, as Bob noticeably paused.

"Oh… s'nothin'," he said, "just thinkin' s'all."

"'Bout what Boudine might've said 'bout?"

Bob blanched a bit, but answered, "Yes. What she said, 'bout me."

Millie Mae looked directly at her son, "Already knew long before here."

Bob looked at Millie Mae for a moment, then said, "How'd you know?"

"Oh, mother's know things. You'll see." She then smiled at Bob and turned back and went inside her cabin, as Stubs and the hound bounded in behind her.

===

Bob held one of the babies and rocked it. Boudine sat at their kitchen table and nursed two others. "How're we gonna tell'em apart? They all look alike," Bob said.

"Well, all ya have'ta do with one of'em is take his nappy off."

"But the two girls?"

"I can already tell'em apart."

"Oh…"

"Oh, what?"

"Nothin'," Bob uttered. "Just somethin' my mother said, s'all."

Boudine looked down and saw that one baby had fallen asleep. "Switch'em," she said to Bob who switched the baby in his arms with the sleeping one."

"Meanin' to ask you somethin', Boudine."

"S'at?"

"Back when I was 'bout to be hung by that Sheriff O'Banyon. Why'd you come after me?"

Boudine looked at Bob, then down at the babies, then said, "Who the hell else was I to go after?"

Bob was quiet for a moment.

"What was that there package you mailed at the Wells Fargo Office last time we was in Deadwood?" Boudine asked.

"Um…" Bob said.

"You ain't gonna tell me are-ya."

"Sure. I'll tell-ya."

"Well?" she said, as she adjusted the nursing babies.

"I sent a story into the Beadle book-makin' company in New York City."

This rather took Boudine back a bit, "You…. You been writin' a story in that notebook of yourn?"

"Yes."

"Well, all be," she uttered. "What's it about?"

"They like stories 'bout the Western Frontier. Pay three-hundred dollars if'n they take it."

"Good Lord. All this time, you wasn't lyin' 'bout what you done for work. You really was writin' stories there, Bob."

"Well, some… yeah."

"What's it called?"

Bob hesitated a moment, then said, "Hangin' With The Truth."

A quiet smile came to Boudine, as she looked at Bob. Then she said, "Well, Bob Duncan… there'ya go then."

ACKNOWLEDGMENTS

A sequel? I'd never written one before. But, my second novel, "Hangin' With The Truth" had ended with, "…Or did it?" which almost begs for a continued story. What was I thinking? But there it was, "…Or did it?" Ok, I'll bite. Did it? So, I started and then a few pages in, my most serious critic said, "The book has to stand on its own." Meaning that someone who hadn't read "Hangin' With The Truth" could read the sequel and be satisfied. So, I tossed those first pages and thought, "Do I really want to dive into this?" Well, I did and here it is…

"DON'T CALL ME SLYE"

Thank you, Melinda Riccilli Slade for your pushing, shoving and intelligent nagging along the way. And, for the title itself! Without your input, who knows where this would have ended up. Also, thank you, once again, artist Morgan Riccilli Slade for creating such a unique cover and book design. And Mitchel Slade for all of your encouragement and solid and unwavering support. You guys are the best!

ABOUT THE AUTHOR

Mark Slade is an author, artist, and actor. DON'T CALL ME SLYE is his third novel. It continues the story of Bob Slye and Sally Mae Boudine from his second novel, HANGIN' WITH THE TRUTH. His first novel, GOING DOWN MAINE was set in New England, where he grew up. He has also authored two books of poetry and art OF PAIN AND COFFEE and SOMEONE'S STORY which reflect his unique perspective on everyday life. He lives in Northern California Wine Country with his wife, Melinda.

For additional biographical information:

www.marksladestudio.com
www.imdb.com
www.wikipedia.org
Facebook
X (twitter)

Printed in Great Britain
by Amazon